A DOCTOR
IN THE FAMILY

A Doctor
in the Family

Elizabeth Seifert

A FOUR SQUARE BOOK

To the Memory
of My Grandfather

© ELIZABETH SEIFERT, 1956

First published in Great Britain by Wm. Collins, Sons & Company Ltd., in 1956

*

FIRST FOUR SQUARE EDITION, MARCH 1966

*Four Square Books are published by The New English Library Limited from Barnard's
Inn, Holborn, London, E.C.1. Made and Printed in Great Britain by Hunt Barnard & Co.
Limited, The Sign of the Dolphin, Aylesbury, Buckinghamshire.*

PART ONE

THIS WOULD BE a crisp winter's day, blue and white and golden, with snow crunchy underfoot, the sky a canopy of azure satin—and so much to do that Linda was up at sunrise to get her duties aligned, hoping only to accomplish a major part of them.

To-day was again an anniversary, with a family dinner to mark it, and once more the country was at war, with the problems of young men heavy upon the hearts of women— Linda sat thoughtful before the fire, remembering that other time, that other day.

That time was the winter of 1942-43, a time of war and priorities and ration books. Of fears and doubts, and an urgent feeling that life was over short.

The place was the small town of Valhalla in the Missouri Ozarks, a beautiful little town built into a fold of the wooded old mountains, its edges touched by a brown, swift river. Not a very progressive town; admittedly it was ruled by the wealth and the prestige of one family, the Thorntons, whose home, a columned, porticoed affair of white-painted bricks, stood serenely aloof at the end of Main Street, its dignity challenging the curiosity of the townspeople, and defending the privacy of its occupiers. The gardens of Fiddlers Green ran down to the river; its farms and horse paddocks stretched widely out through the valley and ran up the sides of the mountain. At the other end of Main Street stood the fifty-bed hospital where Dr. Alan Thornton was the surgeon-in-charge.

Old Jasper Thornton ruled the farmers of the community, and its stockmen, by virtue of his own big farm, his blooded stock, his horse stables, his feed mill—his character and his personality.

In November of 1942, Jasper Thornton was a bit past seventy, a huge man, as strong as an old oak, and as mighty. He wore a wide-brimmed hat, and looked strange without it on the back of his head. He wore a beard, too, salt-and-pepper-grey by then, and he walked with a rush and a plunge, his step uneven as if he rode always over the hummocks of a mountain-side meadow. A completely physical man, Jasper Thornton. In great measure, he thought and spoke in the terms of animals, of horses. His eyes were keen, grey-green under bushy brows. He spoke to all people in the same loud tone with which he shouted "Haw!" at one of his huge Belgian stallions being put through its paces in a sales barn.

Jasper was tremendously rich, yet he could be friends with any man, and was. He himself was as picturesque, if not as strange, as some of his friends. He liked to ride a big buckskin horse with a white mane and flowing tail; to the town's people, he looked odd away from his horse.

For almost fifty years, this man had been married to Seretha Merritt, a tall, erectly slender woman, with masses of dead-white hair, and a coldly correct face and eye. She was a quiet woman, and firm, leaning heavily upon the statistical fact that her family was a bit older than Jasper's old family. She was called Ma'am by her children, and by her servants.

In the big house, too, lived Ma'am's brother, Arthur, a thin stick of an old man, as delicate as the tinkling glass which he lifted too often to his lips. And there was Aunt Flora, silly, too fat, and unhappy to be reminded that her memories extended so far, so many years, behind her.

Then there was Alan, the rock to which the whole family was anchored. Dr. Alan Thornton, the younger son, was a very tall, thin and loose-jointed man; he had Jasper's keen eyes, a big and sensitive mouth, a dark skin and long, restless hands. He was strong enough in his convictions as a Republican, a Protestant, a vestryman, a board member, a committee man—but he was primarily a doctor. A good doctor, and an idealist. He was a drawling, slow-spoken man who talked little and thought much.

Linda was Alan's wife. She was small, with red hair, dark blue eyes and a pointed face—often called pretty. In the fall of 1942, Alan and Linda had been married for ten years, and had no children. The lack was a source of pain within their hearts, and, lately, of unhappiness between them.

There had been another Thornton son, John, older than Alan, and Seretha's favourite. Jasper claimed that she'd spoiled the boy. In any case, there had, years before, come a black time of error and shame to the family. And John Thornton no longer lived in Valhalla, his name was seldom spoken, though perhaps Ma'am knew if he fared well or ill.

The youngest of the Thornton children was Margaret, who had been a widow for almost nine years. Slender, dark and lovely, she was like Jasper's little prize mare, showing her good breeding, her good lines, and cleanly passing them along to her children: Silas, who was an Army flier, and the twins, Jim and Ann, born seven months after a cranky horse had killed their father. The twins were healthy little beasts, with straw-coloured hair and a few teeth missing.

This was the family in wartime, in 1942.

It was Linda's wedding anniversary, and Alan's—their tenth. Seretha, whose pleasure it was to gather her family about her at regular intervals, had seized upon this excuse to have a family party. Except for Silas, lately, she saw each one of them every day, but she liked the feel of having all the threads in her hand at once. Jasper, too, of course, loved to see his "get" seated about the big mahogany table.

That morning Linda woke with the thought of the party before her. She stretched and yawned, and tried the feel of the pillow against her other cheek. It was still dark beyond the window. The fire was not yet freshened, but the room was not cold. Alan had closed the window, and the thermostat of the new furnace started to do its job at six.

"None of this!" she said aloud, and sat straight up, swung her legs to the side of the mattress, fished down and down—she was not tall—until her toe felt the cool white fur of a slipper. She slid down into it, and then into the other, then stood upon the floor and reached a hand for the robe which lay upon the nearby chair. She knotted its sash firmly around her waist and set the screen aside so that she herself might stir the warm ashes upon the hearth, and put a log or two across the andirons. Frowning, she knelt there, waiting to see if the fire would catch—and her ear checked upon the state of things. The household and the farm were waking, even as she had, to go about the day's work before the sun had brought that day into reality.

The house was old and sturdily built. In 1942 it was as much as a hundred and ten years old. Slaves had laid its rock foundation and had raised the hand-made brick walls to the magnifi-

7

cent height of two storeys and an attic. Built around four chimney-stacks and their fireplaces, the ash-wood floors and carved walnut woodwork had well withstood the years. There had been some remodelling, but not much. In the '70's, some of the mantels had been lowered, and since, various concessions to modern heating, lighting and plumbing had been made. It still was a very old house surrounded by its orchards, its pastures and the stables.

As the first blue flame licked upwards about the hickory log, Linda could locate Jasper already out at the stables; his lusty *Haw!* had served as reveille on every morning she had lived at the Green. Smiling, she set the screen in place and turned to the bathroom for her warm shower.

The bathroom had been new, made especially for her when she came to Fiddlers Green as a bride, but the plumbing was "laid on." Through the holes which imperfectly fitted the pipes, as well as through the air ducts of the furnace, came smells and sounds which Linda could trace to the far reaches of this big house. The smell of coffee which richly perfumed the bathroom came from Seretha's big bedroom. With Clew in attendance, the old lady would be sitting up in bed, relishing that first cup of the day. "Ma'am wants her coffee strong enough to float an anvil." No amount of rationing would change this demand. With so many servants and ration books on the place, Ma'am surely could count on having her strong coffee.

Intrigued by her little game of locating the family members through sound and smell, Linda wrapped herself in a thick towel, and decided that poor Uncle Arthur must be feeling squeamish this morning—the coffee smell had probably reached him directly from the kitchen.

Down in that kitchen, Ruby had the big yellow stone-ware bowl cradled into one bare brown arm, and was beating up the buckwheat batter, singing above the noise of her thwacking spoon. "Hammer's a-ringin' on somebody's coffin . . ." she shouted happily.

Linda smiled and shook her head, tidied the bathroom, noting and liking the way the water smelled of clean brown gravel, wrinkling her short nose at the sharper smell of ether which drifted upwards from the clothes hamper when she put her towel into it. She looked out the window—it was getting light. Tree branches and shrubs, the edge of the veranda roof, were

8

etched now darkly against the grey. Down towards the river, Victor, the mastiff, barked deeply within the swirling mist.

Back in the bedroom where the fire now pranced and chattered behind the screen, she laid sheet and blanket and eiderdown back over the foot of the bed, plumped the pillows, her own and Alan's. She had only a faint memory of his departure an hour earlier. By now he would be lost in his work at the hospital, happy to be so lost.

Linda selected a flannel skirt, a crisp white blouse, a cashmere cardigan, brown pumps. She sat down at her dressing-table to comb the tangles out of her red curls and look at the day's page in her memo book. 21st November, 1942. Her wedding anniversary. This particular page was scribbled tightly with tasks to be done, the menu for that evening's dinner, the guest list, flowers—a dozen tasks. But Linda took a minute to sit back, her eyes scarcely seeing herself in the round mirror.

Ten years ago she had been a bride, rising on the morning of her wedding day, her pansy eyes dark with dreams, her red lips trembling with joy. Alan—she had loved him so dearly, had gone to him so eagerly as a bride.

That was ten years ago! The town's librarian was such a pretty girl, people had said when she'd come to fill the position. They said it again, probably, when it became known that she would marry the young doctor, the *Thorntons' son*! What a catch for an outside girl to make!

To Linda it had seemed like a fairy tale come to life—though not because Alan's family was rich. Alan himself, the dark and gentle man, with his own dreams and plans, had become Linda's single dream. She wanted only to do the things that Alan dreamed of, to accept Alan's decision—because she loved him.

His successes had become her triumphs, his disappointments . . . With his hand in hers, they had together faced what the hospital meant to them. Jasper meant well; hundreds of thousands of dollars had gone into the building and its equipment. It was a fine thing for a man to do, both for his community and for his surgeon son. Except that that son had wanted to be a brain specialist, to be free to work and to study elsewhere towards that end.

But here was a fifty-bed hospital, built and equipped during the year Alan and Linda had spent in England while he studied brain surgery. Could a man refuse such a gift from his father? Perhaps.

"It was your mother's idea," Jasper had said.

"I—don't know what to say to either of you," had been Alan's first comment.

But he had talked to Linda. They had talked it all out. For that purpose, they took their lines and poles and reels and drove into the hills, engaged a boat and guide to make a float downstream. That was a fine way to think out a knotty problem, with shadow and sunlight on the clear brown water, the searing burn of the sun on a man's shoulders, the sweet cool of the shade— to make camp upon a sand bar, to sleep beneath the stars, and think—and talk.

There was mention of John, and his parents' disappointment.

There was consideration given to Alan's interest in brain surgery as being real and compelling. To give that up would be a painful wrench. Yet there were other things, perhaps more important, to consider and weigh. The struggle to reach a decision was long and difficult. But it came at last to an end.

"Here I would be working among my own people," Alan told Linda on that last night. "A healing hand is valuable wherever there is humankind. A doctor works from within; he uses his own skill, his own ability—and draws most heavily upon some inward power with which to handle each case as it comes to him. I could be my own doctor, my own man. . . ."

"And will be," said Linda. (Regretting that effort must be required.)

"D'you suppose," asked Alan, troubled, "that Father knows what Ma'am wanted?"

"To keep her remaining son close by? Of course he knows. That's why the decision can be yours."

He turned his head to look at her. In the firelight, his eyes had flashed green. "That's my girl!" he'd rewarded her loving and unquestioning loyalty. And so the decision was made, with no regrets.

The baby—that had been different. To lose her first baby before it ever took form—oh, that had been a very hard time! Alan, too, had grieved, but for Linda it was more than the hurt of loss. It was defeat and failure as well. So much had depended on her having a child! Seretha's acceptance of Linda as a member of the family; Alan's wife should have perpetuated the

Merritt and the Thornton blood and, certainly, the Thornton name! To have failed in this was bad, and grew worse, because in the years that followed, no other child was conceived. The hunger of being childless grew and grew into a gnawing aching hurt within Linda's heart. She *wanted* a child! For the feel of it in her arms, for the pride and satisfaction which a child would bring to her and to Alan. It would be an expression of their love, a means of continuing their union. . . .

But in this she had failed Alan, just as she had failed his family. She knew the full measure of her failure there, and the yearning to belong, to do her part, grew to be as unbearable as the emptiness of her arms.

More than she realised the family loved her, the family leaned upon her. Often Alan protested at the way they imposed upon Linda.

But, she told herself, a really good servant, a housekeeper, could do all that she did. More was expected of a wife than to be a housekeeper. Not having produced the expected Thornton child, Linda felt herself not truly a Thornton.

Alan loved her, Alan was good to her—but often it seemed that he needed Linda much less than he needed his operating-room nurse, tall, handsome and efficient Mrs. Dunham.

The two women had a little joke between them. Meeting upon the street, or in the vestibule of the church, Linda would say gaily to the nurse, "How is my husband these days?" And Mrs. Dunham would answer, smiling, "He's very well, thank you."

Both women knew that Alan was spending the larger part of his time at the hospital. From the minute he had decided to go in as surgeon-in-charge, Alan had become completely absorbed in his work there. And now the war——

Another period of mental travail had ended in his decision to stay with the hospital rather than go off to work in some surgery tent, to go on caring for the people of his district—a district which had come to extend as far as a hundred miles around them—in cases of difficult surgery. And now he was trying to do the work of five men! He promised that it would be ten, should the war continue more than a year.

This would mean—it already meant—that he was too busy, too absorbed, to know that he had a wife.

Linda tied a blue scarf around her red curls, and looked

11

sternly into the mirror. She had no child and, for much of the time, she had no husband either. *Why celebrate a marriage like that?* her stormy eyes demanded.

Jasper would cut down a barren tree in his orchard, or sell a mare that did not produce good foals. He had driven his wastrel son from his house.

Why then was a union between a man and a woman any good if it failed to produce even companionship? What use was Linda as a wife to Alan? What good was she to the family?

Not realising the absurdity of calling her busy self useless, Linda quickly made the bed, and smoothed the striped chintz spread—to save the upstairs maid for other duties on this busy day. Briskly she then went out into the hall, down the stairs, straightening a picture as she passed, tidying a tabletop, smoothing a rumpled rug.

Pad and pencil at hand, she ate her breakfast and talked to the cook. This done, she moved on to other tasks.

This was the day, Saturday, to arrange new flowers throughout the house. A knot of spicy red carnations for Jasper's chest of drawers, something pink for Aunt Flora. Rust-coloured chrysanthemums for the big parlour, creamy ones for the smaller room. And, of course, a special arrangement for tonight's dinner table.

"I had to git the glads and some fern from the city, Miss Linda," the gardener told her, his eyes apologetic. "Please don't tell Ma'am. She expects so *much.*..."

Linda reassured the old fellow. He kept the grounds and the little greenhouse beautifully; if Ma'am expected more, it *was* too much. Linda took a flat basket of flowers back to the house, to the dining-room where the banquet top had already been placed upon the table, and Jacob waited on her decision as to the cloth and china which she wanted used. He, too, spoke to her as "Miss Linda." She was never called *Mrs. Thornton*, even down-town. *Mrs Alan* sometimes, but more often *Miss Linda*. Seretha was *Mrs. Thornton*.

Well, what matter? She helped the butler spread the satiny cloth, then asked for paper and towels to protect it while she arranged the flowers. She would use the red and white English china, cut glass—and put the spikes of white gladioli into the ruby vases. Two vases, with smilax trailing. Ivory candles, she decided. She glanced, questioningly, up at Jacob. He nodded. "You got a hand, Miss Linda," he said approvingly.

Pleasure flushed into her cheeks, and sparkled in her eyes. She began to fold the spread papers neatly inward, careful not to leave a crumb of leaf upon the cloth.

She caught the way Jacob's hand stilled even before she realised that the soft murmur of voices from the breakfast room had risen to the sharpness of charge and countercharge.

"Oh, dear," she breathed.

"I'll keery it out, Miss Linda," Jacob offered discreetly.

"Thank you, Jacob." One could not discuss the family and its affairs with the servants, even with a boy who'd been born and raised on the place. The coloured folk knew their work-family with an intimacy of detail, a keenness of judgment and a tactful ability not to interfere, far beyond the talents of the family itself.

Linda turned, crossed the small passage and went into the pleasant breakfast room. A fire burned upon the hearth, misty sunshine came through the east windows and Aunt Flora and Uncle Arthur sat at the corner of the table, a coffee urn and plates and cups before them, their whole attention upon the quarrel which was mounting into a furious frenzy. Poor, fat, foolish Aunt Flora—poor, thin and equally foolish Uncle Arthur: as correct and precise in his neat tan suit, starched white collar and baby-pink skin as Aunt Flora was fussy in her negligée and lacy cap, her beads and her twinkly rings.

Linda stood unnoticed in the doorway, looking in on the pleasant room. The firelight danced on the plates and dishes within the cupboard, twinkled from the silver on the side table.

Aunt Flora was complaining, tearfully, about her husband's attentions to Miss Little Mae Honeycutt.

Miss Little Mae had been *Mrs. Liddell* for forty years, and widowed for ten, but she still was called by her girlhood name. She had been a great belle, and was still a pretty little old woman.

"She always was silly!" declared Aunt Flora, sniffling, "and you never could see it! I recall so well the time she chose to attract attention by ridin' an unbroke horse side-saddle. All swishy skirts and petticoats. The animal rared, and she went down—with you men most concerned! She came out, of course, bein' not ready yet to die—and she wasn't hurt beside! I remember so well how you left me sittin' lone in the democrat, and made over her. . . ."

Uncle Arthur murmured something about that being fifty years ago, and this dissolved Aunt Flora into tears. He produced a crisp white handkerchief, wiped her cheeks and patted her plump shoulder. "Don't weep, Flora," he begged, "that's all done and gone."

"It's not, though," claimed Aunt Flora in a suffocated voice. "Just yesterday—I saw you pat her hand, and bend your back and scrape your foot. . . ."

"Oh, for the good Lord's sake, Flora!" cried her exasperated husband. "That was jest manners, and you know it! I'm too old for it to be anything else! And you're too old to think so. I can't get into trouble with a woman, and just as certainly you're not in danger from any man!"

To announce her immunity from amorous involvements was the unforgivable sin with Aunt Flora. She rose, weeping, from the table, and stumbled towards the door; defiantly, Uncle Arthur said no word to detain her.

Linda's arm comfortingly circling her shoulders, she led the old lady down the passage, across the wide hall to the chintzy little morning-room with many a murmur of *there, there*, and *poor dear*.

"Don't you ever trust any man, Linda!" sobbed Aunt Flora, sinking into the depths of an arm-chair. "Don't expect them to give you *anything* for all you give them."

"I know," said Linda, in a practical tone, "they're beasts." She laid the newspaper across Aunt Flora's lap, moved the little table closer, with the lid off the box of chocolates. "I wonder . . ." she said, then broke off, her fingertips across her lips.

Aunt Flora dabbed at her eyes, sniffed and selected a chocolate. "What do you want, dear?" she asked in a bruised tone. "Anything poor old Aunt Flora can do . . ."

"Well, as you know, the party to-night is for our anniversary. I wondered if you would want to write one of your little poems?"

The old lady sighed in a shuddering way, "I'll try, dear," she promised. "I'll sit here and collect myself, and then I'll try."

Linda went to the secretary for some paper and a pencil, and, a few minutes later, when she left the room, Aunt Flora was bent over the page, lost in the throes of romantic composition.

14

The morning went swiftly, crowded with innumerable household tasks. Towards noon, Jacob came to the kitchen to tell Miss Linda that Dr. Alan was on the phone. Linda looked up, smiling radiantly, and the Negro smiled too, happy in her pleasure.

Ruby and Jacob watched the swift manner of her going. "She sure love her man," said Jacob contentedly.

"Ev'body love Dr. Alan."

"Ev'body ain' his *wife*," Jacob pointed out.

"What an arrangement that would be!" laughed Ruby.

The downstairs telephone sat upon a small table in the rear end of the wide hall. In the summer, one seated in the needlepoint chair could look out through the screen door, across the back veranda to the sloping lawns and gardens, clear down to the river. To-day the big door was closed, and Linda had a view only of its carved panels or of the scenic wallpaper brought from France before the Civil War.

She spoke softly into the phone, and leaned back, smiling, pleased to hear her husband's firm voice. He talked exactly like his father—Alan was like Jasper! If he'd worn a beard——

Her smile trembled in Linda's voice as she answered his inquiry as to how she was, and was she busy?

"What's funny?" he aked quickly.

"Nothing really." But she told him, quickly, of the jealous quarrel between the old folks.

"They haven't heard then of Miss Little Mae's accident?"

"Oh, dear, no. Did she have one?"

"Yes. She was brought in this morning, about eight. I'm afraid her hip is fractured."

Linda expressed her concern, asked for details, mentally rearranged her dinner table—and again appreciated Alan's voice, his manner. He was so sure of himself, so self-sufficient. She could see his dark, strong face as he talked, the line of his white collar against his throat, the way his big capable hand would be holding the phone.

"I'm so glad you are there to take care of her," Linda told him.

"Thank you, darling, but she's more likely to be Ernst's patient. I have to go to Kennerly. That's why I called you. I'm starting in ten minutes, I hope."

"But, *Alan!*" Kennerly was seventy-five miles from Valhalla. And if he was going to operate there——

"Yes, dear," he agreed to all the things he knew had come into her mind. "I am afraid I shall be late for dinner. I'm terribly sorry to do this, Linda, but——"

"Don't worry about me! I feel sure I can celebrate even a wedding anniversary alone. But your mother, Alan——"

"Ma'am won't like it," he agreed, his dry tone indicating to what extent Seretha disliked any disrupture in her plans.

"Can't they get someone else, Alan? Kennerly is nearly a hundred miles away——"

"It's seventy-five—and they do have a surgeon, Linda. He called me. But this case—she can't be moved. I'm closer than any city doctor. It's a young woman, dear. Hurt in a head-on auto crash. Cochran says it's the worst he's ever seen—I have to try to correct all that I can, dear. She—she's pregnant besides."

"Oh, *dear!* But can you . . . ?"

"I don't know. I'm going to try. If they could find another surgeon closer, I reckon they would have him by now. I—I am sorry, darling."

"Of course you must go," she agreed quickly. Then in an effort to send him off on as pleasant a note as possible: "But don't pretend, young man, that you are sorry to leave me. I know your real love!"

Alan chuckled. "You do, eh? Red-headed, isn't she?"

"All colours. Assorted. Patients come that way."

"I'll grant the assortment," he told his wife. "But I'll argue the identity of your rival. I'm only sorry for my patients, dear Linda; it's their ailments that I love!"

She laughed, "I can't see that it makes much difference. Be sure to get your lunch, Alan."

"I'm eating it now. . . ."

"Then let me talk—no, that won't do, because I want to ask about the little Medley boy."

She sensed the quickening of his interest. "Yes!" he said eagerly. "We had a confirmation this morning! Definitely sickle-cell, Linda. I did right, too, in beginning transfusions."

"You always do right where your patients are concerned." She would have qualified the faintly bitter statement, but Alan spoke to someone at the hospital, and did not comment or answer Linda. When he began to talk to her again, it was to say

16

sadly that things were bad for the Negro child. "What shall I do, Linda? Tell his mother that Oscar can't live—that he'll surely die before he is ten, and probably sooner?"

"Oh, no!" Her protest was richly compassionate. "Let her hope, Alan!"

"She can't *look* at the child without knowing. He's six but appears to be no more than three."

"I know. But I still think . . . If a woman can't hope, Alan, she has nothing."

She felt his sigh against her eardrum. "Thank you, Linda," he said gravely. "I'll take your advice. Your understanding surpasses . . . or is it aboundeth? Anyway, it does! Good-bye, dear."

Linda put the phone down, a little smile tucked into the corners of her soft lips. Indeed his real love was his profession. That he let Linda share in that love made the real intimacy of their marriage. She should be content. . . .

After lunch, Linda exchanged her sweater for the short jacket of her suit, put on a round felt hat, took a basket in her hand and went down to the stables with her father-in-law to see a new colt. She and the bearded old man were great friends. She had disappointed him by not having children, yet she knew that Jasper liked her.

"You goin' to be warm enough?" he demanded, as they crossed the back veranda.

She pulled the brown scarf more closely against her throat. "At the pace you walk? Of course!"

The stables were not quite so old as the big house.

They were brick buildings, neat with little turned cupolas pointing skywards. On that frosty noon, Jasper and Linda walked through the orchard rather than along the smoothly-raked drive. As they walked, Jasper told her, again, of the way the orchards used to be. "We made a large part of our livin' by them." He spoke always of his forebears as if they were his contemporaries.

"My father's orchard was the first commercial one in this part of Missouri. He raised good apples, Bellflower and Jenetons, Red Astrakhans and Greenings, Rambos. Don't find those anywhere now. He'd plant an orchard; when it got through its best bearin', he'd clear the land and use it for pasture grasses a while. Hay, that's why we had to take up horses." His green eyes twinkled down at her.

She nodded. "A sacrificing bunch, you Thorntons."

"Yes'm. We see our duty . . . Where was I? Now it's all Delicious apples, and Jonathans. Can't give away the old pie apples, Ganos and Ben Davis. But I remember 'em. You think I'm a horse man, but my earliest job on this farm was to turn the crank on a little machine—had a bellows to it somehow—drew it along on a horse-sled and it blew a fog of lime and arsenate of lead out through a long tin pipe. I always claimed the worms fattened on it.

"Now, sprayin's got to be a danged complicated thing; so's marketin' and packin'—things called Friday packs. Gad! Why, I recall, Lindy, the way folks used to come here for they apples. In wagons, a long line of 'em, rollin' in jest before sundown. They'd build little fires, and cook their suppers. I liked to hear 'em talk about the places they come from—forty, fifty mile away. They would sleep in the hayloft, and next morning they'd pad the wagon-beds with old comforters, load up apples for themselves and their neighbours—wave us good-bye, and start off for home, promisin' to come back the next year. Apples were different then. People ate lots of 'em. Don't now. Too much other stuff to mess with."

They had come to the broad, smooth sweep of gravel which led to the main entrance of the Thornton stables. Horses in the stalls began to stir at Jasper's approach, to nicker softly—one squealed shrilly, and the old man chuckled. "He knows the new colt's a threat. Come this way, Lindy. Wait till you see that boy!"

The stable was as clean as broom and mop and insecticide could make it; it still smelled pleasantly pungent of horses and hay.

Jasper gave Linda sugar for the mare, who was still a bit restive, inclined to roll an eye and lay back her ears. The colt, all legs and head, was curled into deep, clean straw. Jasper's hand smoothing the mother's nose and neck, he and Linda looked over the door, and Jasper ticked off the colt's fine points, the depth of chest, the promise of powerful hindquarters. He traced the ancestry. "I knew I'd get a good one!" he declared. "The important thing in horse-breedin', Lindy, is to depend on *strain*. That goes for folks, too."

18

She shot a laughing glance upwards.

"You think I'm funnin'?" he demanded. "I'm not. But be sure you understand what I mean by *strain*. It ain't name, you know. Or even blood. The kinship of strain can be, and I believe should be, stronger than the ties of blood. D'you understand what I'm gettin' at, Lindy?"

"I'm trying."

He nodded. "I had a Norsky work for me once. He had a proverb—said it once, I've always remembered it. It went, 'Marry not the maid who is the only good maid in the family!' D'you see what that means, Lindy?" He leaned over to search her face, his manner loving and intent.

She wanted to please him, and she *thought* she understood . . . "That it is better to marry the black sheep of a good family?"

"That's it!" he shouted so loudly that the mare snorted, and the colt made a scramble with his long legs. Jasper hissed soothingly through his teeth, and the animals calmed.

"That's it," he said again with satisfaction. "In a bad line, if you get one good foal—or child—it's just luck. That one germ-cell happened to be good. Better chance is that all the others, and their descendants, will be like the original bad line. Same thing goes for a good line—while a fault may show, the chance there is that it'll not be one to persist."

He touched her arm. "Let's go into the tack-room; there's a fire. I'm goin' to let you name this baby for me."

There was no higher award Jasper could make her. Linda tingled with pleasure as she followed him into the big central "barn" and to the stable where the show horses were kept, where the tack-room was lined solidly with trophy cases, and framed pictures. The old man unlocked his desk, rolled the top back, reached for the stud-book and his eight-sided ebony rule.

He explained again about the way a horse was registered and named. "But what we call him—that's for you to say. You don't have to answer right away."

The Thornton Stable was the Golden Feather, and Jasper's horses often were called by names linked to that general classification. His buckskin stallion was Plume; the sire of the new colt was named Pinion. His five-gaited mare was Wing. . . .

"I know what I want him called," said Linda readily. "Quill. Would that do?"

Within the grey beard, Jasper's lips tested the name. His eyes

19

began to shine, and he reached for the pen. "You did it," he said approvingly. "A good name for a good horse. Golden Feather Quill. We'll see his ribbons yonder. . . ." His shoulder hunched towards the glass-fronted cabinet.

Linda sat back in the oak chair and felt glad that she had been able to think of the right name. Jasper would not have accepted the wrong one.

"Will he be a race-horse, Father?" she asked.

The old man snorted. "No, indeed. I want him for a jumper —a show horse."

She drew in her breath. It could take as much as fifteen years for a jumper to attain the peak of perfection! And fifteen years for Jasper Thornton—did he realise that he would then be almost ninety years old? Surely he did.

But the staunch old man was counting on a future beyond his own span of years. He had grandsons to insure that future. Quill would jump for Silas or Jim. And if she and Alan . . .

Every thought must have printed itself plainly upon her face, and the green eyes twinkled at her beneath the hat brim. But all he said was, "I'll have him well trained."

"How do you know what he'll be?" she queried. "I mean, so exactly."

The old man tipped back in his chair, teetered it for a second, gently reflective. "All a part of that business of strain, Lindy," he told her. "You don't gamble too much if you lean on that. Take our family, the Thorntons. I don't have to go clear back to Adam the way Ma'am can and does. But you take my great-*great*-grandpappy. He happened to be the son of a gentleman and a bond servant who had good blood. I don't know if a preacher blessed 'em or not, Lindy. Can't see that it matters. But I know my grandpap took this girl—she'd come over to Virginny about the same time that the Merritts were a-steppin' off the second trip of the *Mayflower*. She bore my grandsire five sons. He got himself a hundred little apple trees and took them and the five sons across the mountains to Kentucky. Lived there. Some of the family still do. But one of those boys brought *his* sons and a hundred apple trees, *and* two horses, here to Missouri. It so happened that the son who came out here showed good strain; I'm his great-grandson, and I'm glad to say that the strain's holdin'."

He spoke without vanity, exactly as he had traced the ancestry of the foal, Quill. Good judgment and chance were calculated in the result attained. But no brilliance claimed. Nor snobbish pride encouraged.

Linda nodded. "I'm glad that the Thorntons are holding up, Father."

"We've been bred primarily for strain, and now I can count the results. Alan and Margaret show its strength, Silas does, and those danged twins. I'm an old man, it's a good feelin' to know that the strain won't soon die out."

But the name . . . Linda sat, increasingly thoughtful. He had not mentioned his son John. And Alan—her head tilted upwards, her eyes probed the old face. "But you're disappointed, aren't you," she asked bluntly, "that Alan and I have no children?"

"Of course I'm disappointed. I counted on your havin' a whole raft of 'em. That's why I was happy when you consented to live with us in the big house. I told myself I'd have all manner of red-headed Thorntons under foot. But——" His heavy shoulders lifted in an expressive shrug.

Linda took her gloves out of the basket and put them on, her face downbent, hoping to conceal that she was shocked cold to be told, in so many words, that her importance to the family, her significance to the patriarch, lay—had lain for ten years—in the possibility that she would continue the family strain. And name.

She wanted children. She had grieved terribly at not having them. But the family, it seemed, had felt even more strongly about her failure. To them it was disaster. Silas, and little Jim, and Ann would carry on the family strain, though with Silas flying overseas . . . But the *name*—Alan had been their hope there! And with Linda his wife——

Gasping sharply in revolt against the tyranny of family ambition and pride, she rose and walked over to the door.

The old man watched her, and sensed her hurt if not her protest. "You and Alan," he said slowly, "are still young. You got plenty chance . . ."

Her hand lifted the door-latch, her head shook from side to side. "Don't hope," she said forlornly. "I've stopped hoping." Then she whirled around, her head up, her dark eyelashes swept up, her lips trembling. "If the family is so disappointed, perhaps you'd like me to give Alan another chance—elsewhere!"

21

"Lindy, Lindy," he rebuked her.

She dashed her hand across her eyes. "It's been on my mind, too!" she assured him, then opened the door and went out.

As she made her way back to the house, she gathered apples from the grass in the orchard. The best apples of course had long since been picked and sold, or stored. But under the old trees near the house, until heavy frost, one could always find apples with which to fill the bowl which she kept beside Alan's chair in their bedroom.

Now, moving slowly along—three that she picked up must be discarded for each one that she kept—Linda let her tumbling thoughts and emotions subside into something like a pattern. She should not have flared out at the old man, and let him feel the sting of this day's frustrations. Being married for ten years marked a milestone. By that time, a wife could judge her success or failure. And if a part of the contract had been to serve as the mother of Alan's children, the propagator of the Thornton name and line, Linda was a failure. What difference did it make that Alan—and his father—were fond of her?

She was fond of Jasper, had always liked him, and she wished she could have pleased him with his "raft" of red-headed children. It would have been a way to pay him for all he had done. It was he who had given Alan his heart's desire, permitted his son to become a doctor. Alan had told Linda of the sacrifice this had meant to Jasper.

"He said if I chose doctorin' instead of horse-breedin' and apple-raisin', he wanted me to be a danged good doctor!"

Linda herself remembered how the old man had come into the library when she was brand-new at her job behind its desk, and had bragged to her about the fine internship which his son had just got for himself. He'd been so proud to have a doctor-son, and had talked to her so proudly of the good which a *good* doctor could do.

Of course Seretha had been proud, too, but her pride was in the prestige attached to the profession. "My people," she had told Linda, that first time when Alan had taken her to meet his family, "my people have always leaned towards the professions —lawyers, jurists and physicians." She was unaware of, or uninterested in, the service which a doctor gives to his fellow-man.

Linda supposed that one's way of being proud was allied

to the differences between blood and strain about which Jasper had talked.

A drop of rain upon her cheek startled her, and she turned to hurry up to the house—she had so many things to do! It was folly, in many respects, for her to moon about down here in the orchard.

There were to be guests at the dinner that night, and cards to be placed around the table. She had had Uncle Arthur write the names several days ago. A fine copperplate script was one of his talents. She went up to her room to wash the apples and put them into the bowl. Doing this, her thoughts darted to Alan, in Kennerly by now. "Please God, let him do the job he wants to do!" She smoothed her hair and ran downstairs again, the little stack of thick, gilt-edged cards in her hand. She had already told Jacob of Miss Little Mae's accident.

Aunt Flora, when told, had gasped and wept a sentimental tear over what had happened to the "dear old lady. At her age, it will go hard with her!"

The correct number of places had been set about the table, silver, service plates, cut-glass goblets. The white flowers looked well with the china which Linda had selected. Now, let's see . . . five women, seven men—thank goodness, the table was oval! Seretha's and Jasper's cards took care of themselves. Linda and Alan should be nearly across from each other—provided Alan was there at all!

Murmuring to herself, she moved around the table, and around it again, placing the cards flat upon the plates until she had her plan set, when they could be put into the holders. It was a task, what with the family likes, and very firm dislikes. Perforce she gave a deal of consideration to the personality of each guest.

Deciding to seat the new doctor beside Seretha, she thought of him. Dr. Ernst was an Austrian refugee seeking to establish his medical licence in America. He had to do a certain amount of resident practice, and attain citizenship. She did hope he would prove a real help to Alan; he needed such help. Old Dr. Cassidy was daily becoming more of a hindrance, though Alan, of course, put up with him.

Tapping Dr. Cassidy's card against her fingertips, Linda thought of the big Irishman. Shock-haired, bushy-browed, with an untidy moustache, it had been this same doctor—thirty

23

years younger, of course—who had first aroused Alan's interest in medicine. He'd let the boy drive him on his rounds, into the hills, and help him, first in an emergency, later with the idea of training his hand and eye. He let Alan read his books and explained the more abstruse matters. Dr. Cassidy had taken his own training in Dublin; his basic medical knowledge was excellent. In his time he had done a good job for the hill people, but now, of course, conditions were changed. Dr. Cassidy was in his seventies. And good roads had altered things in the hills. The boy who had ridden beside Dr. Cassidy in 1912 was now the chief doctor in Valhalla, and Dr. Cassidy was glad to be allowed a place in Alan's hospital. Glad in a grudging, complaining sort of way. Deciding to seat this doctor between Margaret and Alan, Linda smiled to think how patient Alan must be with the old duffer, once a good workman, but stubbornly unwilling to subscribe to modern techniques and practices.

Her next card was that of Russell Bowman, the young house doctor at the hospital, who was leaving this next week for Army service. That was another reason why it was important for Dr. Ernst to be satisfactory.

Linda had barely met the new man; he was exceedingly handsome in a smooth and glossy way. Not Alan's way of rugged, dark good looks. Dr. Ernst was a smaller man. His black hair lay smoothly upon his head. His skin had a gleam as of polished wood, and his dark eyes were somnolent, his manner gravely courteous—courtly.

The town was already a-twitter about him. These hill people could look askance at foreigners, and the men did at Ernst. But the women—they gushed over the new doctor. His good looks! His delightful accent!

Linda frowned, and hoped again that Ernst would get along well with Alan, who needed help so badly. If the war dragged on, that need would not get less.

Looking at the cards in her hand she saw that Bowman was her last doctor and, she laughed a little, tossing her red hair out of her eyes, just about the town's last doctor, too. They had one other who called himself "doctor." Dr. Zeller. A very fat man, with a pursed, red-lipped mouth and unpleasant, small eyes. Linda knew little of him; it sufficed her that Alan called the man, frankly, a quack, and actively resented the way Zeller promised so much to the ignorant hill people—for a price, paid

24

in advance—and so often let them die, or, when their money gave out, would turn them over, hopeless cases, to Alan and his hospital.

Soft-spoken Alan fulminated against this man and his assertion, widely advertised, that he could cure anything by his complicated electrical appliances. He must, he qualified, get the patient in time, and be allowed to serve without interference. These conditions satisfied, he could, he declared, cure cancer and spinal curvature, tuberculosis and impotency. Single-handed, he conducted what he called a clinic in a suite of rooms above the drug-store.

But Linda need not worry over where she would seat *that* doctor! She placed her own card between Dr. Ernst's and Dr. Bowman's—and tilted her head at the sound of a scuffle out in the hall.

With one last glance around the table, she went swiftly across the room, through its door. The wide hall was shadowy in the misty light of a cloudy afternoon, and pressed back against the wide, walnut door, stood the twins. "Those danged twins," Jasper called them. They were nine—James and Ann—with straw-coloured hair, Ann's a bit the longer. Apple-cheeks, bright red this afternoon, and grey eyes, wide and dark now, their faces solemn. They were obviously in trouble of some sort, and had come to Linda for help.

She dearly loved the twins. They had been born during her first year of marriage, at the time when she was expecting her own child—and she had delighted in the babies. With the years, her love had turned a bit wishful, but she had never grudged Margaret the joy of having the children. Margaret had so needed them to help her get over Si's being killed—but why couldn't Linda, too, be blessed?

"What is it now?" she asked the children, snapping on a lamp as she approached them. Ann gulped, and Jim took his grubby hands away from his throat long enough for her to see the red "burn" under his chin.

"Oh, Jim!" cried Linda in sympathetic concern. "How did you do a thing like that?"

Without waiting for his answer, she was leading him up the stairs to her own room, and bathroom. Carefully she washed the abrasion with soapy warm water, and got the story, told in spurts, first by one twin, then the other.

Jim and Ann, it seemed, had taken Victor for a walk.

Victor was the mastiff, and big enough to outweigh both twins put on the scales together!

"Oh, but you *know* . . ." gasped Linda, reaching for the Merthiolate bottle. "Did he knock you down?"

In unison, they winced at the application of the medicine to Jim's injury.

"You look like your throat had been cut," said Linda, wanting them to giggle and so lessen the hurt. "What happened?" she continued inexorably. The children could come to their Aunt Linda for many things; she would be kind, and fair—and they knew they could not deceive her.

"Well . . ." said Ann, spreading out her short plaid skirt against the side of the tub where she had perched. "That old Victor saw a cat . . ."

"Boots," said her brother.

"And he took off up the bank. . . ."

"You were down at the river?"

"Well, just on the path. Not at the water. But you know how the bank goes up?"

"Yes. And, quite naturally, the dog chased the cat. . . ."

"Yes'm. And somehow the rope got around Jim's neck—and —and rubbed—and he fell down——"

"It hurt!" wailed the little boy.

He could have been strangled! Linda's breath caught. "How'd you get free?" she asked.

"The rope came untied."

"And Victor is loose."

"He won't run away, Aunt Linda."

"I hope not." She tilted her head to see if the Merthiolate was dry. It was. "Come out to the fire," she said then, leading the way into the bedroom. Ann's eyes went to the candy-jar, but not hopefully. This was no time for rewards.

Linda sat down in the low pink chair. The children stood side by side at the foot of the four-poster. Jim's face was the cleaner, because of Linda's first-aid measures. "You know that you should not have taken Victor for a walk," she reminded the twins.

They both nodded. "You won't tell on Jim?" anxiously asked Ann.

"I won't tell on either of you. For one thing, you'll have to tell yourself, won't you? Won't your mother want to know what happened to Jim's neck?"

"I guess so," the children agreed. "We probably won't get out of being punished, either."

Linda would have liked to reassure them, but their sin was grave. "Victor," she said quietly, "is not a pet. He is a working dog. You know that. You've had it explained to you, that he is a guard—a policeman—for the stables at night. In the daytime, he is supposed to rest in his yard. You know better than to open the gate, don't you?"

"He isn't cross, Aunt Linda——"

"He isn't cross to you because he knows that you belong to the Green. But he isn't a playmate for you, Jim. Ann. You knew that you were disobeying, didn't you?"

"Yes'm. But other kids have dogs——"

"And maybe you could have one. Have you asked for one?"

"We had one—Tippy, remember? But it got distemper, Uncle Alan said, and——"

"I know. That was too bad. But maybe if you got a dog from the kennels, not a stray dog, and took care of him——"

Ann moved towards her aunt. "Will you ask her, Linda?" she demanded, forgetting her manners in her urgency. "Will you ask Mums?"

Linda smiled, nodded, and got to her feet. "I'll ask her," she promised. "Now, how's the neck, Jim?"

"It doesn't hurt so much."

Linda got her hooded raincoat from the closet, and with it over her arm, she led the way downstairs again. This being no day to invade the kitchen, she led the children to the small morning-room, and produced a bowl of black walnuts, a hammer and picks; she established them on small hassocks before the fire, with an old flat-iron between Jim's knees. They were to take turns, cracking and picking out—she'd go and tell someone that Victor was loose.

Her pointed face framed in red curls under the hood of her green coat, Linda went out the rear door and across the veranda, a little smile on her lips. She liked a misty day, perversely, because she was not a gloomy person. But on such a day, the shadows were delicately etched beneath the orchard trees, the bare branches gleamed in the pearly light, the brown river bubbled under the rain and the weather vane on the stable

27

turret glowed silver against the grey sky. She would go first to Victor's yard; he might already have been found and returned to captivity—but she saw that the gate swung open, and she had gone almost past his yard when, within the arched cavern of his house, she saw the red gleam of the dog's eyes, and the lift of his wrinkled muzzle. Identifying her, the tawny head dropped again to his enormous paws.

Linda closed and latched the gate. The dog had more sense than anyone. This was a day to stay snugly indoors! She laughed to think how often animals did have the better judgment—and turned reluctantly back towards the house, feeling that she'd been cheated of her half-hour of freedom. She glanced at her watch; she still had the half-hour—so she'd walk.

She'd go to see Margaret. She'd promised the children to ask their mother if they could have a dog—she could do that now, and have her breather, too.

Margaret lived in what had once been the milk house of the big farm. The Green still kept a cow, but a dairy establishment of any size was no longer needed. The small stone house had been made into a charming cottage for Margaret and her children.

It had every convenience; there was nothing of the fragile doll's-house about the dwelling. A storm entrance had been added, a kitchen and a bath. But the wide arched doors of the dairy were preserved, and the original beams. Margaret had furnished the place attractively, and kept it immaculate.

Linda was exceedingly fond of Alan's sister, and they had been friends from the first. Six years older than Linda, Margaret was a small, slender woman, dark, and with an appealing, childish eagerness that concealed her many abilities. She admired Linda greatly, and tried to dress like her in well-cut suits, dainty blouses; she endeavoured to pile her heavy black hair upon the top of her head, and grieved that its shining loops did not look more like Linda's feathery red curls.

Margaret's little cottage faced the river, and on that side was two stories high, with the three small bedrooms and the bath on the lower level. But coming upon it from the main drive-way, turning into the old brick path, one walked directly towards the wide windows of the living-room. The vestibule, set with two comfortable benches, served as an extension of the living-room. Pre-occupied with many thoughts, Linda was within this entry, almost through the arched doorway of the main room, when she stopped abruptly—not to spy, nor to listen—but too surprised and startled to do anything but stop still.

Margaret was seated in the chintz-covered arm-chair beside the leaping fire. Behind her, bending over her, embracing her—his face down in the hollow of her cheek and throat, his arm about her shoulders—was a man. An Army officer, in uniform.

Linda knew him. He was Captain Blake, stationed at the Fort, twenty-five miles from the Green. Alan had wanted him invited to the dinner party to-night—he liked Captain Blake. . . .

Margaret sat, dreamy-eyed, gazing into the fire. The man lifted his head, murmured softly into her ear, his hand holding one of hers. Neither of them saw Linda. After the shortest of frozen seconds, she drew one foot back, and the other—carefully she opened the door, slipped through it and was outside again.

They had not seen her. But she—she had seen and heard enough for excitement to beat its wings hard within her throat. There had been an intimacy between those two, urgency on the man's part, sweet submission on the woman's.

At the crest of the hill, Linda cast a troubled glance back at the little house. "Oh, dear!" she breathed.

Those two were deeply in love. As brief as her glimpse of them had been, it was enough to tell her that much. They were in love, and hopelessly.

For Captain Blake was married. Stationed at the Fort, he had rented a little frame cottage down in Valhalla. There he had established a nurse-housekeeper, and his invalid wife. Various stories were told about Mrs. Blake's condition. Few in town had seen her. She'd been very ill, or had had an accident which had affected her mind. A clouded mind, said some. Frenzied, and in need of restraint, said others. It didn't matter. . . .

What did matter was that Captain Blake had a wife, and one whom he could scarcely divorce. Unless the woman's death should free him, he would not be able to marry Margaret, however much they were in love!

Slowly, Linda walked along the glistening brown gravel of the drive. She gazed down the hill at the dark satin waters of the river, and glanced up into the arching branches of the trees;

29

she watched a flock of ducks drop chattering from the sky—
they'd spend the night in the cat's-tail beds downstream. She
flicked one glance back at the little cottage, then looked hard
at the wide lawn splashed with the red of barberry bushes.

And wherever she looked she felt the pain which was due
Margaret if she loved Fred Blake. "Oh, dear," said Linda again.
"Oh, *dear!*"

She let herself into the house, checked on the children and
suggested that they should be going home soon.

They were on their stomachs, looking at the coloured plates
in the *Britannica*, and absent-mindedly they agreed that they
would leave "soon."

She went to the dining-room and then to the kitchen, and
asked Jacob hopefully if there'd been any word from the
Doctor. There had not been.

Out in the hall, she smiled to hear sounds that indicated a
stirring throughout the house of the old folk rising from their
afternoon naps.

"Miss Linda?" It was Clew, at the door of Seretha's room.

Linda shrugged out of her coat. "Yes, Clew?"

"Ma'am askin' for you."

"I'll come."

Seretha's maid took Linda's raincoat. Both women knew
what Ma'am was up to. She held the reins of family control
capably in her hands, and tightened each leather as she considered it necessary or wise. "It's her ha'r," said the Negress.
"Seems I can't please her."

Linda shot her a blue-eyed smile, crossed the hall to the
closed door, rapped briefly upon it and turned the silver knob.

Linda had seen her mother-in-law at lunch, and in the morning when she'd taken flowers to the room, yellow button
chrysanthemums for the candle-stand, and pink rosebuds for
the piecrust table beside the wing-chair. But now she greeted
the old lady as if this were the first encounter of the day, and
asked how she was.

Ma'am was seated before her dressing-table, tall, slender,
and erect, wearing a long, dark red flannel robe. Her white
hair hung in a loose cape to her waist. She looked at Linda in
the mirror, and did not turn. Ma'am had an alert mind, a crisp
voice, a firm will, and she was greatly respected—but she was

not a woman one could imagine loved with any warmth or passion.

"You're badly blown, Linda," she said now, bluntly.

Linda brushed the back of her hand over her tumbled curls. "I know," she agreed. "I had an errand outdoors, and the hood of my raincoat played hob with my hair."

"Indeed!"

"Clew said you wanted me, Ma'am?"

Seretha indicated the hair-brush. "She's all thumbs to-day. I thought if you—my arm is bothering me." Mrs. Thornton suffered somewhat with arthritis. It was an ailment which often served her purposes.

"Yes, of course." Linda moved closer, took the brush, and then the comb. She smoothed the long, fine, straight hair, as white as goose feathers, and as unmanageable. Linda had had practice in twisting the stuff into the complicated knot which Seretha wanted, and fastening it tightly with an array of tortoise-shell pins.

Mrs. Thornton rewarded her with a wintry smile, and asked if she would help with her dress. Clew, she said again, was so clumsy. The black woman had come back into the room. Her face inscrutable, she helped Linda bring out several of Ma'am's gowns, and spread them out for her to make a selection. None of the dresses was new; Seretha was the kind to keep exact mental files of anything she owned, down to the last button—but she demanded this sort of service, and she got it.

Now she carefully surveyed her gowns, the purple velvet, the black crêpe, the grey lace. "What will you wear, Linda?" she asked.

Linda looked surprised. "My blue."

"With the jacket!" declared Seretha.

The "blue"—palest, silvery blue—was of satin. It was an expensive model which Alan had insisted on Linda's buying when they'd attended the last convocation, and indeed there was a jacket to it, as well as the bustle-sash of vivid green velvet.

"An off-the-shoulder frock looks very naked above a dinner table," said Seretha in the tone which settled all things here in the family. Linda said nothing. She could wear another frock.

Seretha moved to the wing-chair, and leaned back, showing no intent to select her gown, or put one on. "I suppose you've checked on Ruby and Jacob?"

31

"Everything is fine," Linda assured her.

"I thought I smelled turkey."

"Guinea," said Linda. "So close to Thanksgiving, I decided on guinea. The table looks very nice. I am using the red and white china, and I put white gladiolas into the ruby vases."

"Gladioli," corrected Seretha. "I have a gift for you, Linda. I remember that it is your tenth wedding anniversary." Her white hand took a small, rubbed velvet case from the table, snapped it open, and extended it towards her daughter-in-law. It contained a short necklace of carved gold beads.

Linda looked up in pleased surprise. "Why, it's *beautiful*! I've never seen it before."

Seretha glanced at the small worn leather chest which stood at the foot of the four-poster; Linda had never seen its contents. "I have many treasures," said the old lady. "Some—my China shawl—this chain—came to me through the Massachusetts branch of our family. They had shipping interests, you know. My valuable jewellery will, of course, go to Margaret and then to Ann—though if you had had a daughter——"

Linda bit her lip, and caught back her impulse to say, "I'm sorry." She *was* sorry, but——Without ever openly defying Seretha, from the first she had set up certain barriers against the woman's tyrannical rule of her family. That rule should not, and would not, engulf Linda!

Now she busied herself with the examination of each bead. No two were alike. "I hope Alan won't be late for his own dinner party," she murmured. "You knew that he'd been called to Kennerly?"

"You told us at lunch. Did you send flowers to Miss Little Mae?"

"Yes. Alan said they would probably operate—he called it pinning her hip."

"She'll be a cripple. I dread such a fall."

"Alan seemed quite hopeful. He said that Dr. Ernst was very skilled."

"Does he like that new doctor, Linda?"

Linda smiled. "I don't know about liking, Ma'am. He hasn't said much about him in any respect. I am sure Alan hopes that he'll be a good doctor."

"He's coming to-night?"

"Oh, yes. I put him at your left, so you'll have a chance to find out if *you* like him."

Seretha's eyes snapped. "I'll wear the mauve," she threw at Clew. "But I won't put it on until later. You might see if you could help in the kitchen." She turned to Linda. "Who is my other partner?"

"Also young and handsome. I put Captain Blake there."

"Why did you ask him?"

"Alan suggested it."

"Oh," said Seretha. "Is he so young?"

"About forty, I think. He came to see Alan about his being available should the Fort hospital need him. Alan likes him very much."

"Will your table balance?"

"Oh, no. Seven men, five women. Dr. Bowman is a bachelor, and Captain Blake's wife is an invalid."

"Seems a bit odd to invite a gentleman without his wife."

"Alan seemed to think the Captain should go out socially."

"And so he should. If he remembers that he has a wife ill at home. But—I understand that he doesn't always remember. Nor, I'm afraid, does my daughter."

Startled, Linda jerked so that the little purple case slipped from her lap. She bent over to retrieve it, reflecting ruefully that she might have been prepared. Seretha had a way of knowing everything, almost before those things took place.

She straightened, and stood up, murmuring something about its getting late. . . .

Her mother-in-law was not finished. "Margaret," she declared in her thin, icy voice, "has always been a fool. She doesn't gain wisdom with years, either. I am glad to hear that *she* did not ask you to invite Captain Blake. But in any case, I am afraid she may bring scandal upon us, with her open infatuation for the man. She's entirely without shame."

Linda looked down at the old gentlewoman in the grey and white toile chair. "If she loves him," she asked curiously, "don't you feel sorry for her?"

Seretha's white head tossed in disdain. "I feel sorry for the family! Why, Margaret has absolutely no *finesse*, Linda. She couldn't handle an *affaire*!"

In shocked revulsion, Linda turned away.

"What Ma'am wishes to tell you, Lindy," boomed Jasper's

big voice from the opened door into his dressing-room, "if she would but speak the truth without fiddle or farce, is that adultery is only a sin when publicly discovered."

Ma'am sniffed, and Linda, still shocked yet somehow amused, too, by Jasper's frankness, went swiftly over to the old man, both to hide her smile and to fix his tie.

"Your beard," she chattered gaily, "makes this a complete waste of my talents, and squanders your haberdashery as well."

He patted her arm. "Thank you, Lindy," he said warmly. "We may not say it often, but we all depend on you."

She flashed him a smile, said something about needing to dress and was up in her bedroom before she remembered that she had left the gold beads behind. Well, she could get them later; she wouldn't wear them to-night. Though what she *would* wear was now a matter for immediate decision.

The ice-blue satin was out. She did not want to appear in it without the jacket; she had never openly defied Ma'am, and this did not seem a point important enough to justify defiance now. Yet she would not be told.

She selected a flower-splashed taffeta skirt, and a black sweater-blouse, sloping off her shoulders, the sleeves tight to her wrists. She looped several strings of fake pearls around her throat, and twisted a long strand into many rows upon her left forearm. A rose-red length of satin made a cummerbund about her waist. Ma'am would say, again, that a redhead should never wear the colour.

Completely dressed, she laid out Alan's things. She hoped he would come home in time to bathe and change, to get that much rest! At the head of the stairs she met Clew. "I was comin' to help you," the old Negress panted. "Ma'am said . . ."

"Am I late?" Linda knew that she was not. It still was twenty minutes before the set hour.

"No'm," said Clew. "But she said . . ."

Linda nodded. "I know. I'm going right down."

"Yes'm." The maid went along the hall to the back stairs. So Ma'am had publicly sent her up to "help Miss Linda." It was one of Ma'am's many little disciplinary measures.

"Hey, *Linda!*" she rebuked herself and, head up, her eyes glowing, she swept on down the stairs and greeted those of the family who already were assembled under the crystal chandelier of the "big" parlour. Ma'am and Jasper—Margaret cameo-pretty in blue-green, and the twins, scrubbed and brushed within an inch of their young lives, as uncomfortable as they looked, seated primly side by side upon the brocade love-seat.

Before she could more than greet each one, Uncle Arthur and Aunt Flora came in. Uncle Arthur looked more spidery than ever in his high collar and old-fashioned tails, and Aunt Flora was "wearing everything she could lay hands to," Jasper chuckled to Linda, "includin' the crew's washin' and the cook's mop."

"Hush!" she rebuked him.

"Why should I hush?" asked the old man, his green eyes twinkling. "I feel a talkative evenin' comin' on me, Lindy."

"Heaven help us!" she breathed, then turned to say something about Aunt Flora's pretty dress. The old lady's hair had been freshly curled.

"Look like you slept on a flutin' iron," shouted Jasper.

Linda choked down her laughter and regarded her father-in-law with new respect. How had he lived beside Ma'am for more than forty years, and still maintained his manner of irrepressible mischief? That alone made Jasper Thornton a big man!

The guests began to arrive, and now Alan's voice was heard out in the hall. "Hold it ten minutes . . . can be down . . ." Linda smiled, and would have gone to him, but Uncle Arthur stepped between her and the wide doorway. "I'll go and help the boy," he offered.

There was really nothing Linda could have done, for Alan's clothes were laid out and ready. And she had her duties downstairs—but she would so much have liked a minute with Alan. . . .

All Uncle Arthur did for Alan was to get in the way, but Alan put up with the old man's fumbling, talked to him with interest while he showered and shaved and began to dress. "Raining hard," he called, "had to watch the hills. Linda mad?"

"Linda never gets angry," Uncle Arthur informed Linda's husband.

"Don't count on that," chuckled Alan. "Red hair, y'know." He waited for the old man to step out of the doorway.

"You go by the hospital on your way home?" asked Uncle Arthur, watching Alan tilt his head to knot his tie and complete the bow.

"Oh, no. Why?"

"I—I——"

Alan turned to look at him sharply. "You have something on your mind," he accused. "Might as well get it said. We haven't much time." He reached for his trousers.

"I—I wanted to inquire about Mrs. Liddell," said Uncle Arthur primly.

"Miss Little Mae? I imagine she's all right. Ernst is coming to-night. He'll tell you."

"Oh, please don't mention—I mean, Flora—well, it wouldn't do to bring up the subject, Alan." Uncle Arthur's porcelain cheeks were pink, his hands trembling against his black coat.

Alan laughed. "Is your interest in the lady catching up with you?" he teased.

"Her accident has somewhat complicated things," Arthur Merritt replied with dignity. "A very estimable lady, of course," he added, his voice breaking and quavering.

"At least estimable."

"I was ready to terminate the affair—but it's always difficult, you know. I mean, when a lady has been enjoying a man's attention and favour——"

"Yeah," agreed Alan gravely. "It's a delicate move. I always think the best way is to be kind. Not interested any more, or generous—but just kind. It gets the ladies, Uncle Arthur. Gets 'em every time—kindness. You try that."

Uncle Arthur's faded eyes stared at his nephew.

Alan started for the door, winding his watch.

"Wait a minute!"

"Can't. We're late as it is."

"Yes, but I want to find out how a boy like you knows so much! Have you had enough *experience* . . . ?" He sounded and looked startled, and somewhat outraged. *Affaires,* evidently, were not for "boys."

Alan chuckled, and pushed the old man through the door ahead of him. "I don't need the experience you have in mind," he said. "But a doctor, Uncle, looks on at a lot of life, and gets a lot of experience second-hand." They started down the wide stairs. "A good thing, too, because I don't have the time, really, for personal investigation."

Among the groups gathered that night in the silver and white parlour, Rupert Ernst was the lion. His personal success was instant and great. A very attractive man in a dark smooth way,

36

he had charming old-world manners. On his arrival, he had stood for a minute surveying the room, then he had gone swiftly across to Seretha.

"Madame Thornton," he said, "Dr. Rupert Ernst, at your service!" He bowed, took Ma'am's extended hand, and lifted it to his lips.

Seretha's white head tossed in triumph, her cheeks turned pink. She made a place for the new doctor at her side, undertook his introduction to the other guests and to her family.

Linda was standing before an old mirror hung between two brocade-draped windows. In the glass could be seen the back of her head, the little red curls against the white nape of her neck, the sweet curve of her shoulder.

Dr. Ernst looked first at the reflection, and then at Linda's glowing face. Whenever Seretha distracted his attention for a minute, his gaze always returned to Linda's beauty. Seretha saw this, and her face was cold when he finally excused himself so that he might "speak to the *honorée* of the evening." Swiftly he made his way to Linda's side; bowed and smiled at her, his eyes intent.

They stood in conversation, and something in the man's manner, or hers, made each one of the family look anew at Linda. Within any family, the fact of actual physical beauty becomes obscured, and goes unnoticed. But to-night, first one and then another *saw* that her hair was a halo of brightness about her vivid face, that her eyes were the colour of pansies, and that her smile was pretty and gay.

They saw those things because this strange doctor saw them, with eyes accustomed to beauty as the world rated it.

"I'd say the new man was smitten," declared Aunt Flora, fluttering with vicarious excitement.

"Why not?" demanded Captain Blake.

"She's just as lovely as she looks!" declared Margaret.

"I hope Alan doesn't resent his attentions," twittered Aunt Flora.

"A man," declared Margaret, "should be flattered to have his wife so admired."

"Poor Linda is quite flustered," said Aunt Flora enviously.

Linda *was* somewhat flustered; she acknowledged to herself that it was definitely exciting to have drawn the marked attention of this man whose every word, and every glance, was flattering. At last someone was noticing her as an individual apart from the family! Dr. Ernst was the sort to stand close to a woman, to hold her gaze with his own intentness, to speak low, and intimately. He smiled seldom. His admiration was a serious thing!

Thus absorbed, Linda failed to see Alan when he entered the room. Everyone noticed that, too, and looked curiously at Alan to see how he would take such unusual neglect.

He took it by standing for a minute to look at the pair. They were still before the mirror and so he had a three dimensional picture of them, of Linda's glowing face lifted to Rupert's downbent one.

Alan's eyes were thoughtful as he moved across the room to greet his mother, and then turned to speak to the guests, stopping, finally, before his young intern who was leaving on Monday for Army duty. He grasped the doctor's hand warmly, and said to those in the vicinity, "To-night, this is one man I envy! I wish that I could put on the uniform waiting for him, and serve my country as he will do!"

"And I know that's not merely a speech," said Russell Bowman warmly.

"You're needed here, Alan," protested Aunt Flora. "You'll do your service here."

"Yes, I shall," he agreed. "Perhaps what I really want is a little glory and pomp. Valhalla doesn't seem too well equipped with those things."

Everyone laughed, and Alan went on to the pair before the mirror. Linda reached her hand to him, and he said a word or two about the case at Kennerly, but his voice was constrained, and his manner brusque. Linda was relieved to see Jacob going across to Seretha.

"Dinner is served," she said softly, and put her white hand upon Dr. Ernst's proffered arm; Alan turned away abruptly. "He's tired," she murmured in apology for her husband.

"But, of course. To drive so far, to do such a difficult work— to return—— It is too much to do, too much to ask."

There was the usual well-bred confusion of a large group moving across the hall to the dining-room, of being seated. Mention was made of the anniversary, and Jasper seized upon the occasion to demand that Alan carve. "Long as we have a Mayo to cut up the birds . . ." he explained, and there was *that*

38

confusion of a place being made before Alan for the silver platter with its row of glistening brown guineas in their nests of crisp watercress garnished with orange slices.

Linda watched this, wishing that the two men had simply changed places. They were wrecking her pretty table! But she also kept an eye on Dr. Ernst. He had made a strong claim upon her interest, and in any case she was curious about the effect which this truly American family and home might have upon a European of cultured taste and discrimination.

He sat quietly in his chair, one hand upon his thigh, the other on the table edge. His bright, watchful eyes circled the table, lingering upon each of the family members, in much the same manner as he thoughtfully, critically, tasted his wine, savouring the bouquet of it, the flavour.

As the plates were served and brought around, Linda saw his finger stroke the smooth white silver of his fork handle, weighing the knife in his hand before he used it.

The thought struck her that this man was considering the people assembled in the same fashion, looking them over for outward appearance, trying thus to determine each one's importance, to assay the pure metal of their characters as against the alloy of their failings. It was a detached and somewhat calculating attitude.

Well, she excused this, perhaps Alan would need to do the same thing if he were set down in a strange land, among strange people; he'd need to be cautious in all ways lest he make mistakes and blunders against customs and standards unfamiliar to him.

The twins had been seated at a small table in the corner of the room, and now they stirred up a small quarrel as their plates were set before them; Ann's serving, claimed Jim, was bigger.

"Oh, it is not!" said Ann pleasantly. "It's just smeared around more."

"Is there a surveyor in the house?" asked Alan seriously. "Or do we have an apothecary's scale? We can't have one grain more —or less—food on the plate of a starving child."

The children collapsed into a state of giggles, and Alan's grin was fully as happy. Linda sighed. He did so love children, and was so adept with them; she felt again upon her heart the weight of her childlessness. Alan had been cheated—by her.

Seretha sat between Captain Blake and Dr. Ernst. Having

talked for the first minute to the Army man, she turned now and directed her full attention to Dr. Ernst. "How long have you been in America?"

"Two years. I was in Italy for a time."

"But you still miss Austria, I am sure. It is so beautiful. At times we must seem young and crude to you."

Dr. Ernst touched his napkin to his lips. "Austria is beautiful," he agreed, "or was. But even Vienna—I would never want to return."

"You don't get homesick?"

"No—I do not."

"Then you must like it here!" said Captain Blake.

"It isn't that so much," said Ernst. He spoke English fluently, and with only a faint accent. "It is more as if a door had been closed behind me. I must consider only what lies on this side of that door. It would be folly to regret what is past. Just as it would be folly to seek to return, ever, and expect to find things as they were before the *Anschluss*. I believe I would do better to seek to change what Madame Thornton calls young and crude in this country."

Jasper's great head was up and back. "What things would those be, sir?" he trumpeted.

Dr. Ernst sent him one of his most charming smiles; it failed to dim the glitter in Jasper's green eyes. Linda glanced across at Alan who was smiling a little. He shook his head at her. *Let them alone*, the gesture said.

She turned her attention to Dr. Ernst's delineation of the things which he felt needed to be changed in this new world so that they would more nearly approach the glories of the old.

Largely they were cultural things, tastes and customs, ways of pleasure. American taste, he said, was naturally naïve, un-tutored. This could be traced, he thought, to the fact that America had no caste system. Oh, some people made a small claim to aristocracy based upon participation in a revolutionary war not yet two hundred years old. But nothing—absolutely *nothing*—indicated the existence in his new homeland of anything like an intellectual class.

"To which," said old Jasper coldly, "I presume you belonged, back home?"

Linda shivered. But Dr. Ernst seemed unaware of what he faced. To him, the bearded man raised horses and apples, owned a fine home and set a good table. He talked in the vernacular, his education probably had been rudimentary. Even had Dartmouth been mentioned to Dr. Ernst, he still would have thought little of that education.

Dr. Ernst smiled indulgently upon his host, twirled the stem of his heavy-cut wine-glass and admitted that he had indeed been a member of what was known as the intelligentsia. "And for that association," he cried, "I *am* homesick!" Seretha smiled compassionately upon him.

"It was that class," thundered Jasper, "your precious intelligentsia—which plunged Europe into the chaos which it knows to-day! You won't deny that, will you?"

"Some of us were at fault, perhaps," said Dr. Ernst pleasantly. "Not all. I won't argue the point. As I told Mrs. Thornton, I have been in America for two years—quite long enough to learn that it is futile to expect here understanding of me as a representative of European culture and standards. The very fact that your medical set-up demands *my* serving an apprenticeship, ignoring entirely my educational background and all my experience, must demonstrate a disrespect and a lack of understanding which I would really have preferred not to mention."

"You would, eh?" growled Jasper. Of course, now the whole table was listening to the interchange, the men eagerly, some of the women blushing for the old man. "How about *your* understanding of us?" he was demanding.

"Does it take understanding to interpret a country where a man is respected only if he can make money, where a woman is a social success if she can marry a European title?" He spoke contemptuously. "And a doctor like me, who has, after all, something to offer——" His hands flew out expressively, his eyebrows lifted, and his shoulders.

"You Europeans," said Jasper bluntly, "are glad enough to seek haven in our wilderness."

"True enough," Dr. Ernst countered suavely. "Yet it is also true that *you* should be glad to have us come."

Linda, and others at the table, listened unhappily. She was embarrassed for Jasper whom she loved, and anxious for the new-comer who did not understand his audience or his adversary. A truly sophisticated person, she thought, could argue

41

without personalities or offence, with another sophisticate. But not here. Oh, dear, not here! Not with Jasper Thornton!

"And instead of bein' glad," Jasper growled, "we don't even appreciate you."

"No," laughed Dr. Ernst. "I fear that you do not. Otherwise . . ."

"We would not only give you succour, we would grant you the high position which you feel you deserve!" Jasper snorted. "You overwhelm me, Doctor. You really do. Because you seem unwilling to understand that in a democracy any position must be earned."

A little smile flickered across Dr. Ernst's smoothly handsome face.

"That word amuses you?" asked Alan quietly. "*Democracy?*"

"Oh, no. It's just that, while I hear it constantly, I never can get it defined."

"Ha!" cried Jasper. "Easiest thing in the world. A democracy is a society based upon the right to think."

"*Everyone's* right?"

"Why not?"

"Because thinking leads many people only to confusion, and since it is not possible, in a practical sense, to transfer most people's thoughts into action, the right becomes simply a superstition."

Even Linda turned to look curiously at the handsome man.

"You've been badly taught," declared Jasper, disgust plain in his voice. "I can only hope you'll work out here. There seems to be an awful gap between you and my son. By way of kindly warnin', I urge you, sir, not to call him a country doctor, and rest upon that connotation."

"Father . . ." protested Alan.

"I know it's none of my business," agreed the patriarch, "but I feel inclined to point out to Dr. Ernst that you're summoned to do surgery for a hundred miles around the little town where you were born, and work. I take a bit of anticipatory pleasure in considering the way you'll work with this man who speaks so loftily about your training and your background."

"The truth is," Alan said, "I myself would like to have had his work in the clinics of Europe—or his university background."

42

"You'd still be a man who uses his brain, who is always thinkin' and studyin' and ponderin' over how to make *use* of the knowledge you do have. While he is the typical culture-veneered European, content in knowin' what is in the books, and demandin' respect, if not pre-eminence, because of the number of those books."

Dr. Ernst may have been offended; he did not betray it. "Our standards are different," he conceded.

"You said you hoped to change our ways," Alan reminded him, without rancour, "while I feel sure that your experience here will have an effect upon you."

That was the end of the argument. A toast was proposed, and drunk, to the celebrating couple. Dessert was brought in, and Seretha—noting with relief that conversation was now properly distributed in small groups around the table and that Jasper was safely regaling young Dr. Bowman with the way he had secured horses for the Spanish-American War—Seretha asked Dr. Ernst to tell about Vienna, and his escape.

Linda found herself listening attentively; the story was dramatic, and well told. "Did you leave any of your family behind?" she asked.

"No. Well—my parents, of course."

"What happened to them?"

"I don't know."

She was sorry that she had mentioned his family. She looked across to Alan for rescue; he sat frowning in a preoccupied manner, but he looked up alertly when Jacob came to his side, and leaned over, murmuring.

With a glance at his mother, Alan strode out of the room, and Seretha decided that the meal was over; coffee and brandy would be served in the parlours. Alan rejoined them while they were moving through the hall. No, Linda heard him tell Ma'am, it had not been a "call."

"It was Cliff Summers asking me if I meant to run again for the School Board. Seems my term expires."

"What'd you tell him?" asked Dr. Cassidy.

"I said I supposed I'd have to. If only to keep Miss Maggie's job for her."

Dr. Cassidy laughed. "Everybody but you thinks she's getting old."

43

"She is getting old. But she still is an inspiring teacher, and I think the town would suffer a great loss if she were retired against her own will. I went to school to her, and I've a pretty good notion that Miss Maggie will be the first one to know when the job she does is no longer good."

"You don't have time for all these outside things you're taking on, Alan," said Cassidy, mildly.

"The School Board won't be the first thing I'll give up, however. I like that chance to keep in touch with the children."

The children. There it was again, thought Linda. His need and his longing. A wave of sadness swept over her as she watched Alan at the front door, telling the twins good night; they were going home to bed. The tall dark man and the two blond children made a pretty picture of affectionate understanding. Alan's finger tipped Jim's chin up to his scrutiny. Evidently the injury was being explained; his dark face mingled laughter with reproof.

Linda sighed again, and moved on beside Dr. Ernst. "I don't know," she said, laughing, "if I could make you comprehend our Miss Maggie."

"I would try to understand."

"Our Public School system . . ."

"I already understand that." His black eyes never left her face. She again felt bubbles of flattered excitement float upwards through her veins. "Well, that's a help!" she said gaily. "As for Miss Maggie, she is the principal of our elementary school; she also teaches the eighth grade, which is important because it is the last step before the children go on to high school. She is a conscientious teacher, and a fine disciplinarian. Alan thinks her sort is rare and valuable; as he says, he feels a great responsibility for the town's children."

"Perhaps he does assume too much."

"Perhaps he does. Especially since the war began. This last year, in addition to the School Board, and his position as Lay Reader and Senior Warden of the church, he serves on the Selective Service Board, on the State Medical Procurement Board, on the County Health Board—— He used not to take on so much, and he hasn't the time now——"

"Does he neglect you?" She could feel the whirling pull of his interest, drawing her, almost hypnotically. In passing, she

44

touched the switch of the record-player, then accepted the chair which Dr. Ernst held for her.

The *Pathétique* was on the turn-table, and the music poured richly into the room. Linda sipped her coffee, looked down at the shimmer of colour on her skirt, sharply aware of her husband on one side, and of Rupert Ernst on the other.

She glanced at Alan; she had seen almost nothing of him on this wedding anniversary day. Their only talk together had been over the phone! He was sunk deep into the down cushion of the silver brocade chair, turning his brandy glass in his hand, his dark head back, and he was listening contentedly to the music. Watching him, Linda could see the lines of fatigue erase from his face. That was good!

He glanced across at her, and caught her expression. "I like that music," he said happily.

"Why do you like it?" demanded Rupert Ernst, contradiction imminent in his tone.

"I don't know," Alan admitted. "It just seems to talk about a man's inner feelings, his hopes and fears, his dreams. It isn't anything I could put into words."

But Rupert Ernst was not so inarticulate. He wafted his big bubble glass under his nose, sniffed appreciatively. "Your taste in brandy, Doctor," he declared, "is *much* better than your taste in music."

Alan smiled. "What's wrong with Tchaikovsky?" he asked lazily.

Dr. Ernst used every arty term to tell this group exactly what was wrong with Tchaikovsky. He was brilliant—and condescending. Gradually he attracted the attention of everyone in the room, except Aunt Flora, who nodded innocently in a far corner.

"One finds the accent of self-pity in all his music—the direct result, of course, of the fact that Tchaikovsky was homosexual. I trust I may speak of such things in a scientific fashion rather than on a sensual plane?" He did speak in a sensual fashion, however, and with obvious relish.

"Homosexuals, you know," he continued, "maintain an interest in normal sex, though of course it is wistful."

"Castrated horses," snorted old Jasper from his high-backed

45

chair, "maintain it, too. And old men." His eyes snapped angrily.

"Oh, dear!" cried Dr. Ernst, in dismay. "I didn't expect, sir, to have you bring the discussion down so close to earth!"

"I live close to the earth, *sir*."

Odd, thought Alan, sipping his brandy, *but Father seems the younger man in this; his clean, healthy realism against Ernst's almost senile quality of delight in his bit of pornography.*

"I forgot," Dr. Ernst was apologising, and with a snicker, "how easily shocked you Americans can be. As I told you at the table, my background is deeply that of the European intelligentsia. . . ."

Old Jasper snorted again, then got to his feet.

Alan calmly sipped his brandy, and watched Ernst, noting his manner more than the things the man said. Alan did not doubt that his father could hold his own.

The old man paced the rug before the fire, every hair of his beard a-bristle; his green eyes flashed sparks. "You make me ask you again, sir," he shouted, "if it was *not* the intelligentsia"—he spoke the word as if he forked manure—"who wrecked Europe?"

"It is a very grave charge, sir."

"I think I am correct in making it, however. Europe had become drugged, and helpless, in her preoccupation with what you call culture. To talk about books, to write unintelligible prose, and even more unintelligible poetry—to paint pictures that depicted nothin'—and to talk, talk, *talk* about them in a way that meant nothin'. To make a fetish of the abnormal, the amoral—and to make that fetish a substitute for honest, clean passion. Of course, your country became weak, and Europe became the easy prey for ideologists! But I wish you would not come over to this country and assume that we want to follow your example!"

"Are you sure that America does not want . . . ?"

"No, sir, I am not!" thundered the old man. "And I am worried sick about it! Our schools and our homes are faced with a tremendous job! Our young folk must be taught to *think*! Not just to study and to memorise! And to *quote*! That's why Alan here fights to keep on a teacher like Miss Maggie. Her pupils learn to think. That's a basic need in a proper education. It applies to everything from the ABC up to philosophy and ideology. My premise is a nation taught to *think* won't accept Fascism or Nazi-ism or Communism. A nation so taught develops democracy——"

"Where every man," said Dr. Ernst, "is like every other man."

"Oh, no!" countered Jasper. "But where each man, accordin' to his ability to *think*, may rise and attain high position. Where he is not automatically given that position by accident of his birth or class. And I am thinkin' of an intellectual caste-system more than an economic or governmental one. You, my dear sir, are marked by the *stigmata* of the class known in Germany, and probably in Austria, as the professor-folk. Am I right?"

"Except for calling it a stigma, you are correct, sir."

"And you're proud of it."

"Naturally."

Jasper's eyes flashed his anger around the room. "I'm a horse-breeder. I happen to be sure that reliance on blood is not enough, whatever you're breedin'. I know from experience, not book-teachin', that dependence on the fact that your father was a Herr Professor Doktor, and that my grandsire fit in the Revolution, won't guarantee a thing. You got to keep strengthenin' what may have been good blood once upon a time, if you want a good strain of people in a nation."

Linda's head was up. Old Jasper was fighting a good fight, but a losing one. He'd never show Rupert Ernst the difference between the blood-tradition of professor-folk and the strain of individual thought and service.

With a swirl of her bright skirt, she was on her feet, her hand extended to the new doctor. "Come," she said gaily, "let me show you the family portraits. Their honest American faces will help you to understand the ways and manners of your new home and friends."

Dr. Ernst rose willingly, went with her out into the hall. Alan resumed his chair, lifting a rueful eyebrow at old Jasper, who grinned back, unregenerate.

"Lindy thinks I was rude," he grumbled.

"You were rude," confirmed Seretha.

"How're you goin' to get along with that fella, Alan?" asked Dr. Cassidy. "He seems a slippery one to me."

"We'll get along," said Alan comfortably. "He knows medicine. And surgery. Of course he's only a fill-in, and I resent that. He'll work from case to case until his required year is up,

47

and then he'll leave." His cheeks knotted into a grim smile. "Hard telling whom we'll get next. I become a little hot in the neighbourhood of my collar when I'm forced to realise that make-shifts, the physically unfit, not to mention the incompetents, are considered good enough to attend to the job of civilian doctoring."

"I can't find you in that bunch," said Cassidy.

"Why do you suppose I didn't enlist?" demanded Alan hotly. "I'm not so shortsighted as the Government seems to be. I realise that civilians are going to be the backlog of the war effort—especially if that effort is prolonged. Their health is important. Why in the devil doesn't the Government see that and make a certain number of doctors stay in civilian work, either by force or by bribery? Let 'em be over-worked, but for Pete's sake, make them respected. Keep that number at a minimum, and let 'em earn their living in the usual way—but it certainly shouldn't be a *shameful* thing for a civilian doctor in good health to stay on the job!"

"Instead of that," said young Dr. Bowman, "Dr. Thornton makes me ashamed of going into service."

"You hadn't any choice," growled Alan. "Right age, no dependants. I'm on the draft board, too, remember."

This brought laughter and a break-up of the conversation into groups. Margaret and Captain Blake were together on the love-seat. Seretha chatted amiably with Mrs. Cassidy, but her cold eyes, her serene face, hid a troubled heart. The whole evening had gone badly; Linda had been on edge all day, Mr. Thornton's stable talk to the new doctor had been a jarring note—and the way Margaret had carried on all evening with that Army man, watching him at the table, sitting there now beside him on the small couch, as blissful and dewy-eyed as if she were sixteen! Surely everyone had noticed.

Alan had. Without thinking about cause and implications, he'd caught his sister's radiant look of happiness, and he spoke gratefully of it to Linda when she returned to the room with Dr. Ernst.

"When a man has an only sister," he explained to the Austrian, "he wants her to be happy. Margaret's had more roughness in her life than was her due. She was widowed tragically, some years ago, and now her older son—not yet twenty-one—is an Army flier. He's overseas, in Africa, we

48

think. That sort of thing is hard on a mother. If only for one evening Margaret can be released from her worry about Silas, I'm grateful to Fred Blake for amusing her."

Linda smiled and put her hand on Alan's sleeve. "Let's give Dr. Ernst a chance to entertain her," she suggested. "He's fascinating, too."

So that little group of five was formed. Captain Blake rose at their approach. During the general talk, Dr. Ernst actually did take the Captain's place. When Linda turned away to recall a name for Aunt Flora, Captain Blake was left standing beside Alan, and the doctor, knowing that the man's wife had been ill, asked about her health.

Captain Blake did not reply at once, and Alan looked up, to see the officer gazing across at Margaret, a troubled expression upon his face. "I"—he said then, his manner hesitant— "I've been meaning to talk to you about that, Thornton. Professionally—not at a party."

He was a nice chap, not actually handsome. Without his cap, he looked his full age, which must have been in the early forties. He was a Reserve officer, and had the trained soldier's erect bearing, and his tightly-contained manner.

"My wife, you know," he continued. Alan had said nothing, but his face was attentive, and receptive. "My wife is a chronic invalid. It's a nervous—or mental thing. Several years ago she was in an accident. Suffered a head injury—they knew at the time that there had been some brain tissue damage. I don't know the terms. . . ."

"I understand," said Alan.

"She seemed to recover, except that she had headaches, and sometimes seemed—well—a little vague. These times have increased. When I was called into service, I put her into a nursing home, but she wasn't happy. Cried. . . . Now, even if the hospital were built at the Fort, they couldn't take a chronic case like hers. She isn't actually sick. I asked the doctors at home; they said that it wouldn't help, or hurt, to bring her here."

"They think that there is no means of improvement?"

"Every doctor says a brain operation might be helpful, but also that it might be fatal."

"That's true of any brain surgery."

"I suppose. It's a hard decision."

Alan indicated an arm-chair, placed a side chair near it, and the men seated themselves, lit cigarettes. Music again was drifting through the room.

"I'll soon have to make some decision," said Blake slowly. "Or have it made for me. She's gradually—getting worse."

"Mentally?"

"Yes. I found a comfortable house here in town, and I have a practical nurse with her. Then, ten days ago, Fern caught cold. She was feverish, and she coughed a lot. I hesitated to bring in a Post doctor—gossip, you know, about a mental condition."

Alan nodded.

"Mrs. Yearsley, the nurse, mentioned a Dr. Zeller who has an office near us. I agreed, and the man came. He made Fern comfortable for that night, and came back the next day. I was at home then, and he discussed her case with me. He brought your name into the discussion."

"Oh?" said Alan. "How was that done?"

"He called Fern's condition a matter of nervous imbalance. He had charts—and he wanted to use some sort of machine on her. I—well, in arguing for his idea, he said—not too flatteringly, I'm afraid—that you probably would tell me that Fern could be cured. He said—his words were, 'Thornton fancies himself a brain surgeon.'" Alertly, the Captain looked across at Alan.

The doctor sat relaxed, his eyes crinkled into a smile. "I do," he agreed.

The Captain's distress only increased. "Zeller——" he said, uneasily. "He's not an M.D., is he?"

"No, he isn't."

"I—I'm sorry I ever called him."

"Did your wife get over her cold?"

"Oh, yes. But the thing is, Thornton, Zeller keeps coming to the house."

Alan's smile faded. "You can stop that."

"He says she needs attention."

"Possibly she does. But Zeller——" He coughed. And said no more.

"Look, Thornton." The Captain was impatient now. "What I'm getting at—I'd like *your* opinion on Fern, as to how much

50

and what should be done for her. Lately—I'm confused. So, would you take over the case, be interested in it?"

Alan stood up. "I am interested," he said. "But without seeing the patient, I could venture no kind of opinion."

Blake was on his feet. "We could go over to-night."

Alan looked at his watch. "It's a little late to disturb your wife."

"Time doesn't mean much to Fern."

"All right, then." He crossed the big parlour to where Linda was changing records on the player. Rupert and Margaret had come to help with the selection; old Jasper sat still in the wing-chair, refreshed by a brief nap, and now alert to what was being said behind him.

Alan mentioned the trip in prospect, apologising to Linda for leaving the party, then he asked Dr. Ernst if he cared to join them. And, after the social amenities of farewell, the three men left. Behind them Jasper was engaged upon a lengthy anecdote about Dr. Zeller.

It was still raining, and they used Captain Blake's car. The little bungalow showed lights, and when the Captain opened the front door and entered the living-room, Mrs. Yearsley, the nurse, rose from a chair near the radio. He explained the purpose of the visit. "Has my wife gone to bed?"

"I got her ready at nine, like I always do. She may be in bed...."

Their raincoats hung upon chair-backs, the men moved to the bedroom. Mrs. Yearsley followed, lifting her voice to call, "Fern, honey, you got company."

The doctors found their patient sitting in a small rocking-chair, her arms crossed at the wrists. She rocked rhythmically, and continued to rock after they entered. When Fred Blake touched her shoulder, she halted the movement of the chair, but did not look at him.

She was a slender woman, and probably once had been pretty. Fred said she was forty. Her brown hair was neatly combed, her hazel eyes stared fixedly before her, a little moisture bubbled at the corners of her mouth. Alan set a chair at her knee, and tried to attract her attention. She finally did look at him, in a dazed and troubled fashion. He asked questions of her husband, and the nurse. "Does her condition vary?"

"Yes. Sometimes she's brighter. Sometimes she cries. Mostly she just sits this way."

He made certain basic tests of her reflexes, and used his stethoscope. Then the three men withdrew to the front porch, the doctors putting on their raincoats. "A superficial examination like this tells very little," Alan explained. "We should have her at the hospital for a time."

"All right." Captain Blake looked worried, and grim.

Alan's hand fell upon his shoulder. "She needs something different from Yearsley and Zeller," he said kindly. "I know you rented this place furnished. My thought was, Fred, let's move her to the hospital for a time; you give up this place and go and live in Officers' Quarters. If we can help your wife, you can establish another home. If we can't—there are places, for her own protection, Fred."

The Captain struck his fist against a white post. "This sort of thing, Thornton—I'd rather be sick myself!"

"Good lord, yes!"

"There is nothing in my past experience—to help me decide things."

"Only what your life has built up in the way of judgment and integrity."

The Captain shot him a keen look. "What do you mean by that?"

"Why—just that your judgment would help you choose the people to give you expert advice, and that your integrity would determine your obligation to your wife."

There was a little silence in which rain dripped from the porch gutters, and the sound of Mrs. Yearsley's turned-on radio came too loudly through the closed door. Each man was thinking of Margaret as she had looked that evening.

"I would suggest that you check up on me and my hospital —our rating," Alan continued smoothly. "You'd feel better about any opinion I'd have after examining your wife. I think time is an element, but so is your peace of mind."

There was a little more talk and the doctors elected to walk as far as the hospital. It was about four blocks, and the rain had resolved into a mist.

"Poor devil," said Alan, as he and Ernst got on their way.

"Yes. I'd say complete idiocy, wouldn't you?"

"Oh—perhaps it's that bad."

"She knows nothing, feels nothing. Did you notice her hands? The collapsed thumb? She would be better off dead."

"But she is not dead," protested his superior.

"And of course euthanasia . . ."

"I do not practise it!" snapped Alan.

"Can you always avoid its consideration?"

"In a case like this, I find myself more curious to know if Mrs. Blake might be helped."

"You would operate then?"

"If there is any chance of survival and improvement—yes. Certainly."

"But, look, Doctor . . ." Still a block from the hospital they had paused before crossing the highway. "In this case, I think a doctor might be excused if he would not—what are the words?—if he would not *bother*. The husband seems—er—reconciled. Your sister is a lovely woman. And, as you explained to me, you like to see her happy."

"Yes," Alan agreed, "I did say that." Then he looked at his companion, at the fine profile beneath the brim of his smartly dipped black hat. "You know," he said, in the tone of discovery, "I would have said you were a doctor to give little consideration to circumstances surrounding a surgical case, while I would be the one to consider the whole picture. Yet, in this——"

Dr. Ernst shrugged. "I would only prefer to see a romantic picture over one of tragedy. It would perhaps be better for both of us to consider only the medical problem."

"That consideration alone will keep us busy," Alan assented. "Good night, Doctor—I'll go along home."

"Home" was at the far end of this same street, a broad avenue with tall trees at the hospital end of it. Alan walked along three blocks of business establishments, the bank, the post office, the Supermarket and Penney's. He passed the Episcopal Church, smothered in ivy, with tall trees again in evidence; another block of homes, and then he was at the gates of the Green. River fog swirled white about the lamps, Alan's own frosted breath rising as if he were propelled by steam.

The mistiness reminded him of his little-boyhood, when ice still had been cut from the pond, and stored in the old icehouse. Smiling, the tall dark man walked on up the avenue, his memory letting him fairly smell the old brick building, the

53

damp sawdust and wet straw, and see the darkly-gleaming ice buried there. He and young Jacob had often been set the task of getting the ice out. The two boys would go down to the spooky old house. They liked sliding down the chute better than going in through the door. The pack had to be removed, and the needed ice hacked out with a hatchet, which had a fiendish way of losing itself in the straw. Then the ragged blocks must be dragged to the door, tumbled into a wheel-barrow—"borra" in the vernacular—taken first to the cistern to be washed free of sawdust, straw and accumulated debris, then on the kitchen porch, and put into the chest there, with woe to the boy who upset, or even moved, a crock of cream.

Chuckling, Alan let himself into the big house. The party had disbanded. The main rooms were dark. Only the night lamp burned in the hall. Alan hung his damp coat and his mist-beaded hat in the closet, looked down regretfully at the stains upon his fine black shoes. He went over to the console and selected a heavy-headed rose from the vase there. With the flower in his hand, he went up the stairs, two at a time, his long limbs moving like pistons, and put both hand and shoulder against the white panel of the bedroom door.

Linda was seated before the fire, reading, but she rose at once and came towards him.

He gave her the rose, his eyes shining. "I always bring my wife flowers on our wedding anniversary," he told her. She laughed and returned his kiss.

Her hair was brushed loosely about her face, and she wore a quilted satin robe of the same purplish blue as her eyes. Alan held her away, and looked at her, loving his wife, and wishing, almost desperately, that he was not so damn' busy, that he did not, as to-day, spend two-thirds of his time away from her! He wished, too, that he was not so thick-tongued. If only he had some of Ernst's polish, and could summon a few of his glossy phrases! The best Alan Thornton could do was to draw his wife somewhat roughly into his embrace, rub his cheek into her hair and kiss her again.

With the image of Fern Blake still fresh in his memory, he held her close, murmuring something about life being short, and full of hazards; he sighed. "We have to make each day count," he said wistfully.

Linda winced. The whole day behind her had been spent in

realising that she'd been married for ten years, that she had no child. And now—if Alan meant that he too realised, and regretted—— She looked down at the rose which he had brought her, then up into his face. "Has something happened?" she asked.

He frowned. "My life is full of happenings," he reminded her. "But in another sense, nothing has happened. We've been married ten years, of course." He moved over to the upholstered chair, sat down and would have drawn her to his knee—she was a tiny thing.

But to his surprise and dismay, she drew free of his hand, and began to talk, hurriedly, tensely. "You're right!" she cried. "We have been married for ten years! And nothing has happened. It's been a waste for you, Alan. Your mother——" She gulped, her hands pressed to her hot cheeks.

Slowly, the tall man drew himself to his feet. He wanted only to make love to Linda, and, if they talked at all, to speak of Margaret and Fred Blake.

Linda stood upon the hearth-rug, confronting him, her face white with her intensity, her pansy eyes dark.

Seeing that her dimpled chin was inclined to quiver, he laughed deeply in his throat, and would have touched her, but she drew back. "Let me say this!" she begged.

"Why, yes," he said softly, "if it must be said."

"I think it must. It seems only honest, Alan. I realise as well as your mother and father that our marriage has been a waste in that I've not been able to give you a child. I don't need them to point out to me that you are the finest of the Thornton line, and should have a chance to bring fine sons and daughters into the world. Well, I'll give you that chance, Alan. I've decided that I should step out, and let you be free. . . ."

His heart constricted, his face was white. Had he failed her? Did she *want* a way out? "But, Linda," he protested, "you're my wife . . ."

"I have been your wife," she agreed. "Long enough to know that . . ." She choked, and tears began to fill her eyes; one pearly drop spilled upon her cheek.

She shook her head impatiently. "Tell me one thing!" she blurted. "*Does* your brother have children?"

"John?" asked Alan, his tone flat with surprise. "Why—I don't know, Linda."

She took a step towards him, staring.

"In any case," he cried impatiently, "he wouldn't figure . . ."

"Oh, Alan."

"Look, Linda——"

"You're not cruel, Alan," she pleaded. "Not really."

"What I am doesn't signify," he said gruffly. "But I think you must know that it was John's own choice to leave here, to cut himself off."

"Your parents . . ."

"Yes, yes! But he, too. Oh, how did we ever get into *this?*" He sounded angry. He was—impatient. And disappointed.

"It seemed the time," said Linda, mournfully. "You're still young—and if John has no children, it is essential that you have them." Her voice began to rise. "Your mother and father think so. And I do, too. That's why I——" She sobbed aloud, trembling. She regarded him between the hands pressed to her temples. "Oh, please don't argue with me, Alan! I only know the way this thing has come to seem to me!"

Alan sighed. All at once, he was desperately tired. As a doctor, he recognised Linda's wrought-up state. She was unfit to be talked to in any reasoning fashion. And within himself, there were grave uncertainties—after all, he'd not been much of a husband. . . . He took a deep breath. "If this is the way you want it, Linda," he said quietly.

Shoulders bowed, he went past her, picked up his night clothes from the foot of the bed, went to the door and opened it. She made no move, said no word, to stop him. He crossed the hall to the guest-room, fumbled for the switch, snapped it, and stood blinking at the radiance upon unfamiliar colours. The green room, it was called. A strange room. A room without Linda.

She let me go, he thought numbly. He stepped into the room, closed the door behind him. *What am I doing here? I want to go back.*

But he did not go back.

Linda stood on the hearth-rug and watched Alan leave her; she watched the door close upon him. Then, slowly, she walked to it, and put her hand upon its white panel, "I let him leave," she whispered, her lips dry. "I didn't say one word to stop him—and he left. Did he want to go? Does he want—to be free? Does he want—a child—more than he wants me?" She whirled and pressed against the door, her eyes enormous. "Oh, God!" she cried, "tell me what to do next!"

Blindly, she stared before her, then, still dazed, she walked across to the window. With the sound of countless stinging whips a gusty wind dashed rain against the glass; the water poured down the pane, silver on black, then drained off, and Linda stared at the twisting, tortured branches of the trees.

What should she *do*? The thought of losing Alan was a sharp blade turning in her breast. Yet he *wanted* children, and fiercely. If his lack had been a pain even greater than her own, he must have his chance. But, oh, dear God, what would Linda *do* without him?

Clew brought the word to Ma'am with her morning coffee, that Miss Linda and Dr. Alan had slept apart the night before. Yes'm, they had! The bed in the green room was all rucked up, and the door to Miss Linda's room still closed tight. Dr. Alan had come downstairs, unshaved, and in the same shirt and trousers he'd worn last night.

Linda still sat before the tilted mirror of her dressing-table when Seretha, with only the warning of a light knock, sailed into her bedroom. Stifling a sigh of protest, Linda stood up respectfully, murmured a greeting and watched the old lady establish herself in the pink chair. Ma'am laid a purple velvet jewel-case upon the side-table, and lifted her handsome head.

The beads! Oh, dear, to have forgotten them—that added to all the rest. Linda was so tired this morning, so drained.

"You forget these," Ma'am was saying. "I brought them as a pretext to talk to you, Linda. This morning the servants are saying very disturbing things."

Linda almost smiled. She should have known she could rely upon Clew's good offices. It was one of the ways Ma'am kept the family reins firmly in hand.

". . . and *I* want to know what all this nonsense is about!" said Ma'am.

Linda took a deep breath. She must not speak impulsively, unguardedly.

But before she could speak at all, Seretha was talking again. "I am not blind to the trouble there has been building up between you and Alan, my dear," she said firmly. "From my first sight of you, I wondered if you would be able to give him

57

the family which every man wants, and which is particularly important to a Thornton. I even mentioned this to my son, but he married you anyway. Now——" She fumbled for her handkerchief. Ma'am was dressed for church, all but her hat and gloves. "I find myself horrified at the realisation that you are in a position to bring scandal upon us!"

Linda leaned forward a little to look at Ma'am. The old lady was "horrified" at nothing but her own deductions. Linda had not said one word.

"You can't be serious about this, Linda," Ma'am was saying. "You mustn't be. There can be no divorce in the Thornton family. Keep that firmly in your mind! Such a thing has *never* happened. No matter *what!*"

Linda was shocked. Her very fingers tingled with shock. But she managed something of a smile, and was able to speak coolly. "I must remind you, Ma'am, that *I* am not a Thornton." She smoothed the bedspread at the corner. "That," she continued, "is part of the trouble."

Seretha stood up. "I'll not listen to any such nonsense!" she cried. "Of course you are a Thornton, have been for ten years. And I shall do all I can to prevent your forgetting that, and setting a precedent of——"

"But, Ma'am," cried Linda, "don't *I* count?"

The tall woman looked down upon her with eyes as cold as frost. "Is there some other man you want?" she demanded.

Colour flushed hotly into Linda's cheeks, but she only shook her head.

"Then," said Seretha, sailing towards the door, "stop talking about divorce!"

Linda had not mentioned it.

"Things might be different if you did love someone else."

Linda's bright head tilted to one side. "How would they be different," she asked softly, "if there were another man?"

Seretha turned full about to look at her, white head erect, her spine as straight as a ship's mast, her eyes as cold as the sea. She seemed ready to speak, but instead—as if any answer were too obvious to need putting into words—she smiled in a wintry fashion, opened the door and went out into the hall.

Once again, Linda stood face to face with the white panels of her bedroom door. Her eyes followed its groovings, its ridges, its wide planes. Then, as if sick of that white expanse, she whirled about, walked swiftly to the table, and stopped.

Her fumbling hands rearranged the apples in the bowl. *Ma'am,* she thought, *was trying to put words into my mouth. Ideas into my mind. She wants me to get out! She'd be happy if there should be something—a man, perhaps—to make me want to leave! She says I'm a Thornton, and all the time she's reminding me that I am not!*

. . . She's a tyrant, Ma'am is. The whole family knows it. Linda had guessed it, but now she also knew to what lengths Ma'am would go to preserve and prolong the family—the name——

Linda looked down at the apple she held in her hand, startled to find it there. Did Alan, perhaps not knowingly, but deep within himself, subscribe to Ma'am's tyrannical doctrine of *blood?* It seemed unlike him. Yet, last night, without argument, or even discussion, he had let Linda go, for the very flimsy reason she had given him. If he did *not* subscribe to Ma'am's ideas, would he have gone so quickly out of the room? Would he have left her at all? Alone! So terribly, miserably alone!

Roughly, she put the apple back into the bowl, and gathered the whole thing up into her arms. Last night, Alan had not had his bedtime apple, nor fresh clothes this morning—she would move his things across the hall! No . . . She stopped short.

She would make *no* move! She would go on, as close to the normal as possible. Now, she would go down and eat her breakfast; then she would go to church, arrange the altar flowers, take her usual place in the Thornton pew—listen to Jasper sing brassily off key, but joyously, in the *Te deum*. She would watch Alan come down the aisle with the alms basin, and she would lift her eyes to his face—as she had been doing for ten years.

But—this morning, would his eyes meet hers? Softly shining?

Oh, *darn!* Here she was, crying again, and her make-up ruined!

PART TWO

EACH DAY must be faced anew, and each night taken up like a heavy and loathsome burden. By resolutely sticking to her usual routine of duties, Linda accomplished the days—and so a month was passed and gone. Thanksgiving came, and Christmas preparations must be begun and carried through, involving Linda in the ritual of the occasion as celebrated in the family. What with family members, distant relatives, servants, the town, even in wartime a Thornton Christmas was a colossal undertaking.

Seretha, however, had time to attend to matters that seemed to her of first importance.

"I had Clew move your things into the green room," she had told Alan. "I'm afraid Linda is not well."

"She's unhappy," said her son. "And so am I. But please, Ma'am, let us work things out."

"But, of course, my dear. You know I want only the best for you."

He'd stood looking at her for a troubled minute, then had gone on his way, saying nothing more.

With Linda, Ma'am found an early opportunity to urge again that she do "nothing foolish," take no step—until the holidays were over.

What answer she made—if she made any at all—Linda could not recall. She had just come downstairs, shaken by the discovery that all of Alan's possessions had been moved out of their room, even to his tube of toothpaste.

The empty closet gaped, the drawers of the highboy—it was a sensible thing for Alan to have done, perhaps, but it seemed very definite and final!

And now Ma'am——

She spoke as if she wanted the way left open for reconciliation—but really, Linda told herself, stamping her foot into her snow boot—really, it was Ma'am who had made a "thing" out of what could have been only a passing emotional flare-up.

She let herself out of the door and went across the "gallery." Jasper was coming in at the far circle of the drive, and he lifted his crop to her, Plume's neck arching, his tail flowing like silver.

Linda was on her way to the hospital to confer with Miss Adamant about Christmas plans there—gifts for the personnel, "house" decorations, favours for the patients' trays on Christmas Day. She would walk—Linda had her own car, but she used it seldom. Now, particularly, she liked getting out into the wintry air, on her feet, to walk briskly and try to think out the things that were troubling her.

Of course, thinking alone about her situation and Alan's brought her always up against blankness. That first night Alan could have talked her down—and during the days since—but he made no move, said not one word. What was *he* thinking? What plans was *he* making?

She went into the warm hospital, conscious of its sounds and smells, its busyness at this time of the afternoon. Visiting hour, out-patients, the three o'clock shift-change. . . .

She went directly to Miss Adamant's office, half hoping that a white-clad Alan would be sitting at his desk beyond the open door. He was not there, and within the first five minutes she heard his secretary say over the phone that Dr. Thornton was in surgery. "I'll take your message?"

Laura Adamant had been Alan's secretary since the hospital first was built. About the same age as Linda, she was pretty; she dressed well and performed her multiple duties efficiently. She was also inclined to boss Alan, and tell about doing it. Alan hated this trait in her, but he was too gentle, or too busy, to express his resentment. Others took Laura at her word, and were amused at the way she handled the doctor. They had, in the course of telling about his bossy secretary, built up a fiction in town that Laura was "soft" on the doctor, and that Doc somewhat returned the sentiment. All on the up and up, of course. . . .

Alan hated that situation, too. But Laura Adamant was a good medical secretary and hospital administrator, and as such would be hard to replace—and, anyway, doctors must constantly meet the occupational hazard of misunderstanding, talk and surmise.

Now Laura quickly got things lined up for Christmas, and

asked Linda for a suggestion as to what the hospital should give its Chief as a gift.

"Goodness," laughed the doctor's wife, "you see more of him than I do. You should know what he'd like."

Laura's excited laughter and her quick blush made Linda regretfully aware that she had contributed to poor Alan's entanglement. The girl would quote her. Goodness, couldn't she do *anything* right these days?

Her own cheeks scarlet beneath her little fur cap, she went out into the hall again, and was ready to push through the outer door when she heard her name called. She turned.

It was Rupert Ernst, in a short leather jacket, a pointed-crowned green hat. "I'll walk along with you," he offered, pushing the door open for her.

When out for a walk, Linda had, on a couple of previous occasions, met Rupert and permitted him to join her, talk to her. In her recent loneliness, she had found his company diverting, and now when he suggested that they walk a little way into the hills instead of going straight down the avenue to her home, she agreed.

"It's cold," she warned. "There isn't much snow, but locally we say that such a day is colder than a well-digger's feet."

He laughed appreciatively, his fine teeth flashing, and they struck off across the snow-dusted field, entered a small copse of cedars, and came out again into the sunlight, having climbed enough of the mountain-side by then to look down at the town.

They talked of the view, of a dozen things, none of them significant or important—but in their talk the dark, slender doctor managed to be gallant, and so deeply attentive to his companion as to bring rosy colour into her cheeks and put a shine into her pretty eyes.

He mentioned their prettiness—he walked with her clear to the gates of the Green, and watched her face closely while she told him about the place's name, quoting the song:

> *"This eternal resting-place*
> *Is known as Fiddlers Green."*

"I like that," he said, his hand reaching for hers. "I like *you*." He lifted her hand to his lips, dropped it, turned on his heel and went off.

Linda went into the house and up to her room. She took off her outdoor wraps, sat down to smooth her hair—and leaned forward to gaze into the mirror. Her cheeks were pink, her eyes starry. She might have been sixteen, all smiling and dreamy-eyed, because some man had called her pretty.

Well, it was exciting, at any age, for a man to like to be with her, and to say so.

She leaned her chin upon her hand, and stared, dreamily, into the glass. What would it be like to be loved by a man like Rupert Ernst? His arms, his kiss—— She wondered . . . No! Obviously he was experienced with women. What difference did it make if he had loved other women? Why should one ask if he would be faithful? Rupert was a man for *romance*. For love as swift and as sweet as the evening moonlight, glowing pink in the eastern sky, spreading into excitement and expectation, mounting into the full blaze of passion—and dimming into a tender memory.

The woman before the mirror drew her breath in sharply—other women knew that sort of love! If it were offered to Linda, would she take it, experience it, and so have her own memory of such a love? Such a swift and sweet interlude would offer no substitute for what she had known with Alan—but——

She dropped her face into her hands, and sighed shudderingly. What *was* it she wanted? What did any woman want? To be loved, of course. And, for Linda, to belong to the man who loved her, to become a strong, bright thread woven into the pattern of his life. She had always wanted that!

And now . . .

The hours went by, the days sometimes on winged feet. The nights went more slowly, but they too passed. The big house began to smell richly of spices and roasting fowl, of oranges and cedar boughs, to gleam with tinsel and coloured globes of blown glass, to ring with the excited laughter of the twins, and the equally excited twittering of Aunt Flora, caught under the mistletoe by old Colonel Chaney.

On Christmas Eve, Alan was held too late at the hospital to go with the family to midnight services. Linda decided that she would wait at home for him. He came hurrying in at a quarter before the hour, and suggested that they still might go—but his face was so shadowed with fatigue, his eyes so dark with weariness, that Linda took his hat and coat, then led the way back to the breakfast room where a fire burned rosily, and some food could be brought in quickly from the kitchen. Hot chocolate, slices of cold meat, some cheese to be toasted between bread held on a long fork—Linda sat on the fender to do this, while Alan stretched his length in the arm-chair. Soon he began to talk to her, as he had always been able to talk to Linda. She listened, with attentive silence, occasionally a grave comment and a rewarding smile.

To-night she was wearing grey, with a spray of holly caught into her hair, and another tucked into the scarf at her throat. The firelight haloed her head. Alan watched her with pleasure, ate and drank—and was refreshed.

And he talked of the hospital, and then of why he had chosen to be a doctor. "But it was a scientist I had in mind," he said gruffly. "Not a hospital executive." Her eyes turned his way, and his big hand lifted. "I know—we thrashed that all out when Father built the place. But, oh, of course, the war has made things difficult, and Cassidy isn't getting any younger."

Linda's parted lips blew her breath outward in a soft whisper of regret.

"Ernst says to kick him out!" cried Alan. "But, of course, I remember the old duffer when I was a little boy, Linda."

He fell silent for a time, and when Linda moved to the small rocker opposite him, his eyes glanced her way. "It was due to Cassidy that I became a doctor," he said dreamily. "One day when his black boy took sick, Cassidy asked if I'd drive for him—and I did. I loved to talk to the doctor, and he was a bit of a talker himself. Still is. I was about fourteen, and I drove for him that whole summer—and at the end of it I knew I wanted to be a doctor, too.

"I couldn't tell you, to save me, what it was that made me decide. Cassidy wasn't an inspired physician, and I am not. Not in the sense of a clear call, or dedication. What little intelligence I possess is in connection with my profession, but that isn't overpowering. . . . No, it was more—I just wanted to set bones, and see if I could make people well. The work to be done—that's what called me, if 'call' it was. I'm sure there wasn't anything noble or idealistic. In fact, I'm so typically the Republican, Protestant, corn-hog-farm product of these hills

64

that I am constantly amazed when other hospitals send for me to operate. They have their own surgeons, and St. Louis is close enough! Yet they send for me, and I go. But I'm not sure I know why, in either case."

Linda smiled. She sat there before the fire, warmly happy, the pressure of the past days lifted from her because Alan was with her in the firelight and talking to her again in this gentle, intimate fashion.

Alan shifted his weight in the chair. "I realise that all general practitioners in a place like this have to become surgical specialists; we're faced with so many accidents. But when I consider the sort of specialist I once *planned* to be, it seems now that I am—nothing."

"I'd argue that," said Linda serenely, "except that the way you feel about your work is the important thing. Brain surgery is a fine field, and I expect you would be good at it. I wish you could have a few years to try it. Perhaps you can, one day."

"Only through Father's death, and Ma'am's," said Alan. "So I truly pray to God that I never may be free to make that try."

"Did it ever occur to you that God may have chosen to put you here, and keep you here?"

Alan's eyes opened to regard her. She sat in profile to him, gazing into the fire, her bronze hair catching the light of it.

"If He has a plan," she added thoughtfully.

"No sparrow falls," murmured her husband.

She nodded. "That's it. He may have put you here, Alan, to care for His fallen sparrows, knowing that the city is well supplied." She glanced up, smiling, and Alan's eyes glowed in the firelight. Their companionship was so comfortingly what it had used to be that each held the minute like fragile glass, carefully.

"We argue quite a bit, Ernst and I," Alan suddenly confessed.

She shot him a startled look. What had made him think of Rupert? "You don't like him, do you?"

"About as well as he likes me. We're *so* different, Linda."

"Yes, I know. I don't wonder that you argue."

"Well, we do. On purely theoretical cases, like whether an allergy does cause a swelling in the brain, due to a lack of oxygen, and what should be done about it. Then things like——" He shifted again in his chair. "D'you remember the night here when Ernst and Father got into it over Tchaikovsky?"

Linda's fingers caught at the folds of her skirt. "Yes," she said breathlessly, "I remember...."

But Alan was thinking only of the example he would cite concerning his difference with the European. "Ernst hates Tchaikovsky. I loved the *Pathétique* at my first hearing, I remember. Without knowing, then, the story behind it of disappointment and probable suicide, I lived it. It seemed to introduce me to an entirely new world where I was content to dwell for the time. I didn't need to understand why the music was written. But Ernst—well——" He laughed a little. "Of course, we're as different as we look. He's trim and suave. I'm easy-going, careless in everything but surgery . . . and, yet——" He shot a green-eyed glance at Linda. "I mean what I say and stand for, and I'm ready to defend those things."

There was a firmly tense note in his manner of speaking. His words held a deeper meaning which both of them felt, without clearly defining their import.

Sharply Linda straightened in her chair, her eyes suddenly alert. Why, Alan was arguing his case to her! He was too proud to make a more personal appeal, but he was endeavouring to remind her——

She pressed her hand to her mouth, as if to hold back the excitement which was sweeping over her in waves. Was he telling her that he wanted her? Wanted her more than the children he might have had—wanted her—Linda—for herself alone?

He was still gazing at her. "How good you are to me," he said deeply, "to sit and let me talk to you this way. But, then, you always have been good to me."

He stood up, stretching his long bones. Knowing that he would come to her, and touch her, she sat waiting, thinking of his touch, his warm embrace—his kiss. How Seretha would be confounded! Her lips parted in a little smile, her breath quickened....

In so tenderly pregnant a moment, the noise was shockingly offensive. The siren screaming and whooping, their own telephone ringing....

Fire! Linda ran for the telephone. Alan for his rubber

boots, helmet and coat, which stood always ready in the hall closet.

It was Alan who had organised the system of alarm and casualty stations in the town, and around it. Volunteer groups were ever ready to assist the town's small police and fire departments. This fire, the operator told Linda, was just off Main Street; the feed mill, she thought. . . .

That the feed mill bore the Thornton name made no difference; half the industries in town could have been so-called. A fire in any feed mill was a serious thing for the entire town. Linda snatched her own coat and scarf, and was in the car seat beside Alan when he switched on the lights, and Jacob tumbled into the back seat. The red searchlight on, the car swept out of the drive and down the avenue.

The night was a clear one, but the stars were now blotted out above the town by the glow of a hundred headlights, and swirling clouds of spark-spangled smoke.

Linda stayed with the car—a warden would tell her where to put it. Alan and Jacob got out and ran, side by side, as they had done things together, when they were babies, little boys and growing ones.

Linda thought of the people in church. Old Jasper would take masterly charge, herding the women and children, sending the able-bodied men off to their assigned places. She craned her neck to see. The main fire seemed to be in an old office building down the side street. The feed mill was beyond, and a stream of water was played upon it. But the fire itself was in the Merritt building, with its double galleries of time-seasoned wood, that would go like tinder. There was a store at the corner, a garage beyond that—and on the second floor was a beauty parlour. And the Fowler apartment . . . *The Fowler children!*

Seretha had arranged for Mrs. Fowler to live in one of the old office suites, and pay her rent by cleaning the halls and stairs. And now flames were curling from the windows of the mansard-roof attic; when the warden came to her, Linda screamed that children were up there——

"We'll git 'em down, Miss Linda," the man assured her.

She put the car where he directed, and then hurried back to Main Street. Excitement was mounting in shouting waves, much as the fire mounted and mounted, painting the smoke clouds with crimson, sending bits of charred paper down upon Linda's coat sleeves while she was still a block away. It was not a windy night, but the flames and heat generated their own power. She fell back against the building—and then climbed upon the curved grilling at the bank in an effort to see.

The ambulance came from the hospital and stopped, mid-block, obeying the rules of procedure. After a bit, Linda ventured to cross to where it stood, and to speak to the driver about the Fowlers. It had been unwise, she cried, to let the widow and her children live in such a firetrap!

"She poor, Miss Linda," said the driver. "Poor folk learn to take chances. They got to live somewhere. An' don' you worry—efn the doctor's there, them kids have ben thought of. Now look there! They gittin' the furniture down offn the gallery! Stands to reason they got the kids out first."

"I hope they save her loom. She earns her living by rug-weaving."

"Well, they'll save it, given time."

Still she fretted. "If I only knew the children were out and safe . . ."

She put the question to each one who came down the street from the direction of the fire. Eventually old Jasper came, plunging along at his usual speed——

"Yes, Lindy," he boomed. "All the kids out and counted. Along with half a set of Sir Walter Scott bound in imitation leather. I left 'em riggin' a rope to let down the organ——"

"What about her loom?"

"Miz Fowler, even with her back hair singed off, seemed mighty concerned about that organ!"

Old Jasper went on his way, and Linda decided to return to Alan's car. Coughing in the arid air, she crossed the street, stepped up on the kerb and was almost knocked down by a running child—a small boy, racing blindly along the sidewalk, bare as Mother Nature except for his nightshirt blown up into a rope around his neck. He carried his britches in one hand; the other arm protected a pink and white china piggybank, in which a single coin rattled lonesomely. He was sobbing in terror, and gasping for breath. His face was streaked with grime, his eyes pale and staring. Linda caught strongly at his arm, and held him. "*Don't run!*" she cried. "Don't run!"

She unbuttoned her big coat, and wrapped one half of it

68

around his bareness. He looked up at her, unseeingly, and gulped agonisingly for air.

"Lady," he gasped finally, "I'm pure *sceered*."

"Well, there's no need now. Here—let's find the car."

He went with her docilely. She was the one sure, firm thing he had found in a world of turmoil and terror.

Gradually, then, the excitement diminished with the flames and smoke. Jacob came with the word that Alan would go on to the hospital. He was to take Miss Linda home.

By that time Linda had talked her little boy companion into sleepy calm. Jacob said the rest of the Fowler family was being cared for. As they passed the night-duty police officer, they told him that they had this one child.

When they reached the Green, Linda wrapped her coat around the child and led him into the wide hall. His eyes were as big as saucers to see lamplight twinkling in a thousand stars upon the Christmas tree. "It's purty . . ." he said, sleepily.

She made a bed for him upon the deep couch in her own room, and he was asleep before he finished the glass of milk and the cookies which Jacob brought.

Linda lay in her own bed, listening to the sound of a child's breathing close by, and liked knowing he was there! Next morning, it was pretty fine to let him dress in some of Jim's clothes, to take his hand and lead him downstairs, to escort him through the glories of Christmas in that house. The family had been told they would have such a guest, and there were gifts for the child beneath the big tree; a book and candy, mittens and a red fire truck with a ladder that cranked up!

His name was Manning, he had freckles across his nose and a cowlick in his straw-coloured hair. He was nine, and once his shyness had melted, full of questions.

Jim and Ann would have taken over his entertainment, but the boy clung to Linda. She saw Margaret explaining the circumstances to the twins. "She's still our really Aunt Linda!" she heard Ann assert jealously. Linda threw the little girl a reassuring smile and wink.

What with the tree, the gifts, meals and callers, Christmas was a busy day, but Linda found the little boy constantly at her elbow. He followed her like a puppy, and gazed at her with adoring eyes. Early she sent word to his mother that he was safe. By mid-afternoon, snow was coming down in thick white flakes, and the children planned excitedly on coasting.

But the servants said that to-morrow would make a good butcherin' day—first real good freeze! The signs were right—the sausage wouldn't frizzle down to nuthin', nor the bacon shrivel up in the pan. The children debated the charms of this development. "Butcherin'," Jim told Manning, "can be most as much fun as slidin'."

On smaller farms, hog-butchering required days of preparation. At the Green it meant only a bringing in of extra hands to help, the early lighting of fires in the trough, the worktable brought out, the beam trussed to its supports.

And early rising, too, of course. But even so, Linda was brushing her hair when the first shot rang out.

Excited by the talk and the preparations, Manning was anxious to be out and away and would scarcely eat his oatmeal. Linda walked down with him far enough to point out where he might go, and where not. The twins came pelting down the hill to join him, and the wide-eyed children stood staring at the first hog being lifted from the vat of scalding water, drawn over to the table, steaming hot, where the men and their sharp knives were all ready to work swiftly at their job of scraping off hair.

Linda gave the overseer authority to send the children back to the house if they misbehaved, and she herself went hastily up the hill again. "Butcherin'" was not *her* first choice of amusement. Margaret had said contentedly that it would keep the children busy the better part of the week's vacation, but Linda did not enjoy it. That night, she knew from experience, the row of naked carcasses in the lantern light would be a sight to avoid—but she must be sure that some of the meat was sent to Manning's mother.

With a final glance over her shoulder to see that the children were still where she had left them, she went into the house, and back to the breakfast room where the family still lingered at the table.

"Hallo, Lindy," roared Jasper, "you get things under way?" She nodded, smiled and slipped into her chair.

"Is it still cold out?" asked Aunt Flora.

"Oh, bitter! The men seemed pleased about it."

" 'Course they are," boomed Jasper. "Takes near a week to butcher for a place this size."

Linda thanked Jacob for the food he brought her, and mentioned her hope that Manning's mother be allotted a share of the meat.

"See you lost your shadda," teased Jasper. "Did he trust you enough to leave his piggy-bank behind with you?"

"I think so—he didn't have it with him. But, Father, that bank holds a whole nickel!"

The old man chuckled. "I knew it was a treasure," he agreed.

Linda nodded, smiling wistfully. "It's rather wonderful to be loved that way," she confessed. "And trusted. I thought, last night, that I'd like, perhaps, to adopt Manning."

She had spoken with a carefully-measured casualness, seeming more interested in the biscuit which she was buttering than in what she had said.

But she waited breathlessly upon an answer, or comment— and none came. The silence was stony, but not so cold as Seretha's voice when finally she spoke.

"Linda, that is a perfectly ridiculous idea!"

Linda's head lifted, her eyes dark. It had been an idea, no more. But Ma'am's tone—— No one considered *Linda!* Her needs—and her desires.

"Why shouldn't I adopt a child?" she asked, her hurt forming in a stubborn, cold mass in her throat. "Every woman needs a child to love, to care for. Manning is a nice little boy."

"He's a nice little boy," agreed Seretha. Linda cast a glance around the table, and saw that even Jasper was agreeing with Ma'am. Her soft chin set. "But you cannot adopt him, Linda."

"But—why not?"

"Well, for one thing, my dear, the other children of the family must be protected against such a move. Their rights . . ."

"If you mean inheritance, it just *happens* that Alan and I don't have six of our own to diminish their prospects."

"Now, Linda . . ." protested Jasper.

"But, Father, I honestly don't see Ma'am's argument."

"I am waiting for a chance to explain . . ." said Ma'am.

"They're mountain folk, Linda . . ." Aunt Flora endeavoured to help.

Seretha silenced her with a glance. "Ignorance may be cured," she declared magnanimously. "But breeding and blood cannot be changed. Manning seems a nice little boy, and he could perhaps be educated—but you still would have a child of inbred, poverty-weakened mountain people, Linda. His background, his tastes, his impulses, all would clash with our standards for such things. My dear, when you adopt a child, you bring his ancestry into the family. It's too big a gamble."

The family! The family! No matter how cold and unfeeling they would need to be, the family came first! "I could educate him and fit him for life."

"I understand. But you can busy yourself in doing those things without *adopting* him."

It was love she wanted, Manning's puppy-like devotion. Her motive was self-centred, and she knew it. Still . . .

"Granted," Ma'am was saying, "that this boy may be exceptional material. That happens occasionally in such families. But are you sure, Linda, that he would be happy away from his own—well—*folks?* Away from the sort of life he is used to?"

"How can you tell so surely about anyone's happiness?" Linda's hurt now displayed itself for all to see.

"I can promise you,' said Seretha calmly, "that none of *us* would be happy! Not even you, Linda. Manning is already well started in his way of life, and his family lives close by. Everyone knows them, and they——"

"They'd be kin to all of us," growled Jasper. "And claim it, too!"

Though not too clearly, Linda recognised that they were right. The family—Seretha—was being much more reasonable than she was.

"Please," she said in a stifled tone, "let's not talk about it any more." She knew she had already lost the fight, chiefly because she no longer believed in her cause.

She went out of the room, salving her dignity by saying to herself that she'd mention the matter to Alan—when next she had a free minute with him. But when would that be? These days he was so darn busy, she scarcely saw him. He'd not made any move at all to renew the mood of Christmas Eve.

Alan was indeed busy—especially at the hospital. There had

72

been a great deal of illness; people had swarmed into the neighbourhood to work on the Army Camp. They lived in makeshift homes. Being covered by hospital insurance, they crowded the Valhalla Hospital with illnesses and minor accidents that scarcely needed hospitalisation. Enough true cases came in to make the surgeon-in-charge sharply aware of how shorthanded he was in all departments.

Dr. Ernst scarcely took Bowman's place. The cheerful young intern had been ready to do any job at any time; this could not be said for Ernst, who considered his title as *assistant* surgeon to be a title only.

Ernst had a way of being outraged at any administrative job which was put upon him. Alan, to lighten his own load, had asked his assistant to take over the supervision of all surgical activities, which of course would include the management of the operating-room. He ignored the way Ernst bridled at the request. "Mrs. Dunham will help you," he said, walking away. He hadn't *time* to persuade people!

But it was only a day or so later when, under a heavy surgical schedule, he found his surgical nurse opening a package of sponges taken from the shelf rather than directly from the autoclave. He frowned, and later asked Dunham what had happened. "It's the first time since we've been working together that you've run out."

Between her tight cap and the gauze mask, the nurse's eyes met his levelly. She was threading suture into an upheld needle. "Dr. Ernst won't let the autoclaves work during operations, Doctor. Of course, they get empty on a day like this."

Alan whirled on her. "Why would he give an order like that?"

"He objects to the heat."

"He does? Well, *I* object to the sponge shortage!"

The nurse continued to regard him through the space between her lifted, yellow-gloved hands. "Yes, Doctor?"

"I'll speak to Dr. Ernst," he agreed. "But you're in charge here, as always."

"Even to the circulating's shoes?"

Lightning no longer flared from Alan's green eyes. "When she gets tired, she can take off her shoes," he agreed. "If I get any busier, I'll come to that myself."

Mrs. Dunham watched his tall person leave the room. "I

73

wish," she said to herself, "I could listen-in when he speaks to Handsome Ernie."

Leaning upon the facts of his European training, Ernst considered himself the better trained man. That the American system required an apprenticeship of him made him unhappy, and quick to criticise that system. He deplored these *gauche* Americans among whom he must live, the doctors without European degrees, and particularly this small hospital in this small town.

Alan appreciated Rupert's position, and took it into account, just as he took into account the man's suave and charming grace, his quick patter of culture and information, and the fact that women liked him.

He always gave Ernst's medical opinion his most courteous attention, sometimes agreeing with him, but being very firm when he must disagree. "I cannot imagine any situation," he said, one morning, to the man at the next scrub-up sink, "where it would be wise to let a patient read a history letter sent to us by a referring doctor."

"My dear Thornton," said Ernst patiently, "only your rural mountain people would read a letter left upon my desk blotter."

There were several answers to that. Alan scrubbed steadily at his left hand, switched the brush. "We got an excessive flareback on Mrs. Patrick," he said then, tightly. "And our relations with her doctor had always been excellent."

The corner of his eye caught Ernst's shrug, and he turned squarely to face the man. "In my book *every* doctor, *every* patient, is important! If you would put yourself in Harg's place ..."

Ernst said something under his breath.

"You wouldn't want to, naturally. Nevertheless, think of this—Harg referred Mrs. Patrick to us, and sent a letter, saying that there seemed to be nothing essentially wrong with her, but that a little assurance would probably be a great help. We examined the woman, and found his diagnosis correct. But you fixed it so that we were unable to reassure her, and help her. And my contention is that, by neglect of one small ethical point, we failed with an important case!"

"I cannot agree," said Ernst coldly, "that she was important."

Alan resumed his scrubbing. And decided to try again . . .

"Dr. Ernst," his deep voice said patiently, "you came here to learn what you could from me."

"I came here in order to establish my degree and licence, yes."

"So that you might practise in America. Towards that end, it would be easier if you would decide that I had a few things to teach you. Easier for both of us. I know that you feel you are already adequately trained in your profession. If that is true, the things I could teach you would have to deal with our *way* of practising medicine, particularly my way—my feeling about it, my attitude to the patient."

"That indeed is different."

"Yes," agreed Alan, "it is different." He could have pointed out to this insolent man that his own membership in the American College of Surgeons would lend weight to his act should he send Ernst away as untrainable.

Instead, he glanced at the timer—he had five minutes in which to make his point. "When I began to practise surgery," he said patiently, "I had to decide if I wanted to work here among my own people, and I made my decision through the argument that a healing hand is valuable wherever there is humankind. In the little town of Valhalla, or the city of New York—or Vienna. A doctor works from within, by his own skill, his own ability, and he must bring that inward power to deal anew with each case, to treat that case according to any ability that is within him.

"That is why, more than for any other reason, I consider each patient important. I try to get the feel of his condition, to know what has led up to his illness, his injury. I want to know what mental and emotional complications there may be —and to know those things I give great personal consideration to each patient, probe as deeply with my mind, and my heart, as I do with my knife."

Dr. Ernst's elbow shut off the water at his sink. "That kind of doctoring must be very exhausting," he said politely.

"You're calling it emotional?"

Dr. Ernst shrugged, and Alan turned away, thinking that it was, as well, exhausting to have to deal so with Ernst. Often he asked himself why he bothered. Give the man his orders, see that he carried them out—and if he didn't, boot him down the road!

But, generally, Ernst did carry out his orders. He was more than a capable surgeon, he was particularly good. Alan was too honest not to see that, and acknowledge it.

Ernst had, for example, done a masterly job of reducing the femur fracture of Uncle Arthur's lady-love. That accident, which had occurred during Ernst's first week with them, had been the direct result of dim old eyes, foolish high heels and a stretch of icy sidewalk. It was, of course, a serious injury to a woman of seventy.

It had taken Alan to persuade the old belle into a belief that she could ever hope to recover from such an injury—but he had coaxed her into an agreement to a double-pin fixation. Then Dr. Ernst had taken over; he had performed the operation, had made the first spica and had, throughout, attended the case, exerting his personal charm upon Miss Little Mae, coming often out of her room to speak of her as a silly old lady—which she was!—and tell in wonder of her concern lest the operation leave a *scar*!

And now, six weeks after the fall, Miss Little Mae was ready to leave the hospital, to go back to her wide-veranda'd home. Her frilly bed-jackets and the array of creams and lotions had all been packed. Her shiny black Packard stood at the door. Miss Little Mae was dressed and seated in her new wheel-chair, ready to make a charming face at the crutches which the doctors urged her to use. Crutches, she said, were so *ugly*!

She distributed gifts to the nurses who attended her, and wanted to say good-bye to Dr. Ernst, as well as to Alan, who had come in for the ceremony of departure.

"You lazy boy!" said Miss Little Mae, coyly. "You let Dr. Ernst do all the work!"

"I certainly did," agreed Alan. "Well, your doctor will be in in a minute. He——"

"Oh, here he is!" cried Miss Little Mae. She fluttered, and she tittered and she bridled. Dr. Ernst, dressed for riding, in brown coat, fawn breeches, glossy boots, crushed his felt hat under his arm, and lifted her hand to his lips.

"We shall miss you!" he assured the old lady.

"You've been just wonderful to me, Doctor!" she warbled.

"Nothing could really repay your interest in me—but I made this as a token."

This was a fat purse of brown satin, embroidered elaborately in pink moss roses and pale blue bowknots. She must have worked the entire six weeks upon the confection—and it was truly a fearsome thing.

Alan, at the window, put his big hand over his mouth to hide his smile. The things a doctor could get into!

But quickly his smile faded. Ernst had stiffened. Above his snowy stock, his handsome face had become a cold mask, his voice——Coldly he was explaining to Miss Little Mae that doctors were paid by a set fee, not by an offering of handiwork!

He was correct. He was courteous. He was as cold as a knife blade. And stone-hard in his lack of understanding.

Miss Little Mae's faded blue eyes clung to his face; she listened until he had finished. Then she said, as quietly and as calmly as Rupert had spoken, but not quite so coldly . . . "I understand, Dr. Ernst. Will you tell me just what the 'fee' amounts to?"

"The surgical charge, apart from your hospital bill, Mrs. Liddell, is five hundred dollars."

"Thank you." Carefully, Miss Little Mae stripped the white glove from her right hand, she bent her curly head and her pretty little flower toque over the purse in her lap. Carefully she slipped the carved gold button out from the loop of brown silk. From the depths of the purse her small hand drew a thick fold of green bills. Carefully still, her lips counting, she peeled five of these bills from the bundle and set them out upon the bed; then she put the money that remained back into the purse, buttoned it, tucked it firmly under her coat and looked around at her Negro houseman. "I'm ready to go now, Eugene," she said with dignity.

He wheeled her out, awful purse and all.

Rupert Ernst's face was a sight to see! Following the chair, Allan told himself that he must remember to tell Linda! How she would laugh! Her bright head back, her eyes crinkled shut . . . Though, of course, she might be only annoyed.

The elevator came, and he stepped into it after Eugene and the chair. Perhaps Alan would not be able to tell Linda that particular story. Lately he could not seem to tell her funny

77

things—not about Ernest. The time or two he'd tried, she'd sprung to the man's defence. She liked Ernst—and with Linda, that liking would be based on deeper things than the exciting effect of a man's good looks and charming manners.

She saw something of him, Alan knew. He'd seen them walking together, and riding—a time or two. A hot wave of anger and jealousy swept over him. He was as jealous as any sixteen-year-old, ready to fist up to his rival over a girl's smile!

Only—this was not a matter of just any girl's smile. And Alan was not sixteen. He was old enough to acknowledge a gnawing doubt as to whether he had any right to be jealous. What was *he* offering to Linda? Why shouldn't she turn elsewhere? He must think this over, and meanwhile he'd better watch himself, both with Linda and with Ernst. Certainly he must not let his personal resentment, his jealousy, influence his professional relationship to Ernst here in the hospital.

Neither were these happy days for Linda. It was a time of confusion and doubt. She missed doing little intimate things for Alan, the close companionship there had always been between them, the way they'd talked, and shared small jokes. She missed him most particularly at night, in her bedroom. Alone in the wide four-poster, she was unable to sleep. She would lie for hours, lonely and bewildered. "Why does he let me do this?" her heart cried. And she sobbed in discouragement and defeat.

A girl's dreams, she thought, dealt with love and romance, with Prince Charming. When love came to her, when she lay all night in the arms of her lover, she regretted that the night must end, and be followed by the day and its duties. But, when one was beloved, there was always another night. . . .

Now—for Linda—the busy days ended only in nights of loneliness and despair. *What was it for? What was it for?*

Could life go on in this way, emptily, without plan or purpose? Just the living through the days and nights—without straining or looking forward? Perhaps—because when one did try to work out the puzzle . . .

On that night of their anniversary dinner, Linda had acted impulsively, but even so she had not said much! She couldn't remember her exact words, but they couldn't have been much —and the little she had said, she had immediately regretted.

But Alan had been tired——

And Seretha, the very next morning . . .

Had it not been for Seretha, Linda could have gone to Alan, spoken the words that might quickly have set things right between them.

But Seretha had immediately pounded a wedge into the thin saw-cut, then had gone on to add others, aiming to split the tree. Linda recognised her process, but seemed unable to do anything about it.

Seretha was clever. So clever that Alan had probably no idea of what his mother was doing. Perhaps Alan thought Linda had moved his things from their room. Often she had thought of questioning him about this, but always held back lest it seem that she was begging him to return. On Christmas Eve he had seemed ready to attempt a reconciliation—but there had been the fire——

When Linda had brought Manning home, Seretha had made a big thing of Linda's suggestion that she adopt the boy; she had spoken of it often and managed to convey the idea that marriage was over for Linda, and for *that* reason she wanted an adopted child with which to fill her barren life.

Why? Why did Ma'am do these things?

Perhaps she resented a second woman in her home, feared the threat which Linda offered to Ma'am's own position as mistress.

Yet Linda had not aggressively taken over any of the multiple duties which she now performed! It had been a gradual matter of "Linda, will you please see about flowers?" Then, "Miss Linda will attend to the flowers, Jacob."

Ma'am herself had first sent Ruby to Linda for orders about meals. Linda was *asked* to go to St. Louis about replacing the brocade on the parlour chairs.

Perhaps Ma'am, realising belatedly that actually Linda was the executive mistress of the house, now wanted to change this. Perhaps Alan was content to stay the width of the hall away from his wife. If both superstitions were true, then Linda feared that she must take herself out of the house. Her own pride would force that step upon her, and the sooner she did it, the better.

For the moment, however, she could not do anything, because old Jasper had caught a cold, and for the first time since she'd known the big man, he was down in bed, ill.

It had begun with a temperature, and a noisy, sneezing head cold. He complained that he seemed to have a "kitch in his gitalong," and Alan suggested the hospital.

The old man baulked.

"You have to go to bed until that temperature is down!"

"But it'll be my own bed, dang it!"

He was not dangerously ill, but the "kitch" showed that he could be, if proper care were not taken. He was not an easy patient; he wouldn't take his medicine, nor eat the "slops" which Alan prescribed. He roared that they were cooking him with the heat lamp.

"See what you can do with him, Linda," Alan begged. "You always have got along with him. I hate to ask it, but——"

"Why, Alan, I'd love to help him. Poor thing, he just doesn't know how to be sick."

"That's the year's understatement. Did you hear what he called me?"

Linda laughed.

"If he weren't my own father, I'd not stay on the case. See what you can do, will you? If the pleurisy advances . . ."

"I'll try."

Almost at once, silence descended upon the house. Linda went into the narrow, crowded bedroom-office and "managed" the crotchety old man, angry that he should be afflicted, frightened that this sort of thing could come to him.

She teased him a little, she talked to him gently and let him talk to her. Under her persuasion, he decided that the heat lamp was a comfort; as his fever broke, weakness laid its hand upon him, and he would have been terrified, except for Linda.

"Whenever I've had the flu," she told him, "I'd be sick three days, and then take three weeks getting bones back into my legs."

That was how his legs felt, and he decided that Lindy was the only one in the family with a lick of sense.

So, of course, while he needed her, she must stay with him. And she did stay, night and day for a time, finding her own satisfaction in looking after the old man whom she'd always liked, and now got to know in a way she had never known any man except Alan. Though Alan, she realised, was exactly like his father, had the same rocklike strength and stability.

It had taken brute force to get Jasper into bed. Now Alan wanted him to sit up, to walk about—and it took Linda's most deft persuasion to accomplish this. But she managed it, and with the fire built up until the room was roasting hot, the day came when he sat in the big leather chair, his limbs wrapped in a wool comforter, a shawl about his shoulders. "I'm wet as a frettin' horse!" he complained.

"Well, why not? It's ninety in this room—and you swathed like a new-born baby!"

"But, Lindy, I'm sick."

"No, you're getting well, Father.'

His eyes peered at her. "You sure o' that?"

"Why, of course. Don't you want to get well?"

"I figured I'd hit my deathbed."

"Oh, no. You've too much to do. There's Quill to train—and look at your mail!"

He nodded. "Gotta git after that. To-morra, Lindy—I ain't got much steam up to-day."

"I know you haven't. I'm going to fix you a toddy."

"Make it strong."

She winked at him, and went out. When she came back, the old man had dropped the shawl to the floor. She put a stool under his feet, and sat down across from him.

"You been good to me, Lindy," he told her, sipping at the contents of his brown mug.

"I love you."

"Do you, Lindy?" he asked curiously. "Why?"

Her eyes flew wide. "I don't think love is a thing you can explain, Father. But—I guess I love you for the same reasons that made me fall in love with Alan. You're very much alike."

"There's them that would argue the sense of your lovin' us," he chuckled, with so great a return of his old spirit that Linda's heart leapt.

"If I could have had a son," she mused, "I'd hope *he* would be like you, too. That's why my disappointment has been so bitter." She sat gazing into the fire beneath the black iron arch of the grate.

"Yet you talked of adoptin' one of the Fowler wood colts."

"I didn't know they were colts," she said, smiling gently. "Manning was just a nice little boy, and—and—my arms were empty. But you—the family—I realise that an adoption wouldn't do."

"An adoption might do," said the old man, "in some cases. But the Fowler boy—that would-a ben dead wrong."

"And he wouldn't have looked like a Thornton," Linda agreed, trying to laugh. "Not the way Alan looks like you, Father."

The old man snorted, and drained his mug with a smack of appreciation. "Looks ain't what I'm a-talkin' about!" he cried. "Strain goes deeper'n looks. I know that for a fact, Lindy. I know that in one horse you can get stamina, grit and power —and you take the get of a brother or a sister of the same horse and you lack those things. That goes for people. Take my own get. The handsomest one o' the lot . . ." He broke off, his beard dropping to his chest. He sighed heavily. "And then you take Margaret; she's not much to look at——"

"Oh, she's lovely, Father!" Linda protested.

"Pretty, sweet—and puny-sized. But she bred fine kids, Lindy. The intangibles of strain—for want of bein' able to put a better word to it, I'll call it *noblesse oblige*. Margaret had it to hand on to her children. You didn't catch her Silas arguin' whether he ought to go to war—he jest went!

"I could bring the whole matter down to the democratic obligation there's been in my strain, and which I'd hope will carry on behind me. Democracy, Lindy! There's the nub of it. You'll understand me. Some don't. That furrin doctor doesn't —or plain won't.

"About all that man's good for is to straddle a horse; he's got good hands. But he don't understand democracy. That's why he's such a gadfly to Alan down at the hospital. He doesn't understand what it is makes Alan do as he does, not for cash, not for credit, but because he's driven by an everlastin' need to carry out the brotherhood of mankind."

Linda's heart swelled within her breast, warm with sudden joy. It was true about Alan! His sense of responsibility was as big as all mankind! And to love such a man, to have him— and not to lose him . . .

Abruptly, she rose, and went out of the room. She must not, she *could not*, lose Alan!

It was Seretha Thornton's way to hold her children to her

will and wish by means of many small tyrannies imposed upon them. Although she was far from being a helpless person, she demanded a multitude of services from each one. Thus it was Alan's task to make out cheques for Seretha. It was a small task, and he frequently told himself that a man should be glad to do such things for his mother.

Seretha did not, however, hesitate to call him away at some very busy time to write a single cheque, even one that could have been written at any time over a period of a week or more, and thus, like all tyranny, the task became burdensome. On this particular day she had phoned to Miss Adamant, and said that it was important for Dr. Thornton to come home at noon. "If he's busy, I count on your seeing that he does come!"

And, wishing to protect her reputation for being able to "handle" Alan, Miss Adamant exerted herself to clear away anything that might interfere.

So Alan went home at twelve. That was all right—Ruby had made corn fritters, which he loved, and Linda came to the table, saying that Jasper had fallen asleep. But when the meal was over, and Alan said that he'd "look in on Father and get on back to work," Seretha's quiet voice asked him to stop in her room before leaving.

He swore beneath his breath to see the cheque-book set out and ready. Then he turned to smile ruefully at his mother. "Why *won't* you try making them out?"

"Oh, now, son, it's such a little thing—just my church dues."

"It's only Thursday. That cheque can be written any time. Now, suppose you sit down and do it, with me watching to see if you do it right."

"Don't you want to make it out for me, Alan?"

"Oh . . ." he cried, sitting down at the desk. "Hell!" he added firmly. But he was laughing at himself. And Seretha, settling into the fireside chair, laughed, too, contentedly.

Alan wrote the cheque, blotted it, turned about in the small chair to look across at Seretha. "Anything else?"

"No."

"I'll go look at Father, then."

"Linda said that he was sleeping. Sit here for a minute. You may smoke."

Alan made no move to take out cigarettes.

"Linda's made a good nurse," Seretha continued. "I wish——"

Alan's tongue pushed at his underlip. "Yes?"

"I wish you'd do something about Linda, Alan."

For the briefest second, his lips pressed tightly together. "What kind of something?"

"Now, Alan, you know what I'm talking about. Call it a mood if you like. Or a notion. Refusing to let you come to her room, talking about adopting a child. Why don't you *do* something, Alan?"

He rubbed his jaw. "I suppose," he drawled, "because there is nothing I can do."

"That's ridiculous! Why *can't* you?"

"Well, mainly because Linda is quite right in the position she's taken."

Seretha's straight back stiffened; she turned full face to look at him. "What *do* you mean?"

"Just what I say. I'm not a good husband, Ma'am."

"Fiddlesticks!'

"But I'm not. Other than providing shelter for her, and food, I do none of the things for Linda that a husband should do for his wife."

"Did she say that?"

"I know it, for myself.'

"I meant, is that why she put you out of her bedroom?"

"It's why I left her room."

"Well, what's going to come of this—this foolishness?"

"I don't know, Ma'am. Mainly, I don't know because the next move is Linda's to make."

"Is there some other woman?"

Alan laughed. "If I don't have time for my wife, I'd scarcely find it for another woman.' '

"Humph!" said Seretha. "A lot of men do."

"Yes, I reckon they do, Ma'am." He stood up.

"Alan," said his mother sternly, "if you don't do something to prevent it, I suppose you realise that Linda may leave you completely. Will you allow that?"

His jaw was tight, and deep lines etched themselves into his cheeks. "Yes, Ma'am," he said quietly. "I'd have to let her."

His mother sighed in exasperation, and Alan consulted his watch. With the obvious intent of changing the subject, terminating the one which she had chosen, he said, "I'm going to drive to St. Louis for a day or two at the end of the month. So get all your cheque-writing out of the way."

"Why should you go to St. Louis?"

"Business. My kind of business." He smiled. "You see, they're holding a clinic on brain surgery down at Barnes. And Dr. Cabler is going to demonstrate an operation to correct a condition similar to that of Mrs. Blake's. Captain Blake's wife, you know?" He stood with his hand on the knob of the door which led into his father's dressing-room.

"I know Captain Blake," said Seretha, in a tone that finished the man, completely. "But, Alan——"

"Yes, Ma'am?"

"I must tell you, because I am older, and a woman myself, that you should not risk leaving, at this time."

"I have to go when the clinic is held."

"What if Linda leaves the house while you are away?"

Alan sighed, his dark head down, his eyes on the hand which held the silver knob. "Then, Ma'am," he said slowly, "she will —leave." He straightened and turned to face his mother. "I must attend this clinic. Linda knows that I plan to go, and why. It is important in my work—but even if it were not, even if I didn't feel that I had to attend it, I would not stay in town, or in this house, just to hold Linda. She'll do whatever she feels is right—for her own sake, and mine."

He opened the door then, briskly, and went through it.

Seretha sat on in the tall-backed chair, her eyes bright, her cheeks a little pink. The fingers of her right hand beat a tattoo upon the damask arm. "Well!" she said aloud. "*Well!*"

Jasper recovered slowly; his unfamiliarity with illness and its natural progress made him reluctant to trust his body too soon, or too much. But gradually his natural vigour asserted itself, boredom took precedence over such pleasure as he had found in convalescence and there came a spring-like day—the period he spoke of as the January thaw had reached their mountain-side—when the old man announced, somewhat belligerently at lunch, that he was goin' down to the stables that afternoon, to see for himself how much damage had been done.

Seretha made a clicking sound of disapproval and reproach, and Linda laughed gaily. "I hope you won't be disappointed," she told him.

"Be glad to get down there," Jasper declared, a twinkle in his eye, "away from the impudent females in this house!"

"Do you want me to drive you down, Father?" she asked, shaking back a lock of her feathery red hair.

"I ain't able to walk—I ain't able to go!"

"I thought perhaps you'd rather use your strength looking around down there."

"Well, maybe you're right. I reckon there'll be a lot to see to."

So, after an hour's nap, the old man, looking quite himself again in his broad-brimmed hat, got into Linda's little car, and settled back in the seat of it. "You got time for a turn around the whole place?" he asked.

She had time, and they took the "turn," through orchard and woodland, between the horse paddocks and pastures, and finally arrived at the stables. The winter's sky was a clear and tender blue, the sunlight lay like a warm hand upon the pleasant scene. Old Jasper sniffed the air with pleasure. "Alan let me out sooner," he declared, "I'd a-ben well sooner!"

The window of each stall door was open; through every one hung the head of a horse. Plume squealed at the sight of his master, and the other heads tossed, and lips curled back from hard yellow teeth. Hard feet pounded the floor planks. "Should have Plume out and runnin'," growled Jasper, but he was pleased at the greeting from his big buckskin.

Linda watched him go down the line—he had something in hand for each nuzzling mouth—but not for Plume. Plume was no horse to pet. He thought any gesture along that line was an invitation to play, and Plume's idea of play was to take two fingers off at the knuckle. Old Jasper justified his favourite's way by saying that while Plume did sometimes bite, he *never* kicked.

Linda laughed, and shook her head, touched the starter. "Have someone bring you home, Father," she called, "or phone up to me when you're tired."

He waved a hand at her—*exasperated*, no doubt. But he *had* given her his promise not to ride.

He'd look at the horses, and find things to shout about. He already was talking to the trainer as if the man was in the next county, and deaf to boot.

Of course, he overdid it. Linda knew he would. Without

86

any message, she came for him at four, and found him white, tired, relieved to be helped into the car and driven back to the house. He was glad to lie down upon his narrow bed, propped high with his big pillows. Linda fetched him a bowl of milk toast, and he ate it, though grumbling about women and their "fuss." She sat quietly by the fire until she heard his breathing deepen to a snore—and another.

"Miss Linda?" It was Clew at the hall door. Linda rose and went into the hall.

"What is it? I'm afraid Mr. Thornton got too tired."

"Yes'm. Ma'am say she wish you come to the mornin'-room—for tea."

Linda hesitated, then quietly told Clew that she'd be in directly. She went up to her room, put on a fresh blouse, ran a comb through her hair and then went down to the morning-room, where her mother-in-law was seated behind her tapestry frame.

A little fire chattered upon the hearth, and two canaries sang in their cages, cheered by the sunlight which still came thinly through the western windows. Linda greeted Seretha, said that Jasper was sleeping—he'd "overdone it." She picked up her knitting-bag and sat down in the corner of the couch.

Then, seeing Seretha lean towards the window to thread a needle with garnet wool, she rose again to snap on the lamps throughout the room; they'd need them by the time tea was brought in.

"Thank you, Linda," said Ma'am. "The days are short. . . ."

"But it's been like spring outdoors to-day."

"Yes." There was a little silence, marked by the drop of a coal in the grate, the cracking of a seed by one of the birds. Then Ma'am spoke. "I understand Alan is planning a trip."

Linda knitted the stitches from one needle. "Yes," she said in detached tone. "He leaves on Sunday."

"Are you going with him?"

Linda did not look up. "Oh, no," she said readily. "He is going to a clinic."

"I understand there are certain social aspects to those meetings."

"There are. Dinners, cocktail parties, things of that sort. But I don't believe Alan indulges."

For a moment Seretha said nothing more.

She had a purpose in sending for me, ran Linda's thoughts. *I'll wait her out, make her state what she has in mind.*

"I always hate to see Alan go off to a clinic or a medical meeting," said Seretha, in a coolly analytical tone. "Don't you?"

"No," said Linda firmly. "Why should I?"

"Because he always comes home discontented with his position here. And then I have always to persuade him that he is well located. I presume you have the same problem?"

Now Linda lifted her head and looked across at her mother-in-law. The tapestry frame was between them, and Ma'am's white head was downbent to her work. She had not waited for an answer to her question. "I've been fighting Alan for years on that point," she said resignedly. "He thinks he wants to be a city specialist."

"He'd make a very good one, I expect," murmured Linda.

"Now, my dear. You know that Alan would do better to content himself with the fine work he does as a country doctor. And that sort of notion is an especially futile indulgence for a man with his own hospital dependent upon him."

"He realises that, Ma'am," said Linda softly. "The fact sometimes weighs upon him; he says he took on that responsibility too young——"

"Oh, nonsense!"

"Alan is conscientious about his work. We both know that. He is grateful for what you, and Father, have done for him. He knows that it was you who persuaded Father to build the hospital and place him at its head. But one can't blame Alan for being, sometimes, a little overburdened and tired by all that such a position imposes upon him."

"Does he think a city specialist does not get tired?"

"We don't discuss the matter often enough for me to know. He gave up that dream when he accepted the hospital here."

"I don't think he has given it up, however. And that is why I say you should help me keep him here. Where he belongs."

Linda frowned, and said nothing.

"A wife can manage such things, Linda——"

"I'm afraid I am not that sort of wife, Ma'am. I married Alan as a man capable of making his own decisions. And—I still think he is capable. He must be the one to decide such important things as to where he will work, what sort of work he will do. He will decide it, too, Ma'am. He'll do the right thing—the thing that is right in my own mind."

"Humph!" said Seretha, angrily. "That's exactly what *he* said about *you*!"

Linda dropped her knitting, and lifted her head to look at Seretha. Her back straightened; a little smile trembled upon her lips, put a shine into her eyes. How, she wondered, had Alan happened to say such a thing? Under what circumstances? What decision had he and Ma'am been discussing?

Now she was eager to prolong the conversation, but there was the sound of running feet in the hall, childish voices—and the twins plunged into the room, their apple cheeks flushed, their hair—Ann's at least—flying. Their mother, they announced breathlessly, shrilly, had said that they were to come here after school—she would stop by for them.

Linda suggested that they hang their jackets in the hall closet, wash their hands and tell Jacob that they would be present for tea.

The twins scampered off; they could be heard shouting, "Hi, Aunt Flora!" and the old lady came into the morning-room, greeted Linda and Seretha and settled her perfumed, fluttering self into a chair.

"I wonder where Margaret went this afternoon?" mused Seretha.

"Margaret has lots of interests." Linda realised that, these days, she often met with the need to defend her sister-in-law. "Could be the dentist—shopping—a club or committee meeting—bridge party——"

"I expect the twins will know," said Aunt Flora.

Linda put her knitting away, determined to prevent the question—or, at least, its answer.

The twins came back, helping Jacob to bring in the tea things. Ann carried a napkin-covered basket of crullers. "Tangle britches," she announced triumphantly. "Jim's got the milk—if he doesn't spill it."

"Aw, I won't spill it!" her brother protested.

Jacob set the tray before Ma'am, and left.

"You'll pass the crullers, won't you, Ann?" Linda asked.

"Oh, yes, sure," the child agreed. She picked up the basket and took it across to Aunt Flora. "We saw you again yesterday," she said chattily, "with your boy friend."

89

"Oh, my goodness!" squealed Aunt Flora. "Where were you?"

It was Aunt Flora's silliness, her bridling and blushing, her protests and denials, that established the fact of her rendezvous with old Colonel Chaney.

"You twins see too much!" she cried, laughing excitedly, slapping playfully at Ann.

"Well, gee whiz, Aunt Flora, anyone could-a seen you. You sat right there in the trap with him, goin' down the river road. We were over playin' with Lucy, and you went right past."

She bridled, and flushed. "Now," she announced, "I don't want anyone to think that the Colonel and I did, or would do, anything indiscreet. But, naturally, we are friends—with the two estates adjoining. I would hope people would consider that in any comment they might make . . ."

"Silly old fool," said Seretha clearly, flatly.

Aunt Flora chose to ignore her, and turned graciously to Linda with a spirited inquiry about Red Cross classes; could she help in some way?

Deciding that Aunt Flora had, at least, the better social manners of the two, Linda accepted her conversational gambit, then moved the talk on to subjects calculated to engage the children's interest. Seretha sat behind the sparkling tea-tray, watching and listening, but she said nothing more. No further question was asked about Margaret, even when she came in, smiling and pretty and hurried, her furs smelling of the crisp evening air, her eyes shining like deep pools. It was doubtful if she had been to the dentist.

Linda sat back in her chair, sipped her tea and discovered that she was, perversely, enjoying the tea party. Ma'am was in trouble. For all her power, for all her tyrannical hold upon the family, there seemed to be a clutch of problems in the Thornton household which were getting out of her control. She could not prevent Aunt Flora from being an "old fool." She could not enlist Linda's help to keep Alan at work in Valhalla. Margaret was not ready to behave "sensibly," according to her mother's judgment of such things. And—as for Alan's marriage —it might be saved, it might not—but Seretha was not going to be the one to *decide* the matter!

On Sunday, when the family returned from church, Alan's

bags stood ready in the downstairs hall, reminding the family of his trip to St. Louis. "I'm driving," he replied to an inqury. "I'll leave as near two as I can get through here."

The Rector and his wife were dinner guests, so that the family protests were necessarily on a polite level. Linda, watching Alan, was glad that he was a man able to carry out the requirements of his profession without permitting interference from the older members of his family.

We should have established a home of our own, she decided silently, as she watched the plates being handed around. *We'd have done much better*.

Alan was explaining to the Rector in detail beyond his usual custom why he especially wanted to attend the clinic in St. Louis. "I have always had a special interest in brain surgery," he confessed. "This clinic is particularly allied to that subject —and one of the demonstrations is for the relief of bony pressure upon the brain. I happen to have a case like that in hospital—a young woman in her thirties. Some months ago, she was in a bad car accident, and suffered a skull injury which was diagnosed at the time as a crack and concussion. Competent doctors made the diagnosis, and conducted the treatment. I would have done exactly as they did.

"She seemed to recover in a normal fashion, though she was bedridden for some time because she also had a fractured pelvis, and other injuries. But she seemed to progress normally, until—oh, it's a matter of months in which her condition has deteriorated. Her reflexes and mental responses have steadily become weaker. Some doctors think there have been cranial hæmorrhages; some think it is the result of severe shock and possible tissue injury at the time of the accident. In any case, she had been reduced to the place where she is completely dependent upon others for care.

"In the six weeks that I have had this case, I've decided that her condition may possibly be due to a depressed skull fracture. At least, there is some sort of brain pressure. If I am correct, surgery would certainly relieve her, though cure is problematical. There may be excessive brain-tissue injury which would require the delicate neurosurgery which I shall see demonstrated at to-morrow's clinic."

"Medicine as you practise it, Doctor," said the Rector intently, "must be a fascinating thing."

"Would you do the operation on your patient?" asked Mrs. Clark.

"I'd do it, or advise the husband to take her to some brain surgeon and have it done."

"You're talking about Mrs. Blake, aren't you, Alan?" Jasper asked.

Alan laughed. "I mentioned no names."

"Don't need to. Couldn't be anyone else. The Captain comes to services, Reverend. Stationed at the Fort."

"Oh, yes, indeed! Captain Blake—but, my goodness, I didn't know he was married. Let alone—why, that's a most distressing thing, Dr. Thornton!"

"Yes," agreed Alan. "I have the case because medical facilities at the Fort are still not adequate for much except emergency care among the soldiers."

Uncle Arthur leaned across the table towards him. "You can't mean that you plan to try that operation on Mrs. Blake!"

Alan's dark face plainly showed his impatience that the subject should be continued. "That was my idea." He looked at his watch.

"Why, I've seen her . . ." cried Aunt Flora. "And Arthur's right, Alan. That woman would be much better off dead!"

Alan said nothing, coldly and definitely.

"I cannot conceal my surprise to learn that the Captain is married," confessed the Rector. "I'm afraid I've been guilty of a little wishful match-making—between him and Mrs. Giddens. It's a little game I indulge in, I'm afraid. Mrs. Clark says I anticipate the fee." He laughed, his cheeks pink with innocent mischief.

"I hope you've not said anything!" chided his wife.

"Well, I hope not. Of course, I have been casting about on Mrs. Giddens's account ever since I first came to this parish. And the Captain seems such a fine chap."

"He is," agreed Alan. "I'd like very much to help him."

"You won't do it by prolonging his wife's life," cried Aunt Flora. "Margaret is in love with Fred Blake—and if you——" She gulped.

His face sternly blank, Alan looked again at his watch, pushed his chair away from the table. "Don't let me disturb you," he urged the others. "But I said I'd pick Ernst up at two, and I must be on my way. Father—you do what Linda tells

92

you while I'm gone. Good-bye, Ma'am." He bent over to brush his lips across Seretha's cheek. He said a general good-bye and went out into the hall, Linda following him.

The family heard the front door close, car wheels in the drive—and Linda returned. "You may bring dessert, Jacob," she said softly as she resumed her chair.

Aunt Flora evidently had appealed to the Rector for an opinion on Alan's moral obligation in the Blake affair. Mr. Clark was side-stepping the issue.

"I am sure it takes more than surgical spirit to be a doctor. One must have the wisdom of Solomon to handle some of the decisions that arise."

"And the patience of Job," said Linda crisply, "to handle his family."

Rupert Ernst had asked to accompany Alan to the clinic, and Alan had been heartened by the request. He would need Ernst's assistance should he decide to operate on Fern Blake; he supposed that was why Ernst wanted to go.

Alan Thornton used clinics as a means of assaying what was within his own brain and skill, what technical dexterity his experience had trained into him. He could watch the highly skilled men whose ability was kept razor-sharp by specialised practice, and judge just how keen his own performance would be at the times when an emergency arose which was outside the scope of his routine practice.

The two doctors checked in at a hotel near the medical centre, registered for the clinic and received its programme. On this same evening a buffet supper was scheduled and Ernst was anxious to attend it. "I suppose you know everyone," he said to Alan.

"Hardly, since the clinic takes in half-dozen states."

"I meant the *big men* who will be here!"

Alan nodded. "Oh! Yes, I trained here, and I use the Staff men for reference cases. All right, we'll go to their party and I'll introduce you around."

Alan was a hearty man, and he liked people. But he was not a man to disperse his interest. He had come to St. Louis to attend a clinic with a specific case on his mind, an important case. He could not fit himself into the Lions' Convention atmosphere of that first buffet supper as easily as did Rupert

Ernst. Alan stood back and watched his assistant, amused at Ernst's happiness, his chameleon-like transformation into just another of the boys, eating heartily, drinking, telling his own stories, laughing at those of the others. . . .

Alan Thornton had no particular criticism for the holiday attitude of the assembled doctors. They had come to St. Louis from a half-dozen states, all of them leaving their patients and practices to make the trip.

They were busy men; they had made an effort to come for instruction in a difficult subject. But the trip was also in the nature of a vacation, an event rare enough in most doctors' lives. So to-night these men talked, drank and told stories, laughing mightily and uproariously.

The next day they would—and did—attend the lectures and the demonstrations. Afterwards, a lot of them would stand about in the corridors and tell of their own surgical deeds, their personal triumphs.

Alan kept his promise to Rupert Ernst; he introduced him to many of the doctors. After that first evening he seldom saw his assistant. Rupert was busy making "contacts." Alan would glimpse him in one group of men, then in another, Ernst usually doing the talking.

"He hasn't waked up," commented Dr. Cabler, "to the fact that the centre of medical performance has shifted from Europe to America."

"I think he suspects it," drawled Alan. "But our own American snobs help to keep the European fantasy alive."

"In 1938 Hitler killed off all German scientific progress. By the end of this war . . ." The brain surgeon shrugged. He continued to gaze at the glossy-headed man in his well-cut tweed suit. "You say he's your assistant?"

"A refugee, establishing his licence. He's a good surgeon, and he will be an asset to America if he ever acknowledges that even his European education can be added to."

"Doctors who don't grow are dead, eh?"

"You bet! Now in my hospital I have two such men. One is Ernst yonder, who is with us for a year. The other is a man named Cassidy—seventy years old, and I don't give him too many future years. Fifty years ago, he trained in Dublin. He had a fine education as things went in those days. Those men get along like two tomcats on the same fence, and can't see that each blames the other for faults that exist in his own make-up."

Cabler laughed. "Look, Thornton," he said earnestly, "why not abandon your back fence and come and work with me? Here."

Alan's jaw set. "Don't tempt me, Doctor. It's what I've been saying I want."

"Be a lot easier than what you're doing."

"Taking what you want is always easier."

"You won't do it, then?"

"I'd miss my hair shirt."

Alan did his best to forget the offer. He had come to watch Cabler work, and he did watch him. On Tuesday morning Dr. Cabler demonstrated the operation which particularly interested Alan. He came early to the amphitheatre, took a place on the first row of seats and sat there, hunched and uncomfortable, for the entire four hours, his eyes intent upon the robed men around the table, his ears alert to the lecturer's voice. He made a note or two. Mainly, his brain and fingers memorised the technique, down to the anæsthetist's part in it. If he should try the thing on Fern Blake, he'd borrow this anæsthetist. They made all the difference in brain and heart surgery.

When he was free to move, to stand erect, his face was white, his eyes inward-turning. Rupert caught at his elbow. "Join us for lunch at the Jefferson, Doctor?"

Alan looked at him for a moment, as if trying to remember who this chap could be; then he shook himself like a wet dog. "Oh, no!" he said quickly. "That's way down-town."

For a minute, Rupert stood uncertain. "Sorry," he said then, perfunctorily. "Nice demonstration, wasn't it? Now, in Vienna, I've seen . . ."

Alan touched his shoulder. "Will you excuse me?" he asked brusquely. "I'll snatch a bit of lunch, and get to work."

"*Work?*"

"Yes. You see, I——" But Ernst's attention had been distracted and Alan strode away.

He did have work to do. With the demonstration still fresh in his mind, the operator's technique and the lecturer's discussion still clear, he meant to buy the use of a cadaver, and try out the section for himself, train his fingers and his knife.

In brain surgery no guesswork was permissible: the difference of a hair's breadth could mean the difference between success and death.

He worked all afternoon in the anatomy lab, borrowing an interested student's apron, but using his own instruments. He made careful drawings, wrote pages of notes and went back to his hotel room as tired as a hound dog at dawn, and as content. His clothes and hair reeked of formalin, and when he had showered, so did the bathroom.

Ernst came through it from his adjoining room while Alan was bent over, tying a shoe. "You've not taken up embalming, my dear Doctor?" he asked gaily.

Alan straightened and went over to the mirror, caught at his tie-ends. He told Ernst what he had been doing.

The other doctor listened incredulously, and at the conclusion of the tale he put his head back and laughed aloud.

Alan turned to look at him. "I don't think it's funny," he protested. "I wanted to get the feel of the job in my own hand. Seeing the thing done was not enough."

"Then you really do plan to operate on Mrs. Blake?"

"Her case is identical with Cabler's patient."

"Yes, so far as the physical aspect is concerned." Rupert's black eyes watched his Chief alertly.

Alan turned back to the mirror. "What other aspect should concern me?" he asked coldly.

He saw Ernst's shrug, and his knowing smile.

"I plan to start home at noon to-morrow," he said in a manner that would dismiss the other man and his disturbing suggestions. The patient *was* all that mattered: her present condition, her chances for survival and improvement.

They didn't get away quite at noon. For Dr. Cabler hunted Alan out, invited him for lunch and spent the early afternoon trying to get him to consider the offer he had made.

During the drive home, Alan was thoughtful, tired and washed-out—as a person is apt to be when some momentous decision finally is made, and the arguing about it left behind.

It was dark when they were still thirty miles from home. "You'd better come along and eat at our house," Alan suggested to Rupert. "You will have missed hospital meal-time, and we'll be just right for our supper."

"They're not expecting a guest."

Alan laughed, "Except at formal parties, my father always has an extra place set at his table."

"He's a remarkable old man, your father."

"So remarkable that I seldom think of him as old. Or else I myself have reached an age when the early seventies seem quite vigorous."

The car rolled on, through the little towns, past the neon-lighted filling stations and roadhouses, between the silent stretches of farmland, and the even more silent woodlands; and finally their own town began to enfold them. They went past the hospital down the main street to the gates of the Green, up and around the sweeping drive, to the front steps.

The lower gallery was a band of shadow and mystery upon which the front door opened in an outward streaming fan of lamplight, and Linda stood there, framed in radiance.

Alan drew in his breath sharply. He was so glad, so *glad* to see her again, to be within the sound of her voice, the touch of her hand. During the drive home, his thoughts had been like bees swarming in his mind. Fern Blake—Dr. Cabler's offer —his decision—the operation—Margaret. He realised that he had been straining towards Linda, anxious to ask her—to tell her——

Side by side, the two men went up the steps. Linda glanced at Alan's face. "You're very tired, aren't you?" she said gently, lifting her cheek to his kiss.

Then, her hand outstretched, she turned gaily to greet their guest. "Why, hallo," she said warmly. "How very nice!"

Alan had stepped aside. "I asked Ernst to come here for his supper—we were held up, and got off late."

Linda's eyes turned his way, and back to Rupert. "Come in, both of you! I want to hear all about the clinic."

Allan followed, his face darkly troubled. She was only being cordial to a guest. He would want her to be cordial. Yet——

Alan had been a fool to invite Ernst home with him. Why had he done such a thing? Because he feared that Linda's greeting to *him* would be cordial—and nothing more? Had he brought Ernst as a shield against this sort of bright friendliness from Linda, directed to himself, instead of the loving, intimate warmth he so deeply craved?

Supper became a gaily social occasion. The talk centred

around Rupert; he guided it. With his glossy social grace, he included every member of the family—an impudent anecdote to Uncle Arthur, a flattering word to Aunt Flora. He earnestly discussed the possibility of *dressage* for one of Jasper's palominos. He deferred to Seretha as his hostess, and openly diplayed his admiration for Linda.

He even remembered Alan—though that attempt misfired. Alan had wanted to tell Linda of Cabler's offer, in a time of intimate privacy with her. He was neither flattered nor pleased when Rupert spread the whole story out upon the table for family consumption.

"I did well to bring our young man here back to Valhalla," he declared. "Though, of course, I can take no credit for his return."

Seretha stiffened. "What *are* you talking about, Dr. Ernst?"

"I'll explain. If you will permit me to start my story anew?"

"I'd drop it entirely," suggested Alan.

Linda glanced at him. "Is he being modest, Rupert?" she asked.

"Very."

"It is a fault of his," she agreed.

Rupert nodded. "Let me remind you that this clinic which we have just attended was built around the work of a certain renowned neuro-brain surgeon. And we had no more than arrived in St. Louis when I became aware of excitement over the rumour that Dr. Cabler was ready to take on an assistant, a man capable of working with him, and after him. Of course there was a great deal of jockeying and wire-pulling for the position. The man selected would have his reputation and his future assured!

"And then! Do you know what happened? Our Dr. Thornton here was offered the place, the honour—and the man refused it!"

"Oh, Alan!" breathed Linda, proud and regretful at once.

Seretha tossed her white head in triumph.

"What made you do a damn fool thing like that?" trumpeted Jasper.

Everyone stared at him. Then Alan laughed. "I did it, thinking it was what you would want me to do," he confessed. "Wasn't it?"

"Stable boy or top rider," growled the old man. "Each one's got to do his job the best he can, the best way he can."

Alan nodded. "That's what I decided," he said quietly.

It was Linda who gave the signal that dinner was over. Coffee, she said, would be served in the small parlour.

"I'm going to the hospital," Alan told her, before she could speak to him about Cabler's offer. "How has Father been?"

"He's all right, I think. Alan . . ."

He caught her dimpled chin between his thumb and the knuckle of his forefinger. "I did do what I wanted," he said, smiling down into her eyes. "I won't be long."

He let himself out into the night, his mind still seeing the picture of the small parlour—Linda seated in the rose damask chair, her hands busy among the appointments of the coffee table, Rupert at her shoulder, intent, admiring, close.

By eight o'clock the old folk would get sleepy and go to their bedrooms. Rupert would stay on, paying his compliments, Linda listening, her cheeks pink, her eyes bright with pleasure.

He squealed his tyres into the hospital drive. He'd not stay *anywhere* for the purpose of keeping his wife from being excited about another man!

He spent an hour in his hospital, checking on the situation there, what had been done, what was scheduled. Then he went in to see Mrs. Blake, and stood thoughtfully beside her bed. She lay quietly upon the white pillow, without pain, or any response to his voice and touch. Her light brown eyes followed the beam of his flash-light.

He must talk to the Captain about his wife. Some decision must immediately be made.

When he was finished with his rounds, it was just about eight. He could go home, sit upon the Duncan Phyfe settee and join in the talk with Linda and Ernst.

Brusquely he turned his car wheels off the main drive, and down the hill to Margaret's little white cottage. Lamplight streamed from the window. He touched the doorbell and Jim came to answer.

"It's Uncle Alan," he screamed. "Did you bring . . . ?" He gulped, and broke off.

Alan put his arm around the child's shoulders, and went with him into the small, bright living-room where Margaret was busy with a ribbon she was tying in Ann's hair.

99

"It's all right," he laughed. "I forgot to bring anybody anything. Even a box of candy for Linda."

"I don't suppose she expected it," Margaret comforted him. "When you doctor, you *doctor*!"

"I'm afraid you're right." He dropped into a corner of the couch, and stretched his long legs. "Why's everybody so dressed up?"

Margaret waved a hand down the length of her housecoat. "The twins are stepping out," she announced.

"Kinda late, isn't it? On a school night?"

"There's no school to-morrow. Some sort of teachers' meeting. But I agree that the party is late for little children."

"We're not little," disputed Ann. "The party is for nine to twelves—and we're supposed to be there at eight."

"You're going to be late then."

"It's Ann's beau that's late," declared Jim.

Ann made a horrible face at him.

Alan chuckled. "What is this all about? Flounces and frills, and a beau for Ann. A b-e-a-u."

"It's Miss Sadie's Valentine party," explained Margaret. "Don't you remember, Alan?"

"Oh, Pete, *do* I? My goodness, is that old . . . ?"

"Alan!"

The children fizzed off into a storm of giggles, Alan joining them.

Margaret primly swallowed her own laughter, and reminded everyone that this party was one of the high spots of Miss Sadie's dancing class, with the boys and girls paired off, escorts to call for their ladies. Alec was to come for Ann, then Jim would stop next door for Lucy.

"That *Lucy*!" cried young Ann, flouncing around the room. "She *says* she's going to wear a long dress!"

"Some of the girls will, I expect," said Margaret, as if the matter had already been considerably discussed. "But I feel——"

"I know, I know. Mine is hand-embroidered organdy, and a pale blue sash is pretty on *little girls*!"

"On pretty little girls," agreed Alan.

Ann grinned at him. She was going to be pretty—now that her second teeth were coming in, and since the scuffed places on her knees were hidden by the flounce of her organdy frock and the taffeta slip beneath it, she already was pretty. He put his arm lovingly around the child, and she snuggled against his shoulder. But she had not forgotten Lucy, her hated rival and constant nemesis.

"I don't know why Jim likes Lucy Chaney!" she cried desperately. "She can't skate, or play ping-pong——"

"She must have *something*!" teased Alan.

"She sure does," agreed Jim heartily, and Margaret and Alan looked at him, startled.

"Jim sent her a *corsage*!" said Ann derisively.

Alan's eyebrows went up; he was impressed.

"A tiny one of button chrysanthemums," Margaret explained. "Rather sweet."

"Cost fifty cents," announced Jim, torn between pride and embarrassment.

"Huh!" said his sister. "I'd spit in a guy's eye if he sent me a fifty-cent corsage!"

"You'll never get the chance!" yelled Jim belligerently.

The older ones were relieved to hear the doorbell. Alan rose to answer, and followed young Alec Honeycutt into the room. Miss Little Mae's great-nephew was dressed, as was Jim, in blue flannel and white collar; he came bearing a square white box.

"Good evening, Mrs. Giddens," he said, his eyes a little glazed from his effort to remember his coaching. "Here, Ann——"

His freckles covered with a comprehensive blush, he thrust the box towards Ann; she took it to her mother, and together they opened it, folding back green tissue-paper to disclose a truly magnificent corsage. A cluster of violets, surrounded by a circle of tiny pink roses, all bordered by lace, with a dozen fluttery ribbon ends.

Ann gasped with awed pleasure; she seized the confection and whirled about the room in dizzy delight; she waggled it under her brother's nose. "Isn't it *beautiful*?" she lilted.

It was Jim's turn to be jealous—and vindictive. "Aw," he cried, "I'll bet it's the corsage his sister had for last night. There was a picture in the paper of the High School banquet, and she had one *just like that*. A *second-hand corsage*!"

Ann stood stricken, and so did poor Alec. Margaret hastened to their rescue. Ignoring her son, she picked up Ann's coat. "I'd carry it till you get to the party, dear," she said gaily. "It's the kind you can carry. Libby may have carried this last night—but she led the cotillion, didn't she? I'd be very flattered to have her corsage!"

It did the trick. Ann and her freckled escort went happily out to the car, but Alan's hand detained Jim for a minute. "Look here, young man," he said sternly. "Real guys don't go around hurting women."

"Ann made fun of *my* corsage!"

"We men are tough and can take a little hurt. The point is, no guy worth a dime is ever unnecessarily cruel to a girl. Sometimes we hurt 'em without meaning to, but to do it deliberately, that's out, boy! Understand?"

"I guess so," said Jim sulkily.

"Well, get along to your party, then—and have a good time!"

"At Miss Sadie's? You crazy?"

But he dashed out of the house, and Alan closed the door behind him. He joined Margaret before the fire, shaking his head and chuckling.

"Whatever would I do without you?" she asked.

"Well, I take on a bit of extra authority with the twins," he agreed. "They don't have a dad, and I don't have a son."

Margaret looked at him thoughtfully, as if she wanted to ask a question, then—as if she thought better of doing it—she said, "Well, you're certainly a rock of stability for us all, dear. How did the trip go?"

Gravely, he talked about the trip. She already knew his prime purpose in going. He spoke of the people he had met, the good work he'd seen. He discussed the need any man had for a change of scene, a general shaking up.

"I had a letter from Silas while you were gone," she told in her turn.

Alan took out his pipe. "Good! What did he have to say?"

Margaret laughed. "He had a message—a comment, rather —about you."

"Oh?"

"He said that to be a doctor in the Army, on active duty, a man should be a hundred years old to have acquired all the experience required, but no more than ten to have adequate

102

strength and energy. And Silas's comment was that he guessed you could have filled the bill."

"Humph!" growled the young flier's uncle. "At least the hundred-years-old part."

"He meant it for a compliment."

"What else did he say?"

"Nothing, of course, about where he was or what he was doing. He had got his Christmas things, and he asked for some salted nuts. I've already sent some. And—oh, he had a whole paragraph over the arrival of some W.A.C.s at the Base. Said he took back everything he'd ever said or thought against girls in the Army, that—wait, I'll see if I can quote it. 'I can't begin to describe the charm these American women have for me.' What do you think of that, Alan?"

Alan smiled through the smoke from his pipe. "What am I supposed to think? The kid was glad to see someone from home."

"Not just *somebody*, Alan. It was girls—and I don't think he was writing as any kid. Do you suppose he's grown up that much, Alan, that—that the boy who went away from here is —is a *man*, now?"

"What else do you want him to be?" asked Alan comfortably. "He's turned twenty-one."

"Yes, I know . . . I worry about him so much, Alan."

"Of course you do."

"And yet, to be honest, I don't worry as keenly as I used to when he was out late with the young folk here."

Alan nodded.

She sat thoughtful in the corner of the couch, gazing into the fire. Alan finished his pipe. He wanted—he had come to talk to Margaret about Fred Blake, and about his wife, Fern, yet his tongue could not seem to shape the words.

"Alan," Margaret said softly, and he glanced at her.

She flushed, and fluttered her small hands. "I want to ask you," she began again, shyly, "if you think I should go on wearing Si's ring, the engagement ring he gave me, now that I'm in love with another man?"

Well, thought Alan, *that puts a silencer on anything I wanted to say!*

"I did love Si," his sister was saying. "So much! I thought

103

there never could be another man—but, oh, Alan, there is! I am in love again, completely, entirely!"

Her whole person—her glowing eyes, her eager lips, her trembling intensity—testified to her new love.

"Put the ring aside," said her brother deeply. "Put it in your box at the bank, and give it to Ann when she's eighteen; or to one of the boys if he picks the right girl."

"Yes!" said Margaret. "That's a good idea. Oh, Alan—do you think I'm terribly silly?"

"I don't think you're silly at all."

"I'm thirty-eight."

He laughed. "You're a sweet, warm woman. At any age, there's nothing finer on earth."

He rose, came to her and kissed her. "I love you, little sister," he said quietly, "because you are a full woman. Si was a lucky man to have had you and the children you gave him."

She clung to his shoulder. "Oh, Alan," she blurted, "I *wish* that you and Linda . . ."

He straightened, his dark face stern. "I wish so, too, Margaret. But as much as we want children, Linda is dead wrong in thinking our marriage is a failure because we haven't had them."

"Is that the trouble between you?" asked Margaret, her eyes round. "Ma'am says . . ."

"It's a matter between Linda and me."

"Yes, of course, Alan."

"She puts it to me in a way that I can't argue. She says she wants them, too—and if, after ten years, it seems that we'll not have them . . ." He snatched his hat and slapped it against his thigh.

"She's dead wrong, Margaret! She talks a lot of stuff about my producing some strong Thorntons—you'd think I was one of Father's stallions! A man loves a woman, and he wants her in his arms—children, yes, if you are so blessed. But for herself, too, if you are not. Doesn't Linda know that?"

"You could tell her."

He sighed. "I don't seem able to talk to her any more—about anything."

"Of course you can talk to her, dear. She's probably waiting for you to do just that."

104

He smiled wryly, and shook his head. "I hope you're right," he said. "Good night, dear."

He got into his car, drove on up the hill and sat thoughtfully there for a minute before getting out. He was deeply troubled. He should have talked to Margaret about Fern, but he'd not been able to bring himself to dim her rosy glow. Yet, dear God in heaven, it was due to be dimmed! Now, certainly, whatever else he could discuss with Linda, he must talk to *her* about Fern. Of course, he was also going to try to argue with her about her "conviction." If all that troubled Linda was the fact that she had given him no child, that trouble could be argued out of existence. And if there was something else . . .

When, at eight, the old folk rose to go to their rooms, Rupert Ernst gave every indication of an early departure. After they were gone, he stood before the fireplace, smoking, as if he waited only to put the end of his cigarette into the ashes, and then say good night.

But, instead, he turned and came over to where Linda sat in the corner of the settee, and seated himself beside her, very close. She shifted imperceptibly, but there was not room to move far. She could get up and go over to a chair, but that would seem an awkward and rude thing to do.

She felt her cheeks getting hot, and was angry at herself. She certainly was old enough to take any man's talk without getting into a flutter. She acted, and probably looked like Aunt Flora!

Men had always admired Linda, and shown it. Of course, this man—all his mannerisms were extravagant. Other men showed admiration in their eyes, and in their voices, but Rupert's black eyes, clinging to her face, her throat, her bosom—the tone of his voice, softening, throbbing, said that he *worshipped* this woman!

Which certainly was silly! But she didn't need to be silly, too. She'd listen to whatever he had to say, as if he talked of sensible things, and answer him sensibly. That always worked with over-amorous Americans; it probably would help with an Austrian charmer. Let's see, now . . . What was he saying?

Oh, yes! That she was a wonderful person.

"I sense your feeling of obligation to this family, but I also see you being trapped by their increasing demands upon you. Why, they even set you to nursing the old man when he was sick!"

"But I wanted to. I dearly love Mr. Thornton."

He drew a deep breath. "Oh, yes, you love him. You feel that your duty lies in this home, in this small town—that is why I say you are trapped, and urge you to free yourself. Now, don't say that you like doing all the things you do. I sense nothing of the dry and selfless martyr in you, my dear Linda."

"It isn't that——"

"Listen!" He turned a little so that his knee pressed against hers and he took both of her hands in his. Light from the lamp behind them glittered in his black eyes. "Do you ever do anything because it is what *Linda* wants? Be honest with me!"

"Why, of course I do lots of things——"

"What are they?"

She laughed. "I suppose you mean that I arrange my life around Alan's hours. But any wife does that, Rupert."

"Except where the husband gives first consideration to the wife."

"Oh, but, look! Alan is a doctor...."

"And the devoted Laura Adamant is buffer enough for any man! I mean what I say, Linda, you are more slave than free. Your sister-in-law leaves her twins with you while she goes about her interests." His smile was suggestive. "Your crotchety father-in-law uses you; your tyrannical mother-in-law, your nymphomaniac aunt-by-marriage ..."

"No, stop!" she begged. "They are all darlings. You can apply ugly names to almost anyone! But I'm *not* a slave."

"Remember—all slavery is not enforced by the whip."

She turned a troubled face to him. "You're not serious."

"I'm afraid I am, my dear. You see, I come in with fresh eyes, and survey your situation."

"But aren't all people slaves, in that sense? Aren't we all bound by love?"

"It is a matter of degree, my darling. I love and admire you for your unselfish sense of duty—but I love you even more than that, and so I urge you to rescue yourself before that self becomes completely smothered. Be *yourself*, Linda! *Assert* yourself! You have *that* obligation, too. Don't you?"

She put her hands to her cheeks, and regarded him with wide, dark eyes.

"That right to individuality is your democratic ideal, isn't it, Linda? Each man free, equal to another man, slave to none?"

"It sounds right," she said uncertainly.

"It is right! That is why I urge you to free yourself from this house, from this family—from the tyranny of this small-town aristocracy! Be yourself, my darling Linda! Your fine, your beautiful self!" His voice throbbed like the low tones of an organ.

She would have laughed again, but she found herself gathered up into Rupert's arms with a swiftly ardent gesture, his mouth hard upon hers, his embrace . . .

And—for the briefest of seconds—she responded.

In that same brief second, Alan came in through the back door, as was his practice when coming home late at night. He paused to glance at the pad beside the telephone. There had been no calls. He turned, saw that lights still burned in the small parlour, and took a step that way, another—and stopped.

Against the room's pale wall was a shadow, cast by the lamp behind the settee. It showed the sharply etched silhouette of a man and a woman, embracing, kissing. . . .

He stood there, unable to move.

The embracing figures parted, and, at that same instant, Seretha's hand fell upon his elbow. He turned to his mother and moved, forcing her backwards in the direction of her room. She resisted, her old eyes fierce and accusing.

"Do something!" she hissed at him. He put his hand over her mouth, and led her, still unwilling, to her own door and into her room. Then, and only then, he freed her.

She stood outraged, breathing hard. She was in dressing-gown and slippers, her white hair in a braid. Her grey eyes were both hard and hot. "Aren't you going to do anything to them?" she gasped.

A very weary man, he leaned against the door which he had closed. "What could I say? What could I do?"

She beat her hands together. "Almost anything! Almost anything to stop that scandal!"

"Oh," said her son, with a shrug. "Who cares about such things?"

His mother bridled.

"Don't worry, Ma'am," he assured her. "You'll not have a scandal. I'll not lift my hand, nor speak one word. If Linda loves . . ." he gulped. "If Linda loves that man, why, she must have him." He turned and opened the door. "Except for grace in the matter of hand-kissing, I should be man enough to compete with Rupert Ernst. I'll accept the fact that I've lost the contest," he said as he went out, "if and when I *have* lost it!"

His mother could scarcely believe that she'd heard him add that last phrase. What would it take to persuade him that he'd "lost a contest"?

With a grim smile, she walked across the room, and back again, as erect as a steel pole, her face as hard. "I don't think, my son," she said softly, aloud, "that there is any *if* about it!"

She stood for a moment in deep thought. Then, with a swift, decisive gesture, she threw back the room door, went into the hall and up the stairs after her son.

PART THREE

FOR THAT one brief second, Linda's lips were soft beneath the man's bruising, demanding kiss. For that brief time his cheek knew the silken touch of her hair, his arms held her soft body—but then, as sharp as a knife blade, she stiffened and drew back, her hand brushing across her lips, her eyes angry and outraged.

"Don't speak!" she cried.

The man rose, stepped back and bowed.

"Just—go," said Linda, feeling her strength run out of her. She wanted to keep her dignity—she also wanted to cry like a child, sobbing aloud.

She waited until she heard the front door close behind Rupert. Then she did sob a little as she tidied the room, made the fire safe for the night, turned off the single lamp and went out.

She went slowly up the long, curving flight of stairs as if her feet were weighed with lead. If the scene just past was high romance, Linda felt pretty sure she was not up to playing her part.

When she finally reached the upper hall, her head bowed, she started violently to hear Seretha call to her from the door of the green guest-room.

"Linda! Will you come in here?"

She stood for a minute, more surprised to see Ma'am above stairs than anything else. She went across to the door—Alan was standing against the far windows, his dark face grave.

"Come in, please," said Seretha, "and close the door, Linda."

Alan made a move of some sort. Linda closed the door, and walked a little way into the room, her heart weighed with misery and shame. "Has—has something happened?" she asked faintly.

She was wearing a dress of violet wool, her hair was a cloud of red-gold—Alan had never seen her more beautiful.

"I would say that a great deal has happened," Seretha answered coldly. "You are in the best position to say—or know —how much."

"I don't understand . . ."

"Well, *we* understand. But let's stop hedging. I am too old for scenes. I shall remind you, however, that I am not too old to be aware of what is going on in my home."

Linda's dark eyes turned towards Alan, who stood like a man in chains.

"If you've come to tell us that you are leaving the house, that you plan to divorce my son and marry Dr. Ernst, I must urge you immediately to consider our position and feelings."

It's what she wants me to do, thought Linda. *She's been edging me to this position all along. In some way she knows that Rupert kissed me to-night, and she's told Alan. Right at the first Ma'am said that another man would make a difference.* So deep was she in her thoughts that Linda did not realise her failure to speak. She stood, head down-bent, silent.

Perhaps the entire family is with Ma'am, and they all want me to leave. Perhaps Ma'am knows this . . . Her head tipped up, her eyes held a question—and then she all but smiled. *Why, I recognise her tactics! I've seen through them from the first! To-night she had drawn poor Alan into the effort. Ma'am is a jealous woman. She is jealous of the place I have taken in the house, and with Father. I nursed him when he was sick, instead of Ma'am, his wife. She is jealous of my place with Alan. . . .*

Seretha had deliberately developed this situation! By clever suggestion and sly innuendo about her childlessness, the scheming, tyrannical old woman had driven Linda to her foolish declaration to Alan, and her panicky separation from him. Using that as a foundation, she had instantly and grimly, brick by brick, added distortions and half-truths until now she was ready to cap her monstrous edifice!

Her methods were so obvious as to be laughable! Linda would laugh at her, and denounce her. Alan would take his wife's side, and—— But a glance at Alan silenced her. In his face Linda could read only shock. No grim amusement, no anger, nor resentment. Just shock.

Seretha had told him of the kiss, and apparently he was ready to believe anything else his mother might tell him.

Deeply hurt, angry and still not speaking, Linda turned, opened the door, went into the hall and across to her own room. She'd leave if they wanted her to. Of course she would!

Not with Rupert, of course. He had only been behaving according to his idea that a woman wanted men to act so.

She closed her room door behind her, turned and shot the bolt; the sound of metal grating upon metal touched her like a cold, restraining hand. *This was wrong!* She pulled the cylinder back, and took a deep breath.

She would *not* let Ma'am force her into anything! Alan would come to her for an explanation. He *must* come. If she waited—and of course she would wait.

Across the hall in the green room, Alan now was speaking. "Ma'am, I must ask you, again, to let Linda and me alone."

"*Let you alone?* Permit you to stand back and allow her to leave you?"

"'She has not mentioned leaving, has she?"

"That's what she is planning, all right! And she can't do it, Alan!"

He looked at her curiously. He had been deeply shocked by a sudden suspicion that Ma'am was forcing Linda to leave. Linda had thought so, too. He knew that she had—he could read Linda's eyes; she was no dissembler.

Nor was Alan, where his mother was concerned. Seretha instantly had recognised the shock in his face, and knew that retreat would be her better course; so when he said, curiously, "It sounded as if you wanted her to get out," she could put her hand on his sleeve and say earnestly, "Of course I don't want that, Alan. We must not let her do such a thing, son!"

"Why not?"

Her head snapped up. "But, *Alan* . . ."

"Over and above my feelings," he explained.

"Why, for the sake of the family, of course," cried Ma'am. "Remember, Alan, I am an old woman, wise in experience. I know that once a family like ours permits a breach, the whole structure may collapse. If I would allow you and Linda to separate, to break our code, others in the family would feel free to break over. Margaret——"

"You seemed to think it important that Ernst kissed Linda——"

"As evidence of a danger that threatened."

"Oh." He recognised her retreat. "Family solidarity," he said woodenly, "is more important, you think, than individual rights."

"Certainly! You know that the one lasts, while whim and fancy..."

"But, Ma'am," said Alan wearily, "I must remind you that you are speaking of *our* family, not of Linda's. She's been good to us, but——"

Ma'am took a deep breath. "I'm tired," she said. "I'll go to bed. You'll remember what I've said—won't you?"

"Oh, yes," he agreed. "I'll remember."

He took her down to her room, and came upstairs again. For a second he stood at Linda's door. His strongest impulse was to go to her, to take her in his arms and force her to accept him! She was his wife, he loved her and he wanted her!

He could imagine the scene—her eyes would be dark and wide, her body passive and tears would lie upon her cheeks....

He went across the hall and prepared for bed. He was tired and deeply troubled. A man should be able to hold his wife. It spelled failure when he could not—did not. Especially if he loved that wife.

He got into bed, stretched his limbs upon the cool, smooth linen, and stared at the ceiling, his full lips pressed together, his eyes burning, his strong jaw jutted upwards. He sighed, and sighed again. Turned, and turned again. He kicked off the blankets, and reached for them.... He wanted desperately to be with Linda, to love her and talk to her. He had thought to come home and talk to her of the things he had mentioned to Margaret, of the things a man wanted of his wife, besides desire.

Love was another thing entirely. Desire was a part of love, of course—if it was shared. But real love was not just physical union, it was a spiritual communion, as well.

In his marriage, Alan had thought himself blessed with such a love. Had Linda's love for him suddenly died? Or gradually faded until ...

He couldn't be surprised. There was no good reason why a woman like Linda, warmly pretty, gay and sweet, should love Alan Thornton, a country doctor too damn' busy to attend to the little niceties of marriage, so tired when he came home that a warm bath and sleep were his only needs. If he talked to his wife, it was of his work, and its problems. He gave her an

112

account; she could spend the money as she wished; but he didn't even have time to notice the clothes she bought.

Clothes! There was another thing! Linda never saw him, except at church, in clothes that were not rumpled and unattractive from a long day at the hospital. When he came home from such a day, his hair would not be combed; his eyes would be grave from the work he'd done, his laughter drowned in other people's sorrows.

That sort of companionship was nothing to offer a young woman! It was no competition for the glamour of a man like Ernst, with his talk of Vienna, of the opera, the cafés and wine cellars. . . . Ernst could make even his preference for drip coffee seem exciting! His smooth black hair, his courtly manners and his well-tailored clothes—his glossy professional manner—and performance! Against him, Rough-and-Ready Thornton must look to anyone like a bear lumbering up out of the leaves!

Besides all that, Alan had dumped Linda down in the midst of his family, and had let them run their hooks into her. He'd let her nurse Jasper, and run Ma'am's errands, listen to Aunt Flora's ditherings and cope with Uncle Arthur's sodden spells of "illness."

Alan snorted and flopped over, the bed springs grating in protest. For that matter, though, had Rupert Ernst ever spoken to Linda of *his* family? His father and his crippled mother, abandoned in Vienna when Rupert had skipped out to save his own skin? Had he told Linda *that* story of Vienna?

Agh, that was no argument to justify Alan's weighting the girl with *his* family while he himself gave so much of his strength and thought to the troubles of other people that he had nothing left for his young wife.

There was no way he could evaluate things so as to blame Linda. Whatever she did—— If he'd lost her, it was his own fault. No one else could be blamed. . . .

For one black moment he had thought Ma'am—but she would not do such a thing to Alan. No mother would so hurt her son. . . .

The next morning, it was early, still black dark, when he rose and went to the hospital. Deep lines in his face, shadows around his eyes, showed the effect of his sleepless night. He was cross and short-spoken to his assistant in the operating-room; they looked at him, and at each other, in wonder. Doctor didn't act this way! Sometimes he worked without speaking, but Doctor Thornton was never ugly or even brusque. But this morning, even as Mrs. Dunham was phoning to the floor supervisor that his patient was on the way down, Alan brushed past her, and strode out of the room.

He recognised his mood, and deplored it. He was not the first doctor, of course, to resent the impact of his personal life upon his professional performance. Last night he had decided that as a doctor he had neglected his wife. It would be no improvement to let the bad husband he was affect his surgical proficiency.

He stopped at the floor desk, glanced at the Supervisor's census and realised that he had talked to no one about Fern Blake. And he had meant to.

He jerked his head impatiently. What a hell-paver was Alan Thornton! He'd better snap out of this mood, and quick! The first thing would be to eat some breakfast. He'd not even had a cup of coffee before going to the operating-room. He was hungry. Last night he'd slacked supper, had not eaten his bed-time apple. No wonder he was cross!

He dropped down the stairs to the first floor, went swiftly along the hall to his office, asking the floor nurse to have his breakfast sent in. "Lots of bacon!"

"Yes, Doctor."

Laura Adamant had just come in; he greeted her absent-mindedly, opened the inner door, and almost fell over Ann, who was seated in the chair beside his desk, her red snow-suit zipped open in various places, the hood of it slipped back from her head.

"Well, hallo!" said her uncle. "Why aren't you in school?"

"Oh, Uncle Alan! We told you last night there was a teachers' meeting."

He was glancing through a stack of mail. "Yes, so you did. I forgot." He cleared his desk for the tray he could hear coming. "Have you had your breakfast?" he asked the child.

"Sure. A long time ago."

"Where's Jim?"

"Oh, boys are scaredies about things like hospitals." He thanked the maid, lifted the metal domes to check on what he

114

had, poured a cup of coffee and picked up the glass of orange juice. "Is there something I can do for you, Ann?" he asked.

"Sure is." She kicked her heels against the chair legs. "We have to go to school to-morrow."

"Vacation'll be over, eh?"

"Yeah. It was only two days."

Miss Adamant opened the connecting door to ask if Dr. Thornton would see Dr. Carlson on Medical?

"As soon as I finish my breakfast." After his absence, all the personnel would have things to take up with him.

"Now, Ann, tell me. I'm apt to get busy, you know."

"Yeah, sure. Well, we thought—you know Miss Maggie pretty well, and——"

"Are you in trouble at school?"

"Well, sure! Last week we were late three days running—and Miss Maggie said we'd have to bring a note."

"Why were you late?"

"We didn't know we would be. But Fred—we didn't find out till Saturday that he'd set all our clocks right. Mums always keeps them ten minutes fast so we won't be late, and then she—— Our teacher—Miss Heintz, you know?—she got madder each day, and Friday she sent us to Miss Maggie and if we don't have our excuse she'll punish us! She got kinda mad when we told her we didn't know why we were late. That's why we want you to explain, Uncle Alan. You'll do it better. Mums'll get flustered, and fuss at *us*. And we *weren't* to blame!"

"No, of course not."

"Will you write us a note?"

"Well—the note ought to be from your mother. But maybe . . ." He could phone Linda and ask her—— No! By George, he'd not put any more on Linda! *This* he would attend to himself!

"I'll phone to Miss Maggie," he promised. "Or, if I can, I'll walk over to her house and explain to her about the clocks. If you want, you can go with me. Will that do?"

"That will be swell!" agreed his niece, settling back into the chair. "Miss Maggie won't argue with you!"

"Well, I'm not so sure about that," laughed Alan.

He ate his breakfast, and Ann looked at a catalogue from a

115

medical supply house, chattering busily about last night's party, interspersing the account with a dozen questions.

What was a retractor?

What was a snare—with a ratchet?

Why did doctors have to have so many kinds of scissors and stuff? Why—oh, she had been meaning to ask about this for a long time!—why did people say a doctor practised? Was it like music lessons?

A little like it, said Alan. Not exactly, though, because he learned a lot before he practised, while with music——

"I hate playing the piano," said Ann, happily. Then she tipped her head to one side. "Uncle Alan," she asked, "do you think Mums is going to marry Fred?"

Alan took a little time to answer that one.

"All the kids at school," Ann continued, "say he'll be our daddy when his wife dies, and Mums marries him. Huh?"

"Would you like it, Ann?"

"It'd be O.K., I guess. They're kinda old to be so mushy— holdin' hands and stuff. Just the way Silas used to do with Libby Honeycutt. Laughin' and lookin' at each other. Love stuff!" Scorn grated in her voice.

"Wait till your turn comes," laughed her uncle, reaching for the house phone, which was buzzing.

"Thornton here," he said into the instrument, listened to the crackling voice at the other end, then: "I'll be right there." He stood up, glanced down at Ann.

"I have to go to work, honey. I'll call Miss Maggie some time to-day. You run on home now."

And he was gone, through the outer office, into the hall, his face grave, his step long—but not running. Carlson seemed excited, but Alan had learned that excitement was no way to handle any emergency.

Not even his own. He'd not treat his situation with Linda in a mood of anger, or jealousy, or even hurt. He must think about it, carefully, and then do something sensible. But right now he had Carlson's food-poisoning. If it was that.

Carlson was the staff internist, and a reliable man. If he was worried about food-poisoning, Alan could be concerned, too. Last night Alan had made a quick tour of the hospital, but this morning he'd not had time——

He found Carlson on Medical, in the room of two seniles.

116

The doctor was supervising the use of a stomach pump on one patient, and the setting up of a continuous gastric suction on the other. He glanced wildly at the Chief. "We've got botulism, I'm afraid," he barked.

Alan frowned.

"Began last midnight," said Carlson, as soon as he could manage a word or two. "Nausea, diarrhœa—fever, and shock. Patients added—about ten now, all bad. Soft diets, mainly. Milk perhaps. More likely the eggs."

"Eggs?" questioned Alan, helping with the apparatus.

"Frozen eggs—use 'em in scrambled eggs and custards." Carlson rubbed his bare forearm over his forehead. Both doctors looked anxiously down at the old man on the bed; he was in a bad way.

"You carry on here," Alan decided. "I'll get the Supe, and line up the whole situation. Were the eggs used again at breakfast?"

"I'm afraid so."

"Here in the country we should have fresh eggs."

"The farmers are selling them to the Army personnel at premium prices."

"Oh! I suppose so."

Alan had a dozen things to do at once, and did them. He got a report on patients who were ill in this fashion, on ones who might become ill. He called in the emergency staff members, and sent both gastric samples and egg samples to the lab for tests.

Botulism in any case was a serious thing. In a hospital, afflicting people already weakened by illness, or surgery, the situation was grim. By noon, their old man had died, and by evening, a post-operative—and they had twenty-three cases on critical.

Alan ordered the hospital closed against all visitors. He made a terse statement to the press. He attempted to restore calm among the patients, cared for the affected ones, reassured those not in danger. He must also keep a firm hand upon his staff members. After the second death, he was faced with a complete breakdown of morale. Hysterics were evidenced in varying degrees. Everywhere there was a general loosening of tongues. Blame centred first upon the kitchen—the special diet kitchen—and eventually upon Old Cassidy. He was first called that by Dr. Ernst, and the name stuck.

Dr. Cassidy blamed himself. He did supervise the diet kitchen, and ordered the supplies.

"We are all to blame," Alan rebuked them. "No hospital does a single thing through the mind and hands of a single person."

"You and I are not to blame," protested Dr. Ernst. "*We* were out of town."

Alan turned to look at his assistant. His dark face was a little green-tinged with weariness, and there was, perhaps, some fear.

The doctors had gathered that evening for a dinner of sorts in the staff dining-room; there was a great scrubbing and steaming going on in the kitchen beyond. Dr. Carlson sat with his head in his hands. Dr. Cassidy grimly cut his meat, ate it, drank his coffee. Ernst smoked nervously——

Alan looked at Rupert, at this man who, twenty-four hours ago, had known the sweetness of Linda's lips, the perfume and the feathery softness of her hair, which lay against a man's cheek like silk——

Hatred and jealousy swelled in a red cloud behind Alan's eyes; he pushed free of it. He was a doctor, with an emergency on his hands. Ernst was a doctor who could help.

"Our being away," he quietly answered the man, "lays blame upon us."

"You may take that position. I shall not."

"No one cares what position you take," cried Alan. "We're in this thing, and we have to work out of it. We—yes, Laura?"

"I stayed late, Doctor—to help you——"

"Thank you. What is it?"

"Oh, Dr. Harg called. He says he has an o.b. Shall he bring her in? He'd heard rumours . . ."

"Is he on the phone?"

"No, he said to call him back."

"That's way out at Washing Creek," mused Alan. Rupert Ernst gave a hoot of laughter, and Alan's green eyes moved to him. Why, the man was drunk! A little.

His eyes still icy, he turned back to Miss Adamant. "Tell Dr. Harg exactly what is going on here. Tell him it is salmon-ella, not diarrhœa—I am quite sure there is no danger of contagion, but he is to judge his action by his patient's wish to come, or not."

"Yes, Doctor."

"Now," cried Dr. Ernst, getting to his feet. "That is the sort of hospital where I must work! Where a decision is given to a doctor whose mouth drips tobacco juice, concerning the bastard child of a patient on *Washing Creek*. The Chief Doctor calls it *Washing Creek*. The beautiful name of *Joachim* is so corrupted by ignorant, careless people. Not that I am surprised, you understand?" He paced the length of the small room, whirled and further addressed the men seated at the table. Laura Adamant watched him with wide eyes and trembling mouth.

"It is all part of this country!" Rupert declared. "Rough, ignorant, careless! The country, the hospitals, the doctors— peasants and beasts, all of them."

"Oh, shut up, Ernst," growled Dr. Carlson. "We're all tired of your tune."

"There is nothing ignorant nor careless about Dr. Thornton!" cried Miss Adamant, finding her voice on a high, screaming note. "He's the most wonderful man on earth—everyone loves him!"

Rupert's upper lip drew back from his teeth. "I would beg to differ from you, Miss Adamant. *I* do not love him. Of course *I* am not a frustrated woman of——"

"That will do, Ernst!" said Alan coldly. "Laura, go and make that phone call, then go home and get your rest. Put in a call for Dr. James, if Harg is bringing his patient."

"James, of course," said Rupert nastily, "works only when he has a patient. He fancies himself as a specialist."

"I think too many of us *fancy* ourselves," said Cassidy.

"Except you, my dear Dr. Cassidy," Ernst flashed on him. "Certainly *you* have nothing to be proud of—and much to be blamed for!"

Old Dr. Cassidy jumped to his feet, his grey hair tossing.

"I wonder what they are serving in the concentration camps to-night?" he shouted. Carlson glanced up at Alan, who shrugged.

"Why," gasped Dr. Ernst. "You—you *Englishman!*"

Alan stood up, a calm man in the midst of the turbulence of outspoken opinion, wrath and voiced grudges. "That'll be

119

enough, gentlemen," he said quietly. "I've worked out a schedule. We'll take house duty on shifts. I'll stay here round the clock, rest as I can on the couch in my office. Ernst, you're to go to bed at once, and get rid of that fog in your head. Carlson, you go home until seven in the morning; come back then. Dr. Cassidy, will you see me through the rest of to-night? I'll have James take over at three to-morrow afternoon.

"I think that is all, gentlemen. Except to remind you that we have a medical crisis on hand, and that people's lives are at stake. That takes precedence over any fixing of blame, or the possible exacting of punishment. We can take care of those things after we have saved the lives of twenty-three people." He swung sharply about, his eyes blazing green. "What did you *say*, Dr. Ernst?" he snapped.

Ernst shrugged. "I was just wondering why you bothered so much to save some of them—ignorant, poor, foolish. Let them die! Nature means the unfit to die!"

Dr. Cassidy struck an attitude. "And I am the tool of Nature! Is that the charge you would make against me?"

Alan glanced at him. "Will you please go out and check the house, Dr. Cassidy. Particularly that malnutrition case on Children's."

Dr. Cassidy looked at him. "Yes, son," he said kindly. "I'll do whatever I can to help you."

"Thank you." Alan poured himself another cup of coffee. He wanted nothing so much as to fly out at Ernst, to blast away at everything the man had said. His own nerves had taken their beating; that he remained calm and silent amid such winds as had swept this room meant only that he had not permitted himself any relief from his tension.

He was tempted, humanly, to give the Austrian his walking-papers. He had provocation; the man had no right to drink under the present conditions, no right at all to drink when on hospital duty. He could fire him for his ugliness to other staff members. Here, in fact, was his chance to get rid of the man. To take him away from Linda!

Pffagh! Alan got to his feet, dragging his big body erect. He was indeed tired to let such a thought enter his mind! Granted that he disliked Ernst even in a professional way; he could not let the temptation of getting the man out of his personal affairs sway his administrative decision. Ernst was here as a doctor in training. If he could not be trained into an acceptance of American ethics, he must go, but for no other reason!

On the other hand, if he loved Linda—if she loved him—— Had she ever heard his routine about beasts and peasants? Oh, Alan was too tired, and his mind too full, for such consideration, now.

"Let's stop talking, Ernst," he said gruffly. "You go to bed. There may be some surgical call upon us. We can't both be dead on our feet. We won't argue any more, any of us, concerning the regrettable situation now in our hospital. We have the mess; we must handle it as best we can, and clear it up as quickly as possible. Good night!" Tall and stern-faced, he walked out of the room.

It was in the late afternoon of the third day before Alan was free to go home. He was weary to his bones' core—and still worried, because one of the deaths promised to bring a suit for malpractice. The hospital carried insurance, but such a suit was always costly, in money, in reputation, in the peace of the doctors' minds. No doctor can ever say, surely, "I did all that could be done." He knows that he only does the thing he thinks is best—so far as his own knowledge and judgment extend.

Worry had tagged Alan throughout the long days of crisis. *Had* he done his best? Perhaps he had had no business letting Old Cassidy . . . Perhaps he should have come back from St. Louis sooner, not stayed for the talk with Cabler. Perhaps he should never have left his hospital in the first place.

So, on that wintry afternoon, he came home, wanting rest and comfort, wanting reassurance for himself as a doctor, and as a man—wanting Linda! Always before, in any time of stress, she had been near, a glowing light in the darkness, a comforting hand for pain, a reasoning mind, an intelligent comprehension against any confusion or doubt which was his.

But this afternoon he came home, fearful even to ask for his wife lest she already had left him. During the three busy days, his mind had magnified the scene with Rupert until even he recognised its present enormity, its unreality. And yet—a scene had taken place. His marriage, his happiness, had been threatened, and he had felt bound, tied, unable to take the steps which any husband is expected to take to defend his home against raid.

As he entered the hall, Jacob came to take his hat and overcoat. Alan made an effort to speak naturally. "Where is everybody?"

"Well, they about, Dr. Alan. Ma'am, she havin' tea in the mornin'-room. Mr. Thornton, he still down at the stables. Miss Flora ben gone sence noon, and Mr. Arthur, he tuk out a while ago—didn't say where." Alan stood silently regarding the tall handsome Negro. Jacob's eyes twinkled. "Yes, sir. Miss Linda, she had an errand. Seems Miss Ann—and Jim, too—they ben kept in after school all this week, and Miss Ann, she say it all your fault. So Miss Linda went ovah to talk to Miss Maggie."

Alan's jaw dropped; then he smote his forehead. "Oh *Jacob!* It *is* my fault." He told the story of the clocks to the man with whom, when they were boys, Alan had fished and swum and learned to ride.

"Yessir," commented Jacob. "Doctorin' kinda gits in your way sometimes, don't it, sir?"

"It certainly does!" Alan agreed fervently. "And my family suffers. Well—I'm going up to bathe and change. I've washed, and had clean clothes in spots this week, but . . ." As he mounted the stairs, his voice faded. Jacob stood watching him, shaking his head.

"Boy, if you'd do more," he murmured, "and think less . . ."

But Alan went on thinking. His family did suffer for his chosen profession. This matter with Ann was a small thing, but it showed the way the wind blew; Alan had failed the child, and Linda was trying to keep down the cost of his failure.

Alan himself paid entirely too high a price for his profession. Maybe all doctors did. Alan couldn't say. But it seemed that he, certainly, was asked to pay too much—and it was not right to send any of the bills to Linda. He must tell her that, if he told her nothing else! She was to have her happiness—with him if possible, away from him, if—— He sighed, mightily.

He was brushing his hair when Jacob tapped on his door. Miss Margaret was downstairs; she wanted to talk to Alan.

"I think she got special troubles," murmured Jacob.

"Oh? Well, ask her to come up here, then."

"Yes, sir! Right off!"

Margaret came at once, her eyes dark, her breath quick. Alan took her fleecy coat, and led her to a chair. "Jacob will bring us some tea," he said, kneeling to light the fire. He spoke of Linda's absence, its occasion. "I'm really in bad with the twins," he confessed ruefully. He wanted to give her a chance to quiet.

But her urgency was too great. Even as she poured his tea, she began to talk. She'd been waiting, she told him, for a chance to talk to him. Yes, she knew about the trouble at the hospital—it was a terrible thing! But everyone said that Alan had done a wonderful job of clearing it up. Then she hurried on, preoccupied with her own concerns, "I couldn't wait any longer to talk to you, dear. I——" She clasped her small hands against the tucked bosom of her blouse. "Fred tells me that you want to operate on his wife."

Alan set his teacup back on the tray, and stood up, lighting a cigarette. His sister watched him, tall, handsome, dark and, she thought, his eyes smiled a little.

"Alan!" she cried. "*Please* don't do it!"

"Now, Margaret . . ."

"I have to interfere!" she insisted. "I told you the other night that I was in love! And Fern—she—she——"

"She's helpless," said her brother's deep voice. "She can't do anything to help herself."

"But——" Margaret's pretty face sharpened into intensity. "Listen, Alan! Did you know that she was hurt, in the first place, while she was on a date with another man?"

"No," said Alan, looking at the tip of his cigarette. "Fred didn't tell me that. Did he tell you?"

She looked at him blankly. "Oh," she said then. "You mean he wasn't being a good sport. Well, I don't *care*, Alan! Fred and I—we're in love! You snatch at everything when you're in love! You know that!"

"I suppose—I should know it."

"It was a rotten, dirty break that she was hurt! If she hadn't been, Fred would be free by now. As it is . . ." She stared numbly into the fire. Then she looked up at Alan in anguish. "That's why I came to you, to ask you—to *beg* you. He can't. But I can, and I do. I am shameless in my love. I want to snatch at the happiness I could have if—— Maybe I'm wrong. . . ." She gulped and hunted for a handkerchief.

Alan gave her his. "You've nothing to be ashamed of," he assured Margaret. "A woman has a right to happiness. You do. Maybe she has a right to snatch it."

"You always talk, Alan, as if you decided things about your patients with your heart as well as your head."

"That's what I try for," he agreed.

"Well, then, the mere fact that an operation might help Fern Blake—I mean, I can see that it would be a fine thing if you could restore her mind, even partially! It takes a very good doctor to do that sort of surgery, I know. But doesn't your *heart* tell you, in this case——?"

"You think I'm deciding this matter as a scientist, rather than as your brother."

"Well," she said spunkily, "aren't you?"

"No." He sat down. "I am looking even farther into the future than you are, Margaret. I want to give Fern Blake every chance I can give her to know what's going on, and to decide things for herself. If I'd leave her mind clouded, or let her die—— You wouldn't have full happiness based on such a thing, darling. Can't you see that?"

"No," she said stubbornly. "Right now I can only see that I love Fred, and I want to be his wife. You may be right—it's a maddening habit of yours. But don't ask *me* to be noble and self-sacrificing! I just won't make it!"

Alan chuckled, and reached for a teacake, then dropped it to the carpet. He growled at his clumsiness, and scrubbed at the green carpet with his fine napkin.

As if her attention had been called to the colour of that carpet, to notice that it was green broadloom instead of the silky Oriental across the hall, Margaret said, as ingenuously as Ann would have done, "Alan, what's wrong with Linda?"

He tossed the napkin on the tray, took another teacake and bit into it. "Ma'am's talked to you, I expect."

"Oh, heavens, yes! And pointed morals all over the place. My friends have asked questions, too, and I have had to avoid gossip on all sides. That she had put you out of her room, and has taken up with Dr. Ernst. But I'm asking you what has really happened? What's wrong with her, all of a sudden?"

"Same thing that ails you," he said slowly. "She's snatching at life—and happiness."

"Oh, but it isn't the same with her! She's got you. I've been alone for nearly ten years. It's not the same at all!"

"No, it isn't," Alan agreed. "No two people, no two cases, are ever the same. I only meant that Linda wants happiness."

"What about you? Don't you want happiness?"

"Of course I want it. But—well—with Linda, there's a good chance that I'm the one to blame for us both being unhappy right at the minute."

Margaret seemed to gather herself together. "Well, that's good," she said briskly.

Alan stared at her, astonished.

"Well, of course!" she cried. "If you're to blame, you can do something about it! Can't you?"

"I don't know," said her brother. "Do you think I could, Margaret?"

"I think you can do anything you want to do, Alan Thornton. *That's* what I think!"

Seretha had said—not only on the night of Alan's return from St. Louis, but many times—that if Linda should "lose hold," the rest of the family might feel themselves free to forget convention, and do as *they* thought they pleased.

Now—it began to seem as if her prediction of family chaos was justified. Because, on that same evening, disaster seemed to descend from all sides upon the Thorntons. Big and small, tragic and ridiculous, swiftly events piled one upon another within the family circle.

They were only four at the dinner table: Jasper and Seretha, Linda and Alan. Some wonder had been voiced about the whereabouts of Aunt Flora and Uncle Arthur.

"They're certainly old enough not to have to account to us!" Seretha had said brusquely, and the others had laughed in agreement.

The talk had centred largely around the table at the hospital; Jasper asked keenly about the chances of a lawsuit— Seretha disposed of that matter with the remark that, "No one seriously could think that the hospital would try to poison its patients!" Linda took part in the discussion; it was all comfortingly normal, and home-like, until——

"Dr. Alan!" It was Jacob's agitated voice calling to him from the hall.

"Jacob," said Seretha, coldly, "how many times must I tell you not to call out?"

"Just a minute, Ma'am," said Alan. He was on his feet, going out of the room.

Jacob caught at his arm, and pulled him farther away from the door. "There's trouble over at Chaney's, Dr. Alan. Mr. Arthur, he——" He gestured to the coloured boy who was standing bug-eyed at the far end of the hall.

"What's happened, Nick?" Alan asked firmly, going to him.

"I run all the way, Doctor," gasped the boy. "Mr. Arthur—he had some kind of spell at our house. Not drunk, sir. He got hisself a kinda notion that Miss Flora she carryin' on wiv de Cunnel. This evenin' Miss Flora went drivin' wiv de Cunnel, sure nuf—then she come to see Miss Lucy's new doll's house, and stayed for suppah—but Mr. Arthur he come plungin' in wiv a horsewhip, a-talkin' wild about his wife elopin' an' old Cunnel a-seducin'—and—and—he try to whup the Cunnel. Couldn't, o'course. And when he saw he couldn't, he fell down in some kinda spell, wiv the women all a-screechin' for a doctah—and I tuk out ovah here."

"A telephone would have done," said Alan dryly. "But I'll go right over."

Linda had followed him out to the hall. She glanced at him now, her blue eyes dancing. "May I go with you?"

"Sure. I'll need you——"

They went out, leaving Jacob to relay the news as he might see fit. Alan caught Linda's arm in his hand, to help her down the steps and out to his car. He felt a surge of pleasure just to be so close to her, sharing this event—which they hoped was only absurd.

"Poor old things," mourned Linda. "We shouldn't laugh at them. But what got into them?"

"Maybe it's something in the air."

Linda glanced up at him, questioningly. He seemed preoccupied with steering the car out through their gates and into the road. She remembered being hurt that Alan had not called upon her for help in the trouble at the hospital. Usually, in emergencies, he did call on her.

Well—she'd not spoil this minute when Alan was with her again, offering her the old companionship sweet and—and good!

Nick had had to run only a half-mile from the Chaney house to the Thornton one; Nick had cut across a garden, a pasture and the orchard. But to drive was three miles by road, though the car made the trip swiftly.

The red-brick house was alight, and the Colonel himself came out upon the portico to meet them. "Alan, I'm glad you're here!" He wiped his bald head with a fine handkerchief.

"Of course I'm here. I got word that my uncle was ill."

"It's all a mistake, boy." The florid man was badly shaken. "That he's ill?"

"Oh, no. He had a spell. But he had no cause, no grounds . . ."

Alan, bag in hand, went brusquely around the big man and in through the door.

"He thinks only of his patient," said Linda to the Colonel.

Colonel Chaney sighed with relief, and let her into the hall. "Lucy!" he cried, irritably, up the stair well. "I told you to get to bed and stay there!"

"Yes, Grandpapa," said the child. "Oh, hallo, Miss Linda."

Linda returned the greeting, and the pigtailed, nightgowned child reluctantly withdrew into the darkness of the upper stairs. Linda went on into the parlour, where she found Aunt Flora slumped into the depths of a big chair, twittering and repentant.

"I didn't mean a thing," she assured Linda. "Those *men*!"

"Uncle Arthur was worried about your being out late," said Linda. "You should have phoned. Ma'am doesn't like us not to show up for supper. . . ." She was being so very sensible in her explanations that Aunt Flora decided her romantic colouring was going to be entirely washed out, and made a feeble attempt to be coy.

But it was only feeble. She looked tired and bewildered and quite ready, when Alan said they would all go home.

Uncle Arthur was all right, he said. He had a slight heart attack, and at his age, a thing of the sort was a serious symptom—but Alan had decided that he could go home and be put to bed there. Aunt Flora made extravagant promises for his care.

"Old fools!" declared Seretha when finally Linda and Alan came to the small parlour to tell her and Jasper their story.

"I don't think their age has anything to do with their being fools," snorted Jasper.

Linda turned to look appealingly at Alan. When Linda widened her eyes in that fashion her thick lashes lay back against the whiteness of the upper lids. There was a pretty colour in her cheeks this evening, and a small cluster of artificial lilacs tied at the throat of her knitted suit brought out the blue of her eyes. But those pretty eyes were asking a question, and Alan had to answer it.

"Colonel Chaney is anxious to hush this thing up," he said to his parents, "of course."

"Flora will tell it all over town."

"I suppose. Perhaps, Ma'am, that is the tragic part of the matter."

"Sounds more like farce to me."

"Yes—but tragic, too. Poor Uncle Arthur. As brittle as he is, to attempt to defend his home and honour! A man can so often seem comic to others when he himself is most deeply involved in personal drama." He stood as if in deep thought, then glanced across at Linda. Now the pink in her cheeks was poppy red. She gasped a little, and turning, almost ran from the room.

"I'll swear," said Seretha angrily, "I don't know what's got into this family!"

"You don't make sense, son," said Jasper, reflectively. "They's nothin' comic about you and Lindy bein' on the outs."

Alan turned swiftly to meet the steady green eyes of the man who was so like himself.

"Nor tragic, neither," Jasper continued hardily. "You jest, the two of you, put your foot out in the wrong direction. The thing for you to do now is to stop, right where you are in the middle of the dance floor, juggle your feet and start over, go on with the figger. Right?"

Alan picked up the evening paper with a snap and a rattle.

"What if she'd rather dance with another partner?" he asked tightly.

"Well—make sure of that first. Then, Alan, I think you'd be man enough for that horsewhip your uncle must-a left behind at Phineas Chaney's."

128

Alan made no comment, seeming to become engrossed in the printed page which he held before his face.

That was only the first of the events which piled in upon the family in a matter of twenty-four hours. It was early the next afternoon that the clerk in the Western Union office attempted to reach Dr. Thornton.

Laura Adamant was firm. "Doctor," she said, was doing a fluoroscopic; he couldn't come to the phone. She would take any message.

She did take it, with a soft gasp of surprise and regret.

She went to the X-ray room, waited until the warning light flicked off, then opened the door and stuck her head around it. "Doctor?" she said breathlessly.

Alan was still preoccupied with the patient on the table, who was not happy about barium.

"Just wait till I've finished here, please, Miss Adamant," he said. Laura's head disappeared. Another ten minutes passed. Finally, Alan came out into the hall, drawing off his gloves.

"Now, what . . . ?"

"Mr. Wiley called," said Laura, crisply, her tone displaying just the exact amount of indignation to which she felt herself entitled. After all, she should be considered able to judge whether to bother the doctor or not! She continued in the same water-cool voice. "He had a Government telegram for your sister, notifying her that Silas was missing."

"*Laura!*" Alan's hands grasped her shoulders; his eyes blazed.

"It's awful, Doctor," she agreed, her brow wrinkled. "He thought—well, he called you before delivering it."

"Did he send it here?"

"I don't know. I came right downstairs."

"Did you *tell* him to send it here?"

"No—I——"

Alan pushed her out of his way in his rush down the hall. He grabbed a coat from the lobby at the ambulance entrance, was into his car and off before Laura recovered her balance.

"What's got into the Doc?" people asked as he roared down the street. "Acts like his house is a-fire!"

His one thought was to be with Margaret when that telegram arrived. That doggone Laura! Thought herself so dad-blamed efficient—she could at least have phoned Linda! Maybe she had . . .

A car already stood at Margaret's door, an Army car. Alan's speed diminished, but he went on into the house. Everything all of them could do would be too little to help Margaret now.

The gay little sitting-room, the bright, picture-printed chintz —the colour and the sunlight itself—hit Alan like a blow. Margaret had had her telegram; it lay at her feet. Fred Blake sat beside her on the couch, his arm around her shoulders, his voice steady. He glanced up at Alan, then rose. "Oh— Thornton."

Margaret lifted tear-sodden eyes, and stretched her hand out blindly to Alan.

"Oh, darling!" she cried.

"I tell her not to lose hope," Fred Blake said loudly. "These airmen—they often bail out. And they are trained to survive." He stooped for the piece of yellow paper, and handed it to Alan.

He read it, and carefully folded it. "The Captain," he said gruffly, "knows about these things, Margaret."

She drew a deep, shuddering breath. "I know but, oh, Alan —if the enemy has him!"

"Shhhh," said Fred, his arm again drawing her close.

"He's so young," sobbed the boy's mother.

"He's also a big lad, and strong," Alan reminded her.

"Yes, he was. . . ."

"He *is*, dear," said Fred, and she nodded. Drawing calm from his calm, strength from his strength.

Alan shifted from one foot to the other, and finally decided to go on up to the Big House, to tell Ma'am and Jasper. Perhaps send Linda down to stay with Margaret when Fred should have to leave.

For the instant, though, Fred seemed well able to comfort Margaret. If he could dull the edge of her pain one bit, the family owed the man a lot.

"I'll go tell the rest of the family," he said aloud.

"The twins . . ." said Margaret. "Oh, Alan—how will we tell them?"

"It won't be easy. I—I'll send Linda down, if you like."

"I can stay with her for a time," said Fred.

"Good. I'll send Linda, and drop in myself again this evening."

Deeply troubled, he went on up the hill. Linda, he found, was not at home. Seretha took the news quietly. "I'll go to Margaret," she said at once.

Alan said that Captain Blake was with her, and being a great help.

"I still think that I should go!"

"Later, perhaps. Oh, Ma'am—for now, let her have her comfort where she can find it. Let her alone! She's going to need us all—and all that we can do for her. Right now, Blake can be of the most help."

"Well!" said Seretha. "I know I'd want *my* mother at a time like this!"

"She will want you, dear. Now, I'm going out and tell Dad."

Seretha's old eyes dimmed with tears. "He'll take it hard." Alan found him out in the sunwashed paddock, schooling a nervous horse. Jasper no longer rode these jumpers. But now he was holding a lunge line in his hand as a groom took the horse over the piled bales of hay and the white rail a-top them. Patiently, over and around, again and again, teaching the horse to relax, to take the jump in his stride.

Alan climbed the fence and came towards his father. A glance at his son's face was enough for Jasper.

"Take him in now," he roared at the groom. "Rub him down, massage him—put a good half-hour to it, or he'll stiffen on us. Git along, now."

The boy "got along," and Jasper turned to meet Alan. "What's happened?"

Alan told him, quickly, quietly. Jasper smote his gloved hands together. "Nowhere in the Bible, boy," he cried in anguish, "does it tell us why the fit are taken, and the unfit left——"

"Father ..."

"I know, I know. He may still be alive. Just now, that uncertainty but adds to our anguish. What about Margaret?"

"She's your daughter. She'll take what she has to take."

They talked a bit longer, there in the wintry sunlight, then Jasper walked with Alan back to the house. "I'll go in and let Ma'am fuss over me," he decided. "Later we'll walk down the hill."

Alan had told him that Fred was with Margaret, and that he hoped to find Linda to cushion the blow for the twins when they should get out of school.

"She was goin' some place," Jasper told him. "Came past in her car and said something sassy to me—but I've no idea where she was headin'."

Alan glanced at his wristwatch. It was after three, and no one seemed able to locate Linda. His dark eyes drew together. *I'll try to locate her by phone*, thought Alan, driving towards the hospital. *Or set Laura to doing it. I snapped pretty sharply at Laura: she'll knock herself out trying to make up for my irritation.*

He wished he had the courage to replace the girl. It certainly would be easier on him to have less emotion in his office! On the other hand, Laura would make a whopping scene if he fired her—and she was, generally, a good secretary.

She did take things on herself, and too often. He'd been good and angry this afternoon. He could have reached Margaret ahead of the telegram if Laura had used her head and asked Wiley to delay its delivery. He was glad that Fred had been there—surgical obligation or no, perhaps Alan should keep his hands off with Margaret and Fred. . . .

Preoccupied with his thinking, and deeply disturbed about Silas, Alan went into the hospital, to his office, still wearing the ill-fitting coat, with the dark rubber apron still hugging the knees of his duck pants.

Linda, meanwhile, had been having what she called a free afternoon. She had no fixed call upon her time, no Red Cross room-duty, no Church Guild meeting—it was not the day to check linens at home, arrange flowers or plan the week's menus. So—she was free.

About noon, a boy had delivered a dozen pale pink roses in a long box. As she stood trying to decide what to do with them, Seretha came into the hall.

"Did Colonel Chaney send them?"

Linda shook her head. "No, Dr. Ernst. It's his way of saying thank you for the dinner he had with us a day or so ago."

Seretha froze, and Linda flushed. So much had intervened that she'd forogtten about Rupert's kissing her on that same evening, had forgotten that her mother-in-law, in some way, knew that he had. She gathered up the box. "I'm going to take them to Aunt Flora and Uncle Arthur," she decided. "They're really beautiful."

She went upstairs, knowing that Seretha watched her. Linda would have to talk things out with Rupert, explain that European manners could be very much misunderstood in rural America. She'd do that when she thanked him for the flowers.

The small incident made her decide that she would get out of the house for the afternoon. She had kept up her interest in Manning Fowler, and she would go to see the family in the new home they'd found. Ann, yesterday, had told Linda that Manning was out of school with the chicken pox—and that they'd moved.

So after lunch she packed a basket with fruit and vegetables, and a slab of fresh spare ribs, and had her car brought to the back steps. She drove past the paddock where Jasper was training a new jumper; Red Feather, he was called, and in the winter sunlight his coat was red, indeed. She watched them for a minute, then drove on contentedly. She stopped at the Welfare Office to ask where the Fowlers were living; the girl looked surprised. "Why, I thought you knew. . . ."

"No."

Miss Owens directed her, and Linda went on to Woolworth's, where she bought a couple of toys, and some bright picture-books. She must drive back a way, turn into a side street, out along it to the edge of town, to a gravel road.

And there she found the Fowlers, the mother and her brood of children. The little log and frame house sat back within a stake and rider fence. There were some fruit trees; a pig snuffled in a pen, chickens scratched about in the dooryard; a dog barked at Linda as she came through the gate. Mrs. Fowler came inquiringly to the door and sent a couple of the bigger children to help Miz Thornton keery things—not Manning. He had the pox, and a cold wind would send him into spasms, like as not. . . .

"They made me keep all the kids outa school on his 'count," said the mother, leading her caller into the main room of the little house. Half of its small windows looked out upon the mountain slope, the others down to the road. A big bed stood in one corner, with a "truckle-bed" pushed under it. A fire burned upon the deep hearth, and Mrs. Fowler's loom stood at right angles to it. Manning was in the lean-to bedroom, and Linda went in to talk with him. He wasn't rightly sick, explained his mother, jest feelin' puny.

"Has the doctor seen him?"

"Yes'm. The Welfare sent him. But, la, till we got in with the Welfare, we didn't know a doctor's step in my house. I had a doctor for jest one o' my kids bornin'—generally we doctor with things that grow in the hills."

The children scattered about the place, Manning happy with his books, and Linda went to sit in "the rocker" before the fire for a visit with Mrs. Fowler, who sat at her loom; she was threading it, and expanding on the matter of home remedies.

"I don't guess I can tell a doctor's wife much . . . but in the old days every family had to make their own medicines."

Mrs. Fowler was a pretty woman, probably no older than Linda, pillow-fat and good-natured.

"Wasn't no doctors in my grandmammy's time, and no money in my mammy's—so they used black-snake root for fever, to sweat the body, you know—or spicewood tea. Burdock purified the blood—spignard was good for a weak back, and percoon for sore throat. Good for the stummick, too—Seneca tea to break up a cold, and ginseng for sick headache. Oh, I can't call 'em all to mind this minute, Miz Thornton. . . . We used wahoo for bitters, and—and—rue for worms. Slippery elum was used inside and out——" Her laugh came infectiously. "As a tea, or for a poultice. Indian pipe for old sores. When I was little, we kids were sent out into the woods regular to gather such stuff. I aim to git my kids busy at it this summer."

"You're very nicely located here," said Linda politely.

"Yes, ma'am, I am. Dr. Thornton said I could use the house, rent-free—we got us two acres, and we'll put in a garden. I got me my loom, and he say, when the kids are big enough to leave, I can work by the hour in the hospital laundry. We're sure fixed nice."

Linda clasped her hands together, and fought down the little chill of despair which had swept over her. She'd been interested in the Fowlers all winter—and Alan had done all this without telling her! Usually he talked over such things with her, shared them. What was the matter with Alan?

Suddenly her cheeks burned like fire. Nothing was the

matter with *him*! It was Linda. For weeks she'd been distant and preoccupied, until the poor man probably didn't know what he dared talk about to her.

She got up and walked over to the big loom. "I'm glad this was saved from the fire," she said to her hostess.

"Yes'm. I make a little money right along with my rugs and coverlids. I know all the old patterans—in my head, I know 'em. Tennessee Trouble, Cat Trail, Snail Trail—the purtiest is Pine Tree and Snowball. Come I kin dye some wool the right clear blue, I aim to make secha one for you and the doctor."

"Oh ..." protested Linda.

"Yes'm, I aim to. He says he hep me git the wool, and maybe the indigo weed, too. I dye my own yarn, you know. It lasts. I had a couple of coverlids that ben in the family more'n a hundred years, an' the colours jest as *true*! They got burned in the fire, of course. But I got the patterans in my head, and I know what to use for the dye."

She chattered on. Red rock—or ochre, as some called it—boiled in sweet milk, never faded, no matter what! Copperas made purple; "ef you add walnut hulls, you got brown. I use indigo for blue, though some like chamber lye and copperas. I don't! Madder weed and alum gives a bright red; percoon an' alum gives yalla.

"But I'm going to make you and the doctor a blue one. Pine Tree an' Snowball. Ain't *nothin'* purtier!" She laughed slyly. "I told the doctor come he slept under one o' my coverlids, I'd bet he'd made you a passel of kids. ..." She lifted her eyes to Linda.

"What"—Linda asked faintly—"what did the doctor say to that?"

Mrs. Fowler's laughter rang out heartily. "He said he'd like it fine."

Linda left them, and the compulsion of that conversation made her go straight to the hospital. That minute of hurt and anger there in the cabin still rankled and—and—she wanted to *see* Alan, to talk to him!

It seemed to her that she had not spoken a dozen words privately to her husband since before Christmas. And when they were together, they'd been at cross-purposes, or swept along on a tide of other people's affairs. . . . Christmas, the fire, his father's illness—poor Uncle Arthur——

She parked the car and went inside, her red hair blown about her face, her big coat swinging above her slender ankles.

Miss Adamant said the doctor had "stepped out," she thought he'd be right back. It was Laura who told Linda about Silas.

Linda's eyes were still wide with sorrow and first realisation when Alan walked in.

"For Pete's sake," cried Miss Adamant, "whose coat is *that*?"

Alan glanced down at it, frowning.

"And you've still got on your X-ray apron!"

He took off the too-small coat, and the apron. His eyes had touched Linda's face in greeting. He gave the garments to his secretary. "Will you hang the coat in the lobby—I think it must be James's. And then you might take the apron downstairs. I'm glad you're here, Linda. I wanted to locate you." He closed the door upon Miss Adamant, and led Linda through to his inside office, his hand lingering upon her shoulder.

She looked up at him. "I've just heard about Silas."

"Yes." His eyes searched her face. "I went to Margaret—then home."

"Oh, Alan, do you suppose . . . ?"

"I don't know, dear. That's the hell of it. We don't know. He may be all right. We can only hope and pray that he is." They sat, numbly, for a minute, remembering the big, blond boy. Noisy, clumsy—loved by all. His hair had tumbled like straw above his sunburned face, his white teeth had flashed always in a sunburned grin. . . .

"How anyone could kill *him*!" cried Linda in anguish. "Why, they might as well set out to harm *Jim*."

"Not exactly," said Alan, more to quiet her than because he himself believed in any such argument. "Remember, Silas was flying a fighter plane; he was armed."

"I still can't see any good in boys like that fighting! Killing them."

"There isn't any good to *war*! Not even our killing their good boys."

"Oh, Alan——"

"I know, dear." He went on to tell of his going to Margaret. "She'll take this, of course. Margaret has the required stuff."

"D'you suppose there is a chance he may have escaped alive?"

"Until we hear different, we must believe in that chance."

"You mean when I talk to her——"

Alan nodded. He sat back in his chair, his face stern, but serene, too.

Linda sprang to her feet. "*You're* taking it, aren't you?" she cried. "You're just like her. Oh, how I envy you Thorntons! Your strength, and your—your sureness that you have strength! Sometimes I rebel against the family—its—its solidity! But I envy it, too, and wish that I had it—that I belonged." She sat down again in the chair.

Alan heard the tone of hysteria; he knew that she was voicing her grief about Silas. But she was also telling him.

"What you rebel against," he said, "is the restraint which Ma'am imposes on her family."

Linda looked up. Her wet lashes flared back, her red lips trembled.

"She has a patriarchal sense of family," Alan went on. "No matter how weak you are, if your name is Thornton, she categorically endows you with privilege. That's a false premise, Linda. You know it is, and you have every right to revolt against the basic tyranny of blood ties. But, for Pete's sake, girl, don't pity yourself because you haven't that *blood*."

Linda's head now was drooping. She had been indulging in self-pity, and allowing herself to betray her wounded vanity in huffiness to Alan—a silly flirtation with——

She looked up, her cheeks scarlet. "Alan——"

He nodded and said, "There's a difference, you know, in what 'family' can mean. You spoke of it a minute ago, in saying that Margaret could stand up under this blow. You were kind enough to say that I have that strain of fortitude."

"You do have it!" Linda insisted. He was talking like his father, telling a lesson well learned.

"But I think you have it, too," said Alan. "You've not been tested as Margaret has been, but—well, your genuine interest in Manning Fowler shows your acknowledgment of the obligation there is upon you to help your fellow-man; your sense of values is what I consider more important than a drop of Thornton blood in your veins."

Linda gazed at this man who was her husband, and from

whom she had drawn apart. She gasped, a little limp with the realisation of her own folly, and the lengths to which folly could lead a woman. Why, she loved Alan Thornton! It was unbelievable that she had let resentment against Ma'am, accompanied by a state of flattered excitement over Rupert Ernst, lead her into a pronouncement to Alan that she stood ready to renounce her obligations as a wife, to deny the family ties with which her marriage had bound her.

Alan was a man to respect the woman he chose for his wife. He had believed in her sincerity when she said those headlong, foolish things! So—she had lost him!

Rising panic would not let her speak just now of her own folly, so she cast about for a subject to bridge the gap until she could speak to Alan, reasonably, wisely and truthfully. Manning. She told him that she had gone to see the Fowlers that afternoon. "I don't think they're going to need anyone's help much longer," she said. "Mrs. Fowler seems to think, except for sugar and flour and coffee, that they will be pretty well self-supporting."

Alan nodded. "That was my idea." His smile flashed, sweet and warm. "I've generally found, Linda, that it's better to let these people help themselves as much as possible, and on their own level."

"That sounds a bit snobbish, as things go with you, Alan."

He shook his head. "It's not snobbish, however. Their level may be better than my own. They live a much simpler life, for one thing. If they are afraid, they run and hide; if they are angry, they show it. If they love . . ." his mobile mouth quirked ". . . they bring half a dozen bastards into the world. And pretty good ones, too. You know, I suppose, that Ma'am's notion of any legitimate child of an old name being better than a bastard of sturdy stock just doesn't stand up with me. Mrs. Fowler's got a couple of mistakes in her brood, but generally she's bred pretty true."

"But that surely was an accident!"

"Oh, no! She'll tell you herself that she likes a fine, upstanding man!"

Linda laughed a little.

"It's the important strain to breed for," Alan assured her. "Ask Father."

"I don't need to ask him. He's often pointed that out to me,

138

and in his own family. He agrees that you and Margaret and Silas . . ." She broke off, her eyes darkening with remembered pain. "You say she's taking it, Alan?"

"She has to take it!" he said gruffly. "Fred Blake was with her when I got there." He turned to look out of the window, his hands tightly grasping the chair arms. Then he swung back to face Linda. "I've been in a bad spot over those two!" he blurted. "But this thing about Silas makes it worse than I dreamed it could be."

"About Fern, you mean," said Linda softly.

"I've wanted to talk to you about it. You know that it always helps me to talk a problem out with you. But things have seemed . . . somehow . . ." He looked at her appealingly.

"I know. . . ." she said contritely.

"I've been in a turmoil over it," he admitted. "Try as I can to define my simple duty as a surgeon to my patient——"

"Had you reached a decision, before this word of Silas?"

His eyes clung to her face. "I don't know that I had, really," he said slowly. "Have you ever seen Mrs. Blake?"

"No."

"She—isn't alive, except that she breathes and her blood circulates. She is a rather good-looking woman—but that isn't important! Any more than Margaret's big brown eyes and her lovable disposition are significant. Or even the nasty blows which life has dealt her! Or the fact that she's my sister, and I want her to be happy!"

"All those things, however, make this a dreadful decision for you to make, Alan. Why don't you send Mrs. Blake to Dr. Cabler?"

His green eyes flashed. "But even that is a big decision, dear. I can do the operation—he assures me that I can. Or he'll do it if I ask him to. In either case, the problem is the same."

"Will the operation help her?"

"If she survives it, yes. The extent of that help is problematical, of course. So my decision has become one as to whether I should hurt my sister, perhaps disastrously, by helping Mrs. Blake to a few more days, weeks, maybe years, of conscious life."

"If you don't operate . . . ?"

"Cabler says it sounds like complete atrophy within a short time."

"Oh."

Alan pounded his big fist softly upon the desk edge. "It should be a simple decision," he cried in real pain. Then he stood up, as if emotion alone demanded some action on his part. "These days, Linda," he said loudly, "I am forced to acknowledge how seldom life is simple, especially in this big family which I happen to love and consider important. Little things—big things—I find myself physically exhausted by the complexity of existence! It used not to be that way."

Again Linda sat with her head bowed. She knew why Alan was worn by the complexity of his life. For years she had been standing between him and those complexities. Of course, she could not have avoided this problem about Margaret—but he should have been able to talk it out with her from the first. The way ahead might have seemed less obscure, less tortuous. At the beginning, she probably would have urged him to send Fern to Dr. Cabler.

And in many other ways, she had used to insure his rest and relaxation at hime. She had dulled the edges of family troubles, big and little, before they ever reached Alan.

The house phone buzzed sharply and she jumped.

While Alan was talking, she stood up and put on her coat. There was much to be done.

"Yes," he confirmed her preparations. "I'll have to go back to work. Besides, I was going to suggest that you get the twins from school, and help Margaret through the telling them about Silas."

"Oh, yes!" she agreed quickly. She glanced at the clock. "I'll have to hurry." She was out and gone.

Alan went to the receiving-room, aware that their talk again had been aborted. This time, clearly, through no fault of Linda's.

The emergency—a car wreck with several people injured, one critically—held Alan at the hospital until eight that evening, and when he made his rounds before going home he found Captain Blake seated at the side of Fern's bed. She was in a private room, with her own nurse. In every respect, the Captain was doing the right thing by his wife.

Now, when the doctor entered, he rose and stood against the wall. Alan examined the chart, said a few words to the nurse, lifted the patient's wrist. Then he glanced again at the husband, trying to feel what it must be like to be a strong man in his early forties—Alan's own age!—and tied to this log-like creature who was so sick as to be bereft of all personality and sympathetic appeal.

He turned abruptly towards the door.

"Doctor . . . ?" It was Fred Blake, at his shoulder.

Alan stopped. "Yes?"

"I—I must have a talk with you."

"To-night?"

"Some time soon. Of course, if you're too tired to-night——"

"I am tired. But to-morrow I'll be busy, so——"

Followed by Fred, he strode down the lighted hall, turned, went swiftly down the stairs, and again along a shining hospital corridor. Visitors were about; light poured from open room-doors. Finally, they came to his office, and Alan indicated the chair where Linda had sat that afternoon. Alan took the desk chair, and pushed a box of cigarettes towards Captain Blake.

"I presume you know why I'm here," said the man in uniform.

"I've found it safer, as a doctor, not to *presume* I know anything ahead of time."

"Well, to get the matter said and over, I want to ask you not to operate upon my wife."

Alan took the cigarette from his lips, and leaned towards the other man.

Blake returned the gaze, a frown between his eyes, his lips rigid. "Last fall I was told that my wife could not live more than six months—if her condition progressed as it was then doing."

"Dr. Zeller told you that."

"Yes. Yes, he did. Was he correct?"

"So far as any doctor can tell about these things, Blake, I think he was right."

"I——" The Captain was making a great effort for emotional control, and that exertion developed a brusqueness which Alan did not mistake. "This afternoon," he said tightly, "a terrible thing happened to the woman I love very dearly."

The doctor leaned back, his eyes watchful.

"It's too bad that she is—your sister. Bad for you, I mean."

141

Alan said nothing.

Blake looked down at his cigarette. "I—I suppose you and I can only guess at the horrible grief she has now over this uncertainty about her son."

"I know Margaret—and I am sure the grief is cruelly sharp."

"Yes. I am sure it is, too. I am sure of another thing, Doctor."

"Yes?"

"I am sure that Margaret loves me, and that right now she needs me. I could do more for her, if I were free to be with her, free to express my love to her."

"And you think by my letting your wife die . . ."

"I want you to know this—I mean to have Margaret whether Fern lives or dies. I love Margaret and I mean to free myself so that I can marry her."

Alan sighed. "I see. Well, that, of course, is a matter for you and Margaret to decide. I am glad that you came and talked to me. . . ."

"But you still plan to operate?"

Alan's head was up, his face sternly handsome, the lines of emotion and fatigue erased for the minute. "I cannot operate without your consent, Captain Blake."

The officer's hand made an impatient gesture. "You still think you *should* operate—that's what I meant."

He'd put the whole decision upon Alan. The doctor stood up, and after a second Blake rose, too. "Please understand," said Alan, slowly, "that what I decide will be decided, not as a man, but as a surgeon."

Fred fell back a step to look at him. "Then you must have some damned hard things to do, Doctor."

Alan's darkly stern face relaxed. "Oh, yes!" he agreed. "I do."

He walked with Blake to the front door, glad to be told that Linda was with Margaret, and was planning to stay for a few days. That was good—except that Alan . . .

He watched the officer go out to his car, adjusting his cap, tightening the belt of his trench-coat, putting on his gloves.

"I think I've got troubles," said Alan below his breath, and then flushed to discover, when he turned, that Rupert Ernst was standing five feet behind him, watching him with brightly alert black eyes.

142

Alan would have passed him without a word; he had night orders to write. . . .

But Rupert followed him to the floor desk. "I can guess what the Captain wanted," he said softly.

Alan studied the chart he had drawn from the slot.

"What do you now mean to do about Mrs. Blake?"

Rupert stood at the Chief Surgeon's shoulder, handsome and trim in his white garments, his manner respectfully attentive. The Visitors-out gong sounded softly through the hall; Alan hunched over the desk and the chart.

"Did he refuse to sign a release?" prodded Ernst.

"I didn't offer him one for his signature," murmured Dr. Thornton.

"Do you think he will sign one?"

"I don't know—I hope so. I think I should operate."

"But why?"

Alan's green eyes flashed up at him for a second.

"I mean," said the other doctor, pulling a chair to Alan's side, "why should you undertake to play God?"

"Oh, I'm not!" said Alan quickly. Then he sat back and looked beyond the circle of lamplight. They would probably not be disturbed. The floor nurses had their multiple bedtime duties. The medicine nurse and her cart were at the far end of the corridor. "If I seem to be, it is because I want to give Mrs. Blake a free chance—a somewhat *even* chance with Margaret. I strongly believe that Fred Blake should not seek to divorce her in her present condition."

"Oh, *ho!*" said Ernst softly.

"With his wife conscious, able to make her own decision— well, things would be more balanced. We should remember that Fred loved her once and married her—and that the situation with my sister came up while Fern was hurt and helpless. Marriages are often threatened and in need of defence"—his glance flicked across Ernst's face—"against a third person. In Fern's case there has been no chance to defend her marriage, to fight for her rights."

"Was it a happy marriage? Were they in love at the time of the accident?"

"Do you think that is important? Margaret was not in the picture at that time, and there was no need for defence against her. But now . . . I think Fred is a fine person. If he were free

143

I'd like to see him and Margaret marry. But he isn't free."

"He would be, shortly, and without any divorce, if you'd keep your hands off."

"As a doctor, you know that I am pledged to do what I can for my patient."

"As a man, I think you're crazy. But as a doctor, you are crazy, as well. I would strongly advise against the operation, Dr. Thornton."

Alan reached for a second chart. Rupert hunched closer. "Listen to me," he urged. "Perhaps you have not considered one aspect of this situation. It is a complex decision, I will agree. But consider this complexity, my dear Doctor. Consider the fact that you might fail to do a successful operation."

"Fail in what way?"

"Death, of course. Brain operations often result in death. That is usually explained to the patient beforehand, and to the family."

"It will be done in this case." Alan's eyes were shining.

"But failure of that sort would be especially bad for you, after all the significance that has been attached to this case."

"Are you implying that I would go through the motions of operating and then, through some apparent mishap . . ."

"*Ach!*" exclaimed Ernst. "I would not imply any such thing! But you could do your best work—work as good as we saw Dr. Cabler do—and still lose the case."

Alan spoke gravely. "I don't think I shall lose this case, Ernst."

Dr. Ernst stood up then, and set his chair back against the wall. "But if, unaccountably, she should die, you must face the fact that some people will suspect your motives. Whereas, if she survives, success in that sense will be worse than failure, Dr. Thornton. That is why I urge you, caution you, not to play God."

Alan spoke quickly and firmly. "That is precisely why I haven't the right to decide about this case on any basis except that of a doctor making a decision concerning a patient brought to him for such decisions. It is my job to attend this sick woman, to do that job to the best of my medical ability. Then let it be God's decision to heal her—or not."

Ernst smoothed the cuff of his white jacket. "That is idealism rather than science, Dr. Thornton."

"I don't agree. It is what I believe and practise with every case I handle."

"You can't pretend that this is like other cases."

"If I find I cannot be impersonal, I should turn the case over to another surgeon."

"As Chief Surgeon—a man in that position—you must often have to consider the personal angle with cases."

"Of the patients, yes—of their husbands or other relatives, no. As a doctor—any doctor, intern, assistant, Chief—my obligation is to think *only* of the patient. Can I help her? What can I do to help her, to prolong life and health in her?"

He had spoken with conviction to Rupert Ernst, but when, an hour later, he was free to go home, he found himself wearied with the buffeting of the day's emotion, torn between the personal angles which, to Ernst, he had denied existed.

In the little cottage below the drive, a single window was alight. He wanted to talk to Linda—as he had begun to talk that afternoon. But in the cottage the matter of Silas would have precedence, and the light was in Margaret's bedroom. The women would be getting ready for bed—he would only disturb them both.

Linda heard his car wheels. She was lying on the second twin bed in Margaret's room, both women with books in their hands, and pretending to read. Now and then Margaret would speak, and Linda would answer. In between, she let her thoughts move on to her own immediate affairs.

In this time of worry about Silas, Margaret needed her—or someone—to be with her besides the twins. Linda would not have done less—and yet, again the family demands had come between her and Alan.

When she heard Alan's car, she realised wistfully that, had she been in her own room, he would have come to her and continued the talk which had been interrupted that afternoon. It had seemed to her that he was talking with some purpose. If so, he would make an opportunity to talk again to her. A talk there must be. Would be. But not to-night. . . .

Of course, in some respects, it was easier for Linda to be out of the Big House. Since the night when Rupert had kissed her, Ma'am had made life nearly unsupportable. What-

ever she had seen, or been told, Ma'am was acting as if—as
if——

Coming down here to Margaret was better than moving
clear away. It would give Linda a chance to think of what she
wanted to do, of what she could do—should do—must do.

During the past days and nights—and weeks—she had done
a lot of thinking; and, looking back, it did seem that she
should have reached some conclusion by now.

Of course, so many things had happened—Christmas, and
Jasper's illness—she dropped her book, and shifted on the bed.
Evasions! She could pretend to herself that she had had to
stay—but the truth was, she had wanted to stay.

This afternoon, seeking to comfort Margaret, to strengthen
her, Linda had told the sorrowing woman that all things
passed. And they did, indeed. Three months ago, conditioned
by Seretha's suggestion, Linda had acted upon a panicky
moment of thinking, of *feeling*, that life was hurtling past her,
and that she must snatch at her place in it before it was too
late. She had voiced her panic to Alan, and he—he had acted
as if she had come to a soberly considered conclusion, a
privilege which he must courteously permit her.

If he believed the things which Ma'am must have said to him
since——

He had given Linda no chance to explain, or qualify, or
retract anything she had said or done. . . .

No! That was not true. He had been waiting for her to
come to him. She could only hope that he still wanted her to
come.

Alan needed her as much as he wanted her. That night,
going home to the Big House, empty of her presence as it had
not been for him a single night since their marriage, he realised
full force his need of her, and his desire.

Linda had always been ready with advice and counsel—yes,
and praise! His big mouth twisted wryly to acknowledge the
help which that praise had been! But a man's vanity needed
nourishment, too. Linda had helped him in all ways. She had
always been the one to set out fresh clothes for him, against a
night call. Now he must do such things for himself; just as he
must shower and shave without the companionable privilege
of shouting things to Linda over the noise of the water. He

146

must get into the empty bed, with no soft lips to meet his kiss, no red curls silken against his cheek—no receptive ear to his going over the day's problems—and nothing at all with which to fill his encircling arm.

In his loneliness, he realised how much Linda had given him in their early years of marriage, and the next step, of course, was to think of how little he had given her. He hadn't even been with her very much. His days were full, and many of his nights. They'd taken some short trips, but usually on medical matters. She'd not seemed to mind, and yet she must have minded.

He loved Linda—he wanted her. The threat of her leaving him had served to renew, full strength, his desire for her. Without being free to court her as he had done in the months before their marriage, his passion for her was as great as it had been at that time.

It was not, in any sense, a renewal, either. That love had always been there, but while he knew that Linda was his, safe, and surely waiting for his kiss and for his arms, he had diverted his real potency to his work. Such a diversion was neither fair nor right. She had had every reason to rebel, and to turn her eyes elsewhere.

So now, free or not, he must court her anew; he must do everything he could to get her back! He would go to her immediately and tell her how much, how much he loved her. He would beg her—— No! He would not whine to her!

Love had its own claim, its own dignity. He loved Linda and would rest his case on that. She had loved him once, and perhaps that love still cast some shadow upon her; she would listen to him, he thought, when he reaffirmed his love for her.

This afternoon, she had been kind, and ready to listen. He would go to her again, and talk over his problem about Fern Blake. She would listen and advise him as she always had done.

But even that would not be the same! He would not be talking to her as his wife, as he had so often talked over other cases with her, his head upon her breast—and, as often as not, had gone to sleep from pure exhaustion.

No wonder she preferred a man like Rupert Ernst to a *doctor* like Alan Thornton! Rupert came to Linda with flowers in his hand, literally and figuratively. While Alan—actually there had been one occasion when his embrace had bruised

147

her soft flesh with the hard edge of a sample bottle in his coat pocket. A fine lover he was!

Saturday, theoretically, was not so busy a day; though Alan was busy enough. He put an arthritic patient under traction; he did a surgical delivery with James; he treated an injury case for shock and possible skull fracture, certified the cause of death in the man's companion. At noon, he removed a steel splinter from a man's eyeball, and told the Rector's wife on the phone that, as lay reader, he would conduct the next day's service; the Rector was in bed with a cold. He sent Cassidy around to see if hospitalisation would be advisable.

He decided to eat lunch at the hospital, and get through some of the week's accumulated paper-work. To this end, he asked Laura Adamant to have a tray brought to his desk.

"I don't think that's good for you, Doctor," she protested. "You let everything get cold."

Alan's head lifted. "Look!" he cried in exasperation. "Will you quit fussing over me?"

"I was only——"

"I know," he acknowledged. "But you do fuss. And that's not one of your duties. You have plenty without taking it on. Now, how about that lunch?"

She went herself to get his tray, "fussing" a good bit over its arrangement, selecting the exact chop and the particular piece of pie. When she brought it in to him, Alan made an apology for his brusqueness. "I've got a lot on my mind, Laura," he explained.

"I know," she agreed. "Maybe it would help . . ." She broke off and backed towards the door.

"What would help?" asked Alan, filling his coffee-cup.

"Well, I was going to say that it might help if you'd separate personal and professional things—you know, leave your personal problems at home, and keep your medical problems *here*. Then——"

"That'd be fine," he agreed readily. "I'd hope it would work. But thanks anyway—now you go on home. It's Saturday."

Flushed with what she evidently considered a "reconciliation," she offered to stay. "I'd be glad to!"

"There's no need. I'll go over these things you've made out, and sign 'em. You go on. . . ."

It was a darkly rainy day. Alan's lamplit figure was reflected

148

clearly in the window beside his desk. He ate his lunch, and tackled the pile of accumulated papers. Coming to a question which Laura could have answered for him, he leaned back to light a cigarette and consider the little scene with her—and her advice that he separate personal and professional matters. Undoubtedly she'd heard gossip about him and Linda.

In theory, her advice was good. Last night Alan had decided that he was a failure in his personal life.

Perhaps he could do better professionally. He tipped back in his chair, smoked reflectively and began to think again of Fern Blake. Certainly it was a professional item, and so belonged right here in his hospital office.

And yet—through all the convolutions of this particular case, it had become so much more than a medical instance that hardly anyone now considered it as a case.

Fern's husband had rejected the thought of surgery; he had turned in revulsion against the drooling, helpless creature which his wife had become; he had found consolation and joy in Margaret, a small, exquisite person offering him love and pleasure. Whether she topped any memory Fred might have of Fern as she had used to be was not the point. Nor was the fact significant—to the surgeon—that their marriage had been on the skids before ever she was hurt. Fred was opposing the operation on Fern as she now was.

Rupert said that Alan should accept the husband's position, and give the matter no further thought. He pointed out, and truthfully, that the operation in question was a rare and delicate one, a risky one. Alan, he said, had given his advice; the thing now rested with the patient's family. With Fred Blake. Actually, Alan could rest on that, could accept Fred's decision and remain strictly professional and ethical.

He could even argue—as his father might do—that, for the betterment of society, Fern should be allowed to die, and Margaret allowed to mate with Fred, who was a strong man, of good strain.

Even as a doctor . . .

Agggh! Alan got to his feet, stood by the window, peered out at the rain which was coming down hard, flecked with white—they'd have snow, or sleet, by night. He hoped not an ice storm—beautiful as they made the mountains, they played havoc with all concerned.

149

Let's see, where was he? Still arguing with himself, and evading the truth—which was, that the decision was his as well as Fred Blake's. As a doctor, he knew that he should operate if he could. And—he could.

His mind made up, but still with no peace in his heart, he sat at his desk until the gun-metal window-pane, turned satin-black. During the afternoon, there were a few interruptions; the pile of papers moved from the left side of his desk, across the blotter, into the tray on the right, and—as he worked—the Blake case came again and again into his thoughts.

Ernst only guessed at the complete import of this case. But Alan knew. This one operation had come to seem a symbol to Alan Thornton of all that an individual in a democracy could do, the freedom for a man to choose to be a doctor, or not, the freedom to choose to do the abstractly honourable thing, no matter how difficult.

Ten years ago, this same Alan Thornton had set aside his dream of being a brain specialist to work in the hospital which his parents had built for him. But the dream had continued to cast its shadow of frustration, sometimes one so pale as not to be noticed, at other times a dark and ominous cloud over his whole life.

But now, in some way, he knew that he could go on for the rest of his life, contentedly being a small-town doctor for his people, if he could know, surely and *definitely*, that he was *able* to do really important things for them. If, for specific instance, he could do this delicate operation upon the brain of Fern Blake, and restore the woman to something like normal life.

It seemed to Alan that he *must* do this one particular task, or be for ever lost. He must make this decision with honour, with justice to all concerned, and with his best medical judgment. Or he was doomed to be a failure, for ever frustrated, for ever a doctor such as was Cassidy, a man who might once have done real things, and had not. . . .

A doctor could not compromise. He was one thing or the other, and the choice was largely his own to make.

Almost happily, Alan then tidied the papers on his desk, snapped off the lamp and glanced again at the window, cheered to find that the rain had stopped. He went to the doctors' room and changed into his tweed suit, came out to find the

Supe, Miss Fogarty, waiting for him in the hall. She had a clip-board in her hand, and wanted to check the next week's schedule with him. Particularly, she wanted to know if he meant to schedule surgery for Mrs. Blake.

Alan glanced down at the little brown wren of a woman. He took the board in his hand, and wrote firmly upon a certain space. "I want you to phone Dr. Cabler in St. Louis and ask if he can send me an anæsthetist for this case, Miss Fogarty. I'll get the husband's release. We should do that job as soon as possible."

"Yes, Doctor."

He checked the other items scheduled, made one slight change and went on to the records-room; he found Fern Blake's folder—and stopped short to look at the sticker on its cover. "DO NOT KILL," that sticker read.

It meant only that this record was to be kept in the active files—but Alan wondered what a patient, or a patient's family, would make of that blunt demand.

He mentioned the point to the records clerk.

"I reckon," said the girl, with deliberation, "they'd hope you doctors would pay attention to what it says."

PART FOUR

On Sunday, Margaret insisted that Linda go to church as usual. No, she couldn't quite bring herself to go. She'd surely get emotional. She wanted the special prayers, but she herself —"I'll be all right!" she promised Linda. "I'm braver than you think!"

"You couldn't be!" said Linda warmly, and Margaret smiled at her. So Linda took the twins to Church School, then drove home for a different suit, a fresh blouse and a hat.

She sat in the pew with Seretha and Jasper, and intently studied Alan while he conducted the service. He was very handsome in his robes. Linda had given him his cross when he had taken his licence as a lay reader. She thought he seemed not quite so tired this morning as he had been looking lately. That was good—whatever the reason.

He'd had so much to disturb him—his struggle over his obligations in the Blake case, Silas, and Linda was sure that she had hurt him deeply by her withdrawal from him. Alan deserved much better of her; he'd always been so good to her, only to have her fail him in all ways. He had used to discuss his cases with her—not that she was qualified to advise him, but to talk matters out with her seemed to clear his own thinking. He must have missed that particularly in his consideration of Fern Blake.

Linda missed it, she knew. She never, even by word, betrayed the things he revealed to her about his work—that was part of her value to him. Now his failure to talk to her was especially noticeable when everyone—literally *everyone!* —was talking about the Blake case. Seretha—Margaret—the women at Red Cross—even Clew at home. Everyone but Alan. Oh, he had, that one afternoon in his office, begun a discussion —but he'd not finished it, nor had he sought a way to renew it since.

Linda sighed deeply. She knelt and sat and stood, mechanically, but when, as they reached the tower vestibule, Seretha complained that she had not liked Alan's choice of the second lesson, Linda had to look up with wide dark eyes.

"I didn't hear it," she confessed.

"You comin' home with us?" asked Jasper loudly, almost as if he wanted to shield her against Ma'am's brusque comment.

"Oh, no, I'll go back to Margaret's."

"We'll drop you."

"I can walk—really, I'd like to walk."

They left. Alan's ice storm had not materialised, and the day was cold, but fine. Linda lingered a bit on the church steps, speaking to this one and that, half hoping that Alan would join her. Then someone said he had gone over to the rectory to see Mr. Clark, who had a cold.

She started briskly down the block to Main Street, and home.

And at the corner, she met Rupert Ernst.

He was, as always, properly dressed, from the tip of his feathered dark green hat to the toes of his brown brogues. A yellow wool scarf was folded into the opening of his tweed jacket; he carried a heavy stick.

He greeted Linda gallantly, and with pleasure, then asked if he might walk along with her.

"Of course. Why not?"

He walked close at her side, his face turned, his head tipped so that always he gazed at her face, and into her eyes if she glanced his way.

At the corner, Linda paused to wait on an approaching car, and she saw, with a sinking heart and rising colour, that it was Alan's. He slowed a little, then with a lift of his hand, gained speed and passed them.

"Swords and pistols at dawn," murmured Dr. Ernst.

"What nonsense!" cried Linda.

His hand was firmly warm upon her arm. "Perhaps," he agreed. "Though he's quite short with me at the hospital these days."

Coldly Linda said nothing. She was exasperated, with herself, and with this man's suggestion of intrigue and double-dealing. In fact, she decided, she was weary of Rupert Ernst, of his glossy self-pride and air of confident superiority.

He was still talking. Of course! He talked constantly. And now, she realised with indignation, he was talking about Alan.

Patronising him, if you please! Saying that he should really not be a doctor. Of all things!

"As you know," he was saying in his accent-tipped voice, "I admire your father-in-law tremendously. And Mrs. Thornton is a true *grande dame*! But the fact remains that they are not intellectuals, and they should not expect their children to be. Ideally, a doctor—a surgeon—detaches himself completely from family ties, emotional complications, but——"

"Don't you have a family, Dr. Ernst?" asked the small, pretty woman at his side.

He lifted his shoulders in a shrug. As he had shrugged, Linda remembered, the first evening of their acquaintance. Then she had interpreted his shrug to mean, "Please. I would rather not speak of my family."

But now—she stiffened her shoulders a little. "I mean, did you leave anyone behind in Austria? Are they still alive?"

"I haven't the slightest idea."

Last week, Linda had seen Jim and Ann playing with long, thick icicles broken from the eaves of the summer-house, but they had not been so cold and sharp and hard as was this man's voice, the light in his black eyes, the line of his lips.

"Your *parents* . . . ?" cried Linda.

"My dear Linda," he explained coldly. "I had to leave Austria because my mother was a Jew!"

They had reached the gates of the Green, and she stopped now to turn and look at Rupert Ernst. It was as if he hated her wringing that admission out of him.

"But I don't understand," she said in a troubled tone, "your reluctance to mention this. You must know that it makes no difference in this country."

"Perhaps not. But I have never before mentioned it. And I should prefer——"

"Certainly," she agreed, "if you wish."

"My parents——" He ran his tongue across his lips. "The German blood in me has always hated what my parents did!"

Linda stood looking at him in genuine pity. He had rejected his past, and was contemptuous of his present. Here indeed was a man alone. Cast out.

She held out her white-gloved hand. "It was pleasant meeting you," she said graciously.

Before he had his hat back upon his head, she was down

along the drive almost to where she would turn off for Margaret's cottage. Alan's car was standing at the door. Perhaps he would eat dinner with them. Her step hurried.

The twins, Margaret's interests, callers during the afternoon, prevented any talk—but it was *good* just to be with Alan. Linda could treasure now what once she would not have noticed, the natural, casual togetherness of husband and wife.

Linda was staying on at the cottage; she slept there at night, but endeavoured still to attend to her usual duties at home. She went up to the Big House several times a day, and on the next early afternoon she went down the hall to the wing occupied by Uncle Arthur and Aunt Flora. Their rooms were as large as any in the house, but they had become so cluttered up with Aunt Flora's fripperies, with mementoes of happy, younger days, so stuffed with comforts and gadgets added through the years, that Linda had to pick her way carefully among the tables and footstools of their sitting-room to the chair where Uncle Arthur was seated before the fire, a rug across his knees, a silk handkerchief laid tenderly upon his pink bald head.

He looked unlike himself without the stiff white collar which he always wore. His black dressing-gown was handsome, and he had a white scarf folded into the throat of it, but he looked shrunken and as fragile as one of the pink-lined vases on the mantel.

Aunt Flora was taking smothering good care of the old man, and as Linda came in she was in the act of presenting a small painted tray to him; on it stood a little etched glass filled with a clear amber liquid.

Linda gasped a little in protest, and Aunt Flora immediately bridled. "It's only a little dram to warm him," she fluted. "He said he felt a little chill—circulation, you know, dear? It's bad —you know?"

"I know that Alan said particularly he was to have no alcohol."

Uncle Arthur quickly drained the glass. "Just a cordial, my dear——" he murmured, dabbing at his purplish lips.

"Linda loves you, dear," announced Aunt Flora.

"I think Alan loves him, too," said Linda, "but he's trying to get Uncle Arthur well."

155

"But, darling, you give brandy to *babies!*" argued Aunt Flora.

"Now, Aunt *Flora* . . ."

"My goodness, Linda!" cried the plump woman, fluttering her ruffles, tinkling her bracelets, "a drop can't hurt him when he wants it so much! I always say our stomachs tell us."

"But Alan surely knows best. He's a doctor."

"Sit down, dear." Aunt Flora pointed to a little rocker, and Linda seated herself.

"I wish you'd promise me——" she tried again anxiously.

Uncle Arthur pretended to doze. Or perhaps he did drop off; Alan said he was seriously ill.

"Now, listen, my dear," Aunt Flora was saying in one of her attempts to be sensible and brisk. She fell far short of her goal. "You don't need to remind me that my nephew is a doctor. But these modern doctors—there's no comfort to them, you know? Even Dr. Cassidy isn't comforting, the way he used to be. Instead of giving me medicine for my headaches, and telling me that my bed-jacket is pretty—why, he told me last month to take off weight!" The pale eyes popped at Linda in her outrage. "Miss Little Mae says Dr. Ernst has a sweet way to him, but then he did something to make her mad. Though that's not what I started to say. Let's see. Oh, yes. Alan doesn't have time or interest to consider a man's soul!" She leaned back, her ringed hands clasped, as if she had clinched the whole matter.

Linda gazed at her. "I think he was considering Uncle Arthur's liver," she agreed.

"I'm sure of it," said Aunt Flora. "While my husband—— Oh, dear, Arthur's never been strong; he was always delicate as a child—Seretha will tell you—and when he grew up—no children, you know." Her faded eyes widened impressively at Linda. "I think Alan should consider his *need* for a little stimulation—but as I say, sometimes Alan is hard. Take the way he is about that crazy woman. All Alan can see is a chance to carve on her head—and he's just stubborn enough to do it, too. Though I heard that the Captain warned him not to operate, and threatened him if he did. You see, *he* wants to marry Margaret. . . ."

Linda sighed; the story certainly had grown beyond all bounds of truth. She stood up. "Oh, Aunt Flora, that's all hearsay and I don't think Alan's family should discuss his patients. We both of us know that he'll do what he knows is right."

Aunt Flora leaned back, and patted the beads draped upon her full bosom. "Well, of course, he *can't* operate unless Captain Blake says he can!"

Linda turned towards the door.

"And," declared Aunt Flora, "Fred Blake probably—*very* probably—will refuse to give his permission."

"Oh, but he can't!" cried Linda. "That would be a terrible thing for him to do!"

"You'll see . . ." said Aunt Flora confidently. "You'll see! Off with the old, on with the new—that's men. We women can't ever lose our grip."

Aunt Flora was a silly old thing, Linda told herself. She was no judge of people, men or women. And yet——

She hurried through the remaining things she had planned to do, anxious to get back to Margaret. She couldn't talk to her about Fred and his wife, but—well—she was pretty sure Margaret wouldn't love a man who could—or would—— Oh, *darn* Aunt Flora! Why did anyone ever listen to her!

Linda's arms were full, with half of the cake which Ruby had baked for dinner, some books and magazines, a dozen jonquils covered by a protective twist of paper, and her thoughts were still turned inwards, when she pushed open the door of the cottage and went in—to turmoil.

The puppy was barking and running in circles; Jim and Ann were screaming unintelligibly and Margaret was prostrate upon the couch.

"What on earth!" Linda dropped her various parcels, herded the puppy into the kitchen and closed the door, then spoke firmly to the twins. "But, Aunt Linda . . ." gulped Ann.

"I'll listen in just a minute, dear." She indicated the chairs where she wanted the children to sit. Then she crossed the room, and knelt beside Margaret, who stretched a hand out to her.

Crumpled in that hand was another telegram—and this time no one had warned anyone.

It had been determined, the thing told, that Lieut. Silas Giddens had been killed in action. A letter would follow.

Linda stared at the words, wanting to find some of her own.

Not finding any, she put her cheek against Margaret's, and held the stricken mother close in her arms.

The twins began to whimper, and Margaret stirred. "They're frightened. . . ." she said piteously. "Oh, *Linda* . . ."

"Shhhh!" Dry-eyed, her own grief a hard and hurting lump in her chest, Linda cast about for ways to dull the hurt of the children. Because action would be her own best relief, she set them to little tasks. Jim was to bring a box of Kleenex to his mother. Would Ann take the cake out to the kitchen?

They both could let the puppy out, and watch him.

Next, a vase for the flowers, and water. She herself moved about, tidying the suddenly dishevelled room. Alan had left a sedative to give Margaret should she need one; Linda decided that this was the time, and she administered it, comforting the little dark-eyed woman as she would a child who had suffered a strange and bewildering hurt.

She picked up the telegram, smoothed it, glanced at the clock. "I think I'll send this up to Father, dear."

"You take it," urged Margaret. "Or let Alan tell him. Did you phone Alan?"

"Yes, but he was out—Miss Adamant said he'd be back late this afternoon. I thought of sending the twins. It will give them something to do—and—well—they never will take the place of Silas, darling—but it is going to help Father Thornton and all of us, to know that we still have them."

Margaret sighed, her eyes glazed with grief. "I thought anything would be better than not knowing . . ." she whispered.

"Yes . . ." Linda fed the children a slice of cake and a glass of milk, checked on their outdoor wraps and carefully instructed them. "Don't get excited. You don't want to frighten Grandfather. Just take this up to him, and tell him when it came. Let him read it—and then—well, be nice to him. You know you two are going to have to make up for Silas now. You may as well start."

"You mean, now Jim will run the farm?" asked Ann, astutely.

"Yes. With you to help."

She watched them start up the drive, hand in hand, as they had not walked in years. Sturdy, healthy—Jasper being what he was, the twins would help him as nothing else could. Only Jim now was left as male heir to the Thornton line. Linda

158

sighed, and went back to Margaret, sat down beside her, hoping that she would sleep.

But she wanted to talk, and Linda let her. Anything that would help . . .

"Why, *why*," the mother asked, "did it have to be Silas?"

There was no valid answer. The question rang like a gong in Linda's own mind. Had she had sons—if she ever had sons—this same web of circumstances could enmesh her. For that thin reason, Linda was able to sympathise with Margaret, to admire her and to withhold platitudes of consoling patriotism.

Through the wide window, the afternoon light was strong upon her. "Margaret," she said firmly, almost sternly, "Silas went willingly to war, to whatever it might mean to him. Even —death. Young as he was, he decided that his country's value was great enough to make his sacrifice worth while."

Margaret lay white and still, her dark eyes gazing at Linda. Both of them were picturing Silas, the strong, golden lad.

"The cost is big—too big!" Linda continued. "But you have something—a shining memory of Silas that—that——" She broke down then, and Margaret held out her arms to comfort *her*.

"You're right, darling," she said against the cloud of red hair on her shoulder. "I'll get so that I can accept that. But just now—oh, it's hard, Linda! So *hard*!"

It was hard. Much, much too hard.

Then, in a tone of dull acceptance, Margaret continued. "And Fred—I'm going to lose him, too."

Linda's heart stopped, and her breath.

"My own brother," mourned Margaret, "my own brother is taking that chance of happiness from me."

In a moment of blinding-white clarity, Linda knew that she must say the right thing! Margaret leaned upon her, admired her, accepted her judgment in so many ways—so now Linda must speak wisely, and her guidance must be thoughtful and true.

"People," Margaret was saying dully, "may criticise Fred for falling in love with me while his wife—— They forget that she *isn't* his wife, and hasn't been, really—even before she was hurt."

"Many of them think of you," said Linda softly, "and of how his love may hurt you."

Margaret's eyes were dark with protest. "I've never been happier . . ."

"I know, dear. But he came to you, offered his love and that happiness, without either of you being able to know its full expression. So don't blame Alan. . . ."

"But, *Linda* . . ."

"The situation is not of Alan's making, dear. You and Fred got into it, both of you old enough to realise that it had small chance of ending any way but in hurt."

Margaret was calm now. And thinking. "Does Alan say that?" she asked.

Colour swept in a rosy tidy across Linda's face, stained her throat. "I don't know what he says," she confessed. "Alan and I—he hasn't talked to me about the matter."

"I begged him not to operate on Fern," said Margaret in a small voice.

"I expect he understands your reasons. What did he say to you?"

"He didn't make any promises. But I suspect he thinks as you do. . . ."

"You'll come to see it, too, darling. Just as you'll come to accept Silas's loss. When he said he felt that he had to go to war, you did your part by saying nothing to weigh him down. You genuinely did your duty there. And now, with Fern——

"We women—we love our men, and our children—but there is a *way* of loving them that is right! Oh, do you know what I'm talking about, Margaret? We get hurt—so very deeply, dear!—but the hurts do heal in time, and if our way of love was right, we are left with pride and a shining memory that will stay with us, and be a golden glow about us down through the years. . . ."

Margaret raised herself, leaned forward, and kissed Linda's cheek. Later she was to tell that it was Linda who opened the door for her, who set her feet on the way which she could follow, and so go on. . . .

At the particular minute, all that Linda had said and done helped her to a quiet acceptance of this grief which was upon her. Seretha phoned that she was coming down later in the evening. There were other phone calls, and finally Jasper came in, with the twins.

His gathering Margaret into his patriarchal embrace burned

an image into Linda's mind that would take time to heal, and when they both turned to her, and suggested that she go in person to tell Alan . . .

"It's the right thing to do," said Jasper.

"Darling, please?" urged Margaret.

Linda went, glad of a chance to speak to Alan while her purpose was clear and firm in her mind. She would show her regret, voice her love—but firmly, too, she would urge upon Alan the necessity for him to have children. With Silas's death, there were too few strong Thorntons—so she must bravely step upon the little budding tendrils of hope that she and Alan could take up, and go on with their good but fruitless marriage. She must find a way to show him his duty to the family, make him listen to her, and let her be sacrificed. It would in some small degree make up for the sacrifice which Silas had made.

Alan hurried to get back to the hospital to keep an appointment which he had made with Fred Blake. With Fern's operation on the schedule for to-morrow, he must get the husband's release. He would lay things on the line for the man, if necessary.

Fred was to come at five; Alan was "home" by four-thirty, and, he thought, he would catch up on any number of little tasks. He must check on the anæsthetist's coming from St. Louis, read over the tissue report on a burn case—— Eventually he considered the notes which Laura had written upon his memo pad. One was a call from Linda. He glanced at his wrist; his free time was now down to twenty-three minutes.

He sighed, and reached for the phone, then turned his head at a knock on his door. "Come!" he said loudly. It would be Blake.

But it was not. It was Linda herself, glowing and beautiful, her eyes starred with tears as she told him about Silas.

"Oh, no!" he moaned. He turned towards the window, his dark face convulsed in a swift spasm of grief and protest. "They wouldn't let me go!" he cried. "It could have been me—not him!"

She touched his arm. "I don't think—this war—I don't think it's a question of one man in place of another, Alan. Of one man being a hero, and another not. Silas was the man who happened to be in the certain place—doing the certain thing

—to be killed. Perhaps his is the easier thing—and yours the harder."

His arm about her shoulders drew her to his side. "Did you speak wisely to Margaret?" he asked gently.

"I tried." She told him haltingly of the things she had found to say to Margaret. "I don't suppose she heard much of what I said." She told of sending the children for Jasper, and of his coming. She mentioned his size, his beard—— "He made me think of that Michelangelo Jehovah."

"This must have hit Father hard," mourned Alan.

"It did. But—he's like a tree, Alan. Strong—and upright. I—I was thinking——" But she could not go on. Tears welled into her eyes, poured down her cheeks, and he took her into his embrace, his own eyes wet. It was comforting to weep there against his rough tweed shoulder, to feel his strength and warmth, to weep for herself, and for Margaret—for Silas's fine young life drained out upon the sands of Africa—to weep with Alan. They comforted one another in their grief.

After a short time: "I had an appointment with Blake," murmured Alan. "If he's heard this—he won't come. And it doesn't make any difference now. I won't hurt Margaret more than she's been hurt. I simply can't."

Linda stood back to stare at him. "Oh, Alan!" she breathed. "You're not—you don't mean Fern?"

Wearily his hand swept back over his head. "Yes. I had planned it for to-morrow, but—now——"

She caught at his arm. "Listen to me, Alan," she said tensely. "You must go on with that. Operate, if that is what you have decided you should do. You have to do what you think is right, for your own sake. *For your own sake!*"

But he made no promise. He would go to Margaret. He helped Linda into her fleece coat, and they went out through the office. Laura told him that Captain Blake had sent word he'd been delayed.

Alan told her the news of Silas. "I'm going to my sister."

"Yes, Doctor, of course. We're all sorry."

He nodded, started down the hall, then turned back. "I'll write my night orders later," he said in a strange, deadened voice.

Laura and Linda exchanged concerned glances. Alan was taking this very hard.

162

They went to the cottage, and found Ma'am and Jasper there. The little place was overcrowded. "Let's go up to the house," Jasper suggested to Ma'am, "and give Alan a little time with Margaret."

Margaret was sitting up on the couch now; the twins were eating their supper in the kitchen; they could be heard chattering busily with Frankie. When the elder Thorntons had gone, Alan went to sit beside Margaret. He asked if she had sent word to Fred.

"No. I hadn't a chance."

"I had an appointment with him; he was delayed. I—— Margaret, I've decided that I won't operate on his wife."

She looked up quickly. "Is she worse?"

"Oh, no. There's no change. It's just that now—well, you've been hurt enough." His shoulders were bowed, his face lined; he looked defeated, discouraged.

Margaret almost glared at him. "Do you think it's going to help me any to worry about *you*?" she demanded.

Alan raised his head. "How do you mean?"

"Why, you know what I mean! Just because I let myself fall in love with a man I knew wasn't free to marry me— that's no reason, Alan Thornton, for you to go against your own sense of what is the right thing to do for a patient. Is it, Linda?"

Linda had brought them each a cup of hot tea. Now she shook her head. "I told him the same thing."

"Why, of course," said Margaret briskly. "If you had planned to operate, you must go on with it, Alan."

Alan stared at them incredulously. He shook his head briskly, as if to clear it. Then he sighed and tasted his tea; chains had fallen from his limbs, a weight had dropped from his shoulders. "Women!" he said darkly.

Linda and Margaret actually laughed a little.

"One thing certain," he went on. "Never trust them to want what they say they want." He glanced at his sister, who was pale, but serene, then at his wife, who was blushing. "Either," Alan continued thoughtfully, "they are speaking impulsively, or trying to be noble." He stood up. "In either case," he decided, "a man should not take them at their word."

Margaret nodded in agreement. "What sort of appointment did you have with Fred?"

"I was going to have him sign a release for surgery. I couldn't operate without it, you know."

"He'll sign it," said Margaret. "I'll see to that."

Linda said she thought they should eat supper, and when the hospital called to say that Captain Blake was there, she told Alan to have him come over.

"And bring the release with him," called Margaret.

A fourth place was set at the table, and Fred came in very shortly. He did and said just the right things to Margaret. He was a well-contained man, sure of himself, disciplined and with a genuine kindness which showed warmly in his voice and manner. Alan and Linda exchanged approving glances.

"He's so—nice," said Linda softly.

Alan nodded his confirmation.

Fred went to talk to the twins, Margaret with him.

Meanwhile Alan served the plates, and Linda watched him. "Isn't Margaret wonderful?" he asked thoughtfully.

"You Thorntons are all wonderful," Linda assured him. "You can't blame me for wishing I were one of you."

Alan looked across at her, stunned. "But what are you—if you're not a Thornton? Of all the fool tangents, Linda!"

"Yes," she agreed meekly. "I guess it is. But don't be cross."

He laughed a little. "You know?" he said. "It's rather a relief to be cross. I haven't had time even for that with you recently."

She stretched her hand towards him. "I know," she said contritely.

Supper went as well as could be expected, although no one ate very much. Afterwards, Fred signed the paper without comment, and Alan said he must go back to the hospital. He had night orders . . . the operation was scheduled for nine the next morning. Linda thought she'd go up and sit with the old folk for an hour.

So they left Fred with Margaret, sitting before the fire, and it seemed the natural thing for Alan to walk with Linda up to the house. When he left her, it also seemed the natural thing that he should kiss her, warmly, tenderly. Linda clung to him, and searched his eyes. Then she looked away.

"I'll have to stay down with Margaret for a while," she said hesitantly.

His down-bent face was gravely still. "I want you to."

She touched his arm lightly, then turned and went up on

164

the deep porch. She stood there, watching Alan go along the sweep of gravel, passing through the shadows of the tall trees, a strong, tall man, and a brave one. She dashed sudden tears from her eyes, blew her nose, and went into the house.

Again—nothing had happened. She'd neither effected her great renouncement—nor were she and Alan reunited.

The next day, Margaret and Fred sat together in Fern's room at the hospital, waiting until the operation should be done. It took four long hours.

Alan Thornton was an efficient, capable surgeon. His operating-room was at no time a place for tension. On this winter day, this problem of brain surgery allowed no exception to that rule. Of course, the silent, sheet-draped figure upon the operating-table, and the man and women in green who worked about her, presented a dramatic situation. But even with this particular patient, there was no excitement.

That morning the surgical team consisted of Alan, the Chief Surgeon, Dr. Ernst and Dr. James, assisting; the anæsthetist sent up from St. Louis—a dark-eyed young doctor, he was, with the improbable name of Ravenol—Mrs. Dunham and the scrub nurse, with Lucille Gara circulating.

Considering the tensions surrounding the case, they all went about their business in an amazingly relaxed manner. To the anæsthetist, of course, this was only a difficult problem in his own field. He had been in the Valhalla Hospital for eighteen hours, and throughout the long operation he sat surrounded by his tanks and machines, charting pulse, respiration, blood pressure, the depth of anæsthesia. He was using what he called a "tossed salad" of drugs to carry Fern through the surgery. His task was made difficult in that the field could not be screened off from him—though he was well accustomed to that difficulty.

As in most surgery, the patient tended to disappear, with all attention focused upon the surgical field, a small area of flesh and blood and bone, bordered by coloured towels, blue ones and yellow, sharply illuminated by the overhead spotlight. The rubber-gloved hands moved in and out of this lighted field in changing rhythm, quick, deft, then slow, and rigidly disciplined.

Dr. Ernst began the section—and would end it, too—with

Dr. Thornton coming forward for the main task in hand. The first incision was made with one swift stroke—then the instruments took on a more measured pace, moving almost daintily, gently exploring.

The assistant followed the surgeon's hands with his own, clamping, tying off blood vessels as rapidly as they began to trickle—the wound remained clean and dry. There was some lightening of pressure when Alan's towel dropped from around his hands, and he moved up to the table. Mrs. Dunham was a joy to watch, anticipating his every move, selecting the instrument he would want, rapping it smartly into his palm before he could speak. She had some thirty instruments in the tray beside her; she did not err once in giving the right one into the hand Alan stretched towards her without looking up.

There was no lightning speed, no need for it with their expert anæsthetist. Dr Thornton could work calmly and carefully, sometimes discussing the situation with his assistants as he went along. The anæsthetist gave him all the time he would need, as well as providing a wide margin of safety for the patient. The risk of death during brain surgery is always high; Alan's skill minimised that risk.

Everything one might say about the surgery performed on that winter morning in the Valhalla Hospital could be said of any surgical problem executed by Dr. Thornton.

Yet never had so much real drama been packed into his operating-room. Doctors from neighbouring towns had all come in; some had asked permission; some had found it convenient to drop by the hospital that morning, and to stay. Every spare nurse on the staff was present. It was well agreed in the neighbourhood that Thornton was much too good to be a country doctor; this section they were watching quickly displayed itself as the work of a master-surgeon, and an inspired man.

The men and women seated at the end of the operating-room well knew that all doctors do not have a "feel" for surgery, do not possess that extra sense of where to cut, what to do, how much—how little.

But Thornton had it, and that morning his audience could fairly see his God-given power guiding his hand.

Even Rupert Ernst looked at this man with respect, and envied him his skill, his confidence, his inward strength.

Vaguely he came to understand why a man might spend his life in routine work if at one certain instant he could be on hand and have the ability to do this special sort of task.

The operation took four hours. The room became hot, the smells rose upwards and lingered. Valves purred, steam hissed and instruments clicked; pans softly clashed, bodies moved in a rhythmic *susurrus*. Three rows of white-clad people sat at one end of the room, their eyes all sloped towards the one centre, the surgeon's hands. All the glare, all the sounds, all the sight in that room was focused there in an hypnosis of attention. It was as if life itself centred upon that one point, and as if the tall, intent-eyed surgeon held that life like a bubble-ball of blown glass between his two hands.

And then—it was done. The people on the ranked benches could move, and talk and laugh a little, slumping under their relief from strain. They found that their limbs were stiff, their mouths dry, that they were hungry, and tired. When the patient could be moved to her room, Dr. Thornton followed slowly; he, too, knew a relief from strain. The danger was not yet over, but the decision had been made, the work completed and—it was a relief.

Late that afternoon, Linda Thornton took a walk. She had an errand in town; she thought she might go on as far as the hospital, and perhaps she could see Alan.

Margaret, on her return home at one-thirty, had said that the operation was successfully over. No, she said, she had not talked to Alan.

People coming along the street towards Linda threw long shadows upon the pavement, and those who passed her had their faces lit by the setting sun. Rupert's face was so lighted when he came abreast of her, and her own must have been for him.

He seized her arm with his gloved hand, saying how lucky he was to have caught up with her. Linda took a step towards crossing the street; from there she would enter the hospital grounds.

His hand detained her. "I don't need to be back for an hour." His head indicated the hospital. "Couldn't we walk away somewhere? Or perhaps have a drink?"

She shook her head.

"We've always enjoyed our walks," he reminded her softly.

"Yes," she agreed. "Yes—I'm afraid we have."

"*Afraid?*"

She turned to face him. She was wearing a slim, straight coat of heather-toned tweed, a little purple cap cupped the crown of her head, with bright curls springing out around it like a red-gold halo. "Rupert,' she said quickly, hurrying the words, "I have been acting very foolishly and selfishly to encourage you to spend so much time with me."

"But, my dear Linda—I have so enjoyed your sweet companionship, and hoped . . ."

"Yes," she said swiftly, "I've enjoyed it, too. Sometimes you make a delightful companion."

"You must know," he said intently, "that I would be much more to you—that I had even hoped you could love me."

"Oh, no!" Her eyes were like stars on a cold night; her cheeks were pink. This, she thought, was a strange place for a love scene. On a public corner of two well-travelled streets, in the all-too-clear light of early evening.

"You could learn to love me, I think." Rupert's eyes were boldly adoring, his voice was whispering soft.

Her head lifted. She was—actually—enjoying this! "But," she countered, "I'd have to want to learn!"

"And you think you do not?"

"I *know* what I don't want to do," she cried, "because I happen to be the kind of woman who thinks it enough to love just one man."

"You mean your husband?"

Linda almost laughed. He sounded downright shocked.

"Well, of course!" she said gaily.

"But why, Linda?"

"*Why?*"

"I mean—it has been obvious to me since my arrival here that you are—well—disaffected with your husband. I could understand why. He is a busy, absorbed man, a dedicated man, and one who neglects his wife. I think he is a great fool. You are so lovely, so exciting to be with. But because his chief interest seems to be elsewhere, I have felt myself quite free to attempt to take his place in your regard. I even imagined— when I finally dared embrace you . . ." His eyes reminded her of her swift second of response, and in the deepening twilight, her flush darkened.

"We all make mistakes, Rupert," she said with dignity. "I am sorry if you thought—if I let you think——"

"*Expect*," he amended her word.

She bit her lip. "But you had no right . . ." His hand fell to her forearm, and again her head lifted. "All right!" she agreed. "*I* had no right. I am Alan's wife, and——"

"And you lately learned that I am a Jew." He spoke harshly.

"Oh, no!" She put out her hand. "Oh, you must not think that!"

"Then why? Tell me why!"

"I don't think I *can* tell you, exactly," she said anxiously. "Perhaps I myself don't know. . . ."

But suddenly she did know. She couldn't tell Rupert because he wouldn't understand. But Alan would comprehend this exalted feeling of clear strength, of being a person! *Why,* her thoughts ran, *I can have strain, too! Not much, maybe, but it will be enough—and it can grow within me! With blood, one is born with it, or not. Maybe it's good, perhaps it's thinned down. But strain—where that is—call it behaviour, if you like —or conscience—— Well, anyway, it's a thing I want. No running away, nor whining at what life brings—but the strength to do the job as it is set for me to do! The way Margaret is doing—the way Silas did—and Alan.—*

Oh, dear, dear Alan!

She took a step towards Rupert, her thought shining in her face. "It is just, my dear," she said softly, "that I feel for Alan what I can never feel for you."

His chiselled-marble face was cold. "That's certainly a dry crust for a man to gnaw upon. And," he added suavely, "for you, too."

She would not be frightened. "Even if you're right—that it is only a crust, and dry—it is still bread, and that is what we all live by."

"Not bread alone . . ."

"If I need more, I must find it in my own way. But I shall not be so foolish as to cast the bread aside. You think that Alan neglects me—but you are thinking only of externals. Of little attentions that are pleasant when one has them—flowers, and gifts and time spent upon me. But you have no understanding of the core of my feeling for Alan. It has to do with my sureness that Alan Thornton will always know the right thing to do, and do it. You can call it integrity, or bravery—but it's a quality that makes me know that whatever I do for such a man, however small a thing, it will be right, too, and so have its own significance. And however little *time* Alan gives me, he awards me all of the things that matter; his trust, his respect, his love. So, if he wants me . . ."

"He does," said Rupert Ernst bitterly.

Linda smiled softly. "Yes," she said, "I think he does."

The operation upon Fern Blake was a success. Alan knew that it was before he ever finished in the operating-room, before the anæsthetist had complimented him and before the patient had had a chance to show the first signs of recovery.

Twenty-four hours after the operation, he could take Fred Blake to his wife's room, and point to Fern's hand as it lay upon the white spread. The thumb, he explained, was strong—it no longer lay collapsed within the fingers in what was medically called the *baby position*. Before surgery, Fern's hand had shown a loss of will-power and independence. But now——

"Then she is—cured?" asked Captain Blake.

The doctor smiled. "To the point where she will be in control of herself and her emotions. I should strongly advise moving her, when she's ready, to a good convalescent home. She is weak now, of course, from surgery. And she may continue to be weak. Probably will. I removed considerable bony tissue which had been pressing upon her brain. There were clots as well, and one cyst. I am afraid she hasn't much in the way of life-expectancy. I mean, she won't live long. A year—perhaps longer. But she will soon regain consciousness, and some strength. I offer you this hope, Fred. Even if memory is not restored to her completely—and you must face that possibility—or if she does remember you, she may herself wish to be freed of marriage. But at least she is going to be able to decide such things for herself."

"Doctor——"

Alan pressed his shoulder. "I know. You love Margaret. Don't be ashamed of wanting her. But nothing, not even

Margaret, was worth getting 'at all costs.' That phrase——"
He shrugged, and turned towards the door. Fred Blake stood
looking gravely down at Fern. Her head was turbaned in
bandages, she seemed asleep. Before he left the room, he lifted
her open hand, as Alan had done, dropped it and patted it
gently. "Poor girl," he said softly.

That afternoon, Alan went down the street, walking slowly.
He was feeling, he knew, the slump which comes after some
great decision is made, some dreaded task accomplished, some
tragedy met, and passed. People noticed the difference in his
pace—one or two commented upon it. Doc usually, they told
each other, went along in a "burnt hurry." This afternoon, he
sauntered. He stopped to bargain with the little Negro boy
who asked him for a "solid quarter." He crossed the street to
look at a brace of Walker hounds in the bed of a pick-up
truck; he rubbed their velvet ears, scratched their spotted
backs, looked into their eyes—and told their owner that he'd
like to have just such a dog. "One of these days," he promised,
"I'm going to take some time to hunt."

He continued to dawdle along, by easy stages, until he
finally reached the stables, thinking that he would have a rare
hour with his father. But a groom said the Old Man was off
about the Farm somewheres—a mare had foaled out in a
pasture, and Jasper had taken off. "He split the creek, Dr.
Alan. Mare had no call to be out, o'course. I'll bet by now he's
told some feller how the cow et the cabbage!"

"Stem and all," agreed Alan, laughing. People did not make
mistakes for Jasper. "I'll walk down that way—maybe I'll see
the smoke and find him."

It was not a warm day, but the air held the promise of spring.
Tree buds were swelling; the sounds of the land were those of
stirring and waking. A redbird sang piercingly sweet, a little
creek gurgled and spashed on its way downhill to the river.
He saw the horse van going down the gravel road, and he
thought he heard his father's shouting, "Haw!" Of course
that could still be a mile away; it was hard to figure why that
roar should quiet a horse, but it usually did. Scared 'em to
death, maybe.

Alan sauntered along between the white fences. He'd
stopped at the house long enough to pick up a leather jacket.

Now he filled his pipe and leaned on the top rail to watch a young colt kick up his heels. Yep, spring was nigh.

And here came Jasper, across the fields, the white mane and tail of his buckskin like banners in the wind. The big man rode as if he were a part of his big horse. Alan watched them come closer, a smile crinkling his eyes.

Jasper spied him and turned that way, greeting his son loudly and affectionately. Alan went along the fence to open the pasture gate and restrain his impulse to give his father a hand down from the saddle. Jasper's twinkle acknowledged that restraint.

They talked for a minute or two, both tall men leaning on the fence-rail, the buckskin tied at the gate.

Jasper hooked a thumb at the frisking colt. "Lindy named him Quill," he told Alan. "He's goin' to make a good horse. Look at the strength of those hind-quarters."

"What will you name to-day's foal?"

"Makes no difference," declared Jasper. "Claimin' horse."

Alan chuckled. "What happened?"

"I make a mistake now and then."

"I thought you said the foal was all right."

"Holy Jeremiah, son!" cried Jasper. "They's a power o' difference between bein' an' all-right foal and a good one!"

"You can tell that already?"

"I bred this one by the book. Sire and dam all read good—I should-a stuck to Feathers." He meant that he'd bred his mare from another line.

"You have to get new blood now and then, sir."

"I do. But I should give thought to how that blood shows up—not just rely on its bein' blood."

Alan smiled, and Jasper acknowledged the implication. "Maribou's the mother o' this one. She's pretty near all blood-line herself. I took a chance in breedin' her to more blood, and the result is a pretty horse that'll read like *Burke's Peerage* on the book, and not be much else to rely on.

"You see, son, it does work out that way. Horses and people. Us. Our family. The Thorntons. We've got *good* blood, but mainly we're a line for strength and endurance. Now you take your mother—she very strongly believes that blood—just what's set down in the stud-book—is the strength of a family.

172

It's not. That's where she's wrong. She could look at her own family—Seretha, your Ma'am, is herself the strongest of the Merritt line, but her main strength is the way she rules this family. Though—— But d'you ever notice, Alan, that the left hand, which is generally the weaker, is better suited to hold the reins than the right one?"

Alan regarded his father with awe.

"Ma'am knows that," Jasper continued. "She knows where her strength lies. Why else, d'you suppose, she's took out after Lindy lately? She has, you know. First, convincin' the girl that she had failed you and the family by not givin' you children, naggin' at her to let you have another chance . . ."

Alan stared at his father, white-faced. He'd known that Seretha was somewhat in the picture, but——

"All because," the old man swept on, "she knew that there was real strength in Lindy. Ma'am can't rule her, and she knows, too, that it'll be Lindy who will supersede her, with a strength that's quite different from Ma'am's strength—that rein-holdin' I mentioned."

Alan looked away now, but still stared, white-lipped. After a bit, the old man put his hand on the leather jacket sleeve. Alan glanced down at it. Gnarled, like part of an old tree. "Why don't you say some of these things to Linda, Father?" he asked quietly.

"I do a power o' talkin' to Lindy. Ben able to. She knows what she needs to know. *Now*—she knows."

Alan kicked his shoe into the dead grass under the fence-rail. "I had an idea that Ma'am wouldn't mind too much if Linda and I—broke up. But I didn't think that she—— Oh, Father, I don't want to think such things of my mother! What —what shall I do?"

"Nothin'—now. Won't need to. And Ma'am knows that. You'll have no more trouble from her. She's a lady, Alan—a blue-blood. What she did, she did because she believed it was best for the family. That comes first with her—as it should be. I'm grateful by and large for the way she's raised my pups. You and Margaret . . . What about *her*, now, Alan?"

"I had to be the one to hurt her—and deeply, Father. I hate that, coming on top of losing Silas . . ."

Jasper nodded. "She's good stock. She can take hurt."

"I hope you're right," groaned Margaret's brother.

His father walked over to his horse. "I have to be right," he said, almost indifferently. "Or what's going to become of the human race?"

Fifteen minutes before dinner time, Linda and Margaret and the twins arrived at the Big House to share the meal. "To help eat a ham," Jim explained their presence.

Margaret greeted the others, gently smiling, and said she'd run up to speak to Uncle Arthur; she'd not be long. Linda helped the twins with their wraps, and watched their manners. She herself spoke formally to Ma'am, smiled at Jasper and flushed pink when Alan kissed her.

"Everybody kisses everybody these days," complained Ann.

Linda's bright head was up, her eyes starry. "You'll get to an age where you'll like it," she said gaily. She had a snowy-white something at the throat of her grey wool dress. Her black shell pumps and her pretty ankles twinkled as she busied herself with the equal division of the evening paper's funny pages between the twins.

With them settled, she joined the older folk with the soft announcement that Fred Blake had that day received orders. He was being transferred to a Camp in New Jersey, and would have to leave before the end of the week.

"Well," said Seretha, "*that's* a relief!" She tossed her head against the glances turned her way. "Certainly!" she said firmly. "I've been afraid that he and Margaret would do something indiscreet and bring disgrace upon the family. Neither one of them has the *finesse* needed to maintain an *affaire!*"

Alan's laughter, and Jasper's, rumbled. Linda looked across at the twins. They were busy. And Margaret still was upstairs.

"Appearances *are* important," insisted Seretha, answering some word of Alan's. "They're everything—usually."

"Your mother does believe that," Jasper confirmed. "I recall a time when her Pa was buried——"

"Now, Mr. Thornton!" protested his wife, her cheeks so pink as to draw wonder in Alan and Linda. It took a lot, they suspected, to make Ma'am blush.

"That was a time ago," agreed Jasper, accepting his glass of sherry from Jacob. "Burials don't change much, but the grass in the burial plot was longer in those days, and so were

174

the skirts of the women who went to the buryin's. Ma'am's skirts swept the ground that day when her Pa was laid to rest, and o' course she and *her* Ma were standin' nigh the open grave—as was your Aunt Flora. An' all of a sudden Flora began to squeal and slap her hand over her mouth, everybody a-lookin' at her. But your Ma'am didn't make a sound— though afterwards we were to find she was more a-buzz than Flora. Flora got but one bee up under her skirt, and Miz Merritt did, too. But Seretha here, she'd swept full sail right over that bumblebee's nest, which naturally felt a stingin' resentment when confined under a tent-like skirt. But Ma'am and her Ma just stood till the service was over an' the other women could rush to their rescue...."

Alan and Linda leaned against each other in joy, weak with their laughter.

"Ma'am never did forgive Flora for failin' to observe the propriety due a burial," concluded Jasper.

"Oh, Father," laughed Linda, "that's wonderful!"

"You never told that one before," Alan accused.

"No occasion to," explained the incorrigible old man.

"Mr. Thornton," said Seretha coldly, "can always find a tale to point his argument!"

And that set Linda and Alan to laughing so hard that the children's heads lifted in wonder, so they controlled themselves, remembering how Margaret would feel should she come down to hilarity. Though Linda made herself a promise to tell Margaret; she'd love it.

"To get back to Fred Blake," said Jasper, his green eyes a-twinkle, "I believe he is a very good man! The way he's acted, the job he's done at the Fort—he's got good stuff in him, and they still may marry and have children together. I hope to see them—just as I hope to see the ones Lindy will have for Alan."

Linda blushed in confusion, but excitement shone in the eyes she lifted to his twinkly gaze. *Why*, she asked herself, *should I* TRY *to decide things for myself? The family will attend to everything. Ma'am might try to spoil things—but Father—Father won't let her. All I need do is to sit tight!*

Alan was watching her, his green eyes as bright as Jasper's, and a slow smile began to fold into his cheeks, to bracket his big mouth, to spray out from the corners of his eyes.

After dinner, and an hour of quiet talk with her parents, Margaret walked down the hill with Alan, Linda having gone on ahead to get the twins into bed. Margaret clung to her brother's arm, and looked up at the stars; in the light from them her face was wistful and sorrowful, but on the whole serene.

"Did you know," she asked softly. "that Fred is leaving?"

"Yes. Linda told us. It may make things a little easier, dear."

"Yes. It may. What about Fern? How soon . . . ?"

"She can't be moved for at least a month."

"I—Alan, I want you to know—I've no regrets about Fern. I know now more clearly than I did before the operation, that you did the right thing."

"I hoped you'd feel that way," he said quietly.

"Mhmmmmn." She walked along, three steps to his one. "Now," she said contentedly, "if ever I may have Fred, it will be with a clear conscience. And I do love him, Alan!"

"Swell guy!" confirmed her brother.

"Oh, he is! I never thought, after Si, that I'd love just that way again. But—well—now if things do work out, and we can marry, it's going to be right, Alan! A wonderful, honourable thing. You thought of that, didn't you?"

"I thought of it. But, mainly, I was sure I could help his wife."

"Of course. It seems incredible now that we ever argued the matter."

They were walking very slowly, wanting to complete the conversation before reaching the cottage.

"It seems to me," said Alan, "that a person often can spend time and agony puzzling over a situation, and then after it is settled, resolved in some fashion, perhaps without our doing much of anything, we stand and wonder if there was any cause for all the worry—though, of course, there *was* some cause! The bruise of our anguish remains." He was thinking of his months of estrangement from Linda, why their separation had ever occurred, why it had persisted—and why, now, it should be so simply over and done with.

He glanced down at his sister's dark head, wondering if she guessed the trend of his thoughts. But she was thinking still of her own affairs, as she had every right to do. "It will be more wonderful to be with Fred if our happiness can come without

176

hurt to—a helpless and innocent person. Fred and I mean to wait for such a time. We've decided that any love worth the name can stand disappointment and delay. I don't know if it will be easier with him away—but if it isn't, I can take that, too."

They had come to the door of her home, and Alan bent down to kiss her. Without speaking of it, he knew that this chance for her to make her own sacrifice had somehow helped his small sister to survive the loss of her son.

"I hope," he said deeply, "I truly hope you may be happy, darling."

She rested her hand for a moment on his shoulder. "I shall be. Won't you come in?"

"No, I think not." He tipped his head back towards the Big House. "I have some housekeeping to do to-night."

"*Housekeeping?*"

"Yes. I've a mess of stuff—shirts, and cuff-links, and such junk—to move across the hall. Linda's been a little busy lately, what with one thing and another, and my stuff's got scattered all over the upstairs. I'm going to collect it, and put it back into our room where it belongs. Going to see that it stays there, too."

Margaret stood back to look at him. "I wouldn't say you were the housekeeper type," she murmured.

"A man can do anything he *wants* to," he assured her.

Margaret laughed. "You run along, then. Shall I tell Linda why you didn't come in?"

"Do as you like—but she'd be upset if she thought I was neglecting my chores."

"It never pays," said Linda the next day, turning away from the telephone, "to say that you believe things will settle down now."

"What the twins done?" asked Jasper shrewdly.

"They've stirred up something at school," she agreed to Jasper's surmise. "Miss Maggie sent for me instead of Margaret. *Poor Mrs. Giddens,* she called her."

"Margaret's had a bitter blow," Jasper agreed, "but I don't think she's earned maudlin pity. I'd say she was doin' fine."

"She is," said Linda, going towards the coat closet. "Last

night she told me that I was to come up here after this week-end. She was not going to let herself depend on me."

"A good thing," said the old man dryly. "For Margaret—and for Alan."

Linda smiled at him. "Yes," she said serenely.

"You got to go over to the school-house?"

"Yes. Miss Maggie seemed to think I should. . . ."

"Then you better *git*, girl! You want a car or a horse?"

Linda laughed. "I'd walk, except there may be pieces to pick up, if they really have been fighting."

"The *twins*? Or just Jim?"

"If it started with Jim, Ann got into it. You can count on that."

Jasper followed her out to the garage; his beard fairly trembled in delight. "Want me to come 'long?"

Linda flirted a saucy glance at him. "I do not! You have your talents, Father, but smoothing ruffled feathers is not among them."

He was still chuckling when she drove past him.

Miss Maggie had not given any details over the phone, but she was waiting, stiff-backed, stern-faced, when Linda came into her office, drawing her blue scarf from her hair, unbuttoning her big coat.

"I'm sorry to have to bother you, Mrs Thornton," said the school principal, forthrightly. "But I'm sure the time has come when a stand must be taken. I intend to speak to Mrs. Chaney as well."

"Oh, oh!" breathed Linda. *Lucy again*.

Miss Maggie nodded, her smile wintry.

"Yes," she agreed. "Ann is inclined to be jealous of Lucy —where I'd hoped she might try to emulate her. I mean her better qualities, her tidiness, her pretty manners——"

Linda looked down at her folded hands. Old Jasper called Lucy Chaney a *hellion*. She was indeed a neat little girl, and she did have lovely manners—to grown-ups. Her black hair was always smoothly drawn into pigtails tied with crisp rib-bons. She flirted her brief skirts and fascinated the little boys —particularly Jim Giddens. And Ann—poor Ann. A lot of her jealousy was just that, a forerunner of the time when some girl would really transplant her in Jim's affections and company—but, the rest of it—Ann was a sturdily honest child, and honest people were more easily hurt than the other kind.

However, all that really did not explain how Ann and Lucy had come to what Miss Maggie called a pitch-battle in the schoolyard. "Lucy's pretty dress was torn, her hair ribbons—I had to send her home in near hysterics."

"You think it was all Ann's fault?"

Miss Maggie's lips quirked. "Ann feels that we grown-ups judge solely by appearances."

"Well, sometimes we do."

"Yes. Miss Heintz considers Lucy a model child. But I've dealt with children for many years, Linda. I know enough to respect the children's estimate of a classmate. Lucy must be a difficult child, hard for the others to endure. Prigs always are. But—just the same!"

"Oh, you're right. Fighting cannot be allowed. You said you sent Lucy home. What about Ann?"

"Well—— Lucy managed to defend herself. Ann had a bloody nose—but she in no way had hysterics."

"No. She gets stubborn."

"She does, indeed! Which is a good way, if properly directed."

"What was the fight about?"

"I don't know. Lucy said she'd done nothing. And Ann—well, as you say—she's stubborn."

"I wonder——" Linda pursed her full underlip. *My,* thought Miss Maggie, *she is a pretty girl!* "I wonder if I could talk to Ann. I don't mean to condone her fighting. She must stop that! But perhaps if I can find out why, and how . . ."

"Do you think Ann will tell you?"

"I'm sure she will."

"Well, then. She's in the teachers' room. At the head of the stairs. You'd better go alone."

The "teachers' room" was designed to be a restful place. It succeeded in being only dreary. The wicker furniture had been old when someone had donated it. The cushions and draperies were of cheap cotton print, and had faded. But the room was quiet. And in it Linda could talk to Ann, alone.

When she opened the door and went in, Ann was standing at the window, and did not look around. Her small shoulders heaved, and she sniffed a little. Linda went to her, drew the bloodstained face against her bosom, and then led the child to where they could sit side by side on the couch. She waited until Ann had cried for a while—as a boy, or a man, cries, the tears squeezed out, hard and bitter. Soon she began to gulp out phrases.

"That old Lucy!" . . . "I beat her up!" . . . "I sure beat her up, Aunt Linda!"

Linda waited, and soon the whole story came. "You know what she said to me, Aunt Linda?" Now Ann sat away from Linda, her cheeks like red balloons, her grey eyes a-sparkle with anger and tears. "And to Jim, too! I guess he doesn't think so much of goosey-Lucy now! Though 'course he couldn't beat her up. But I sure did. I really give her a goin' over."

"Don't be proud of it."

"But *Aunt Linda*—she called Aunt Flora—she really had the *nerve* to come up to me in the schoolyard and ask me how my Aunt Batty was these days. I asked her, real polite, who she meant, and she said, 'Why, I mean Mrs. Merritt, your Aunt Batty.' And so what could I do? Of course Aunt Flora *is*, but Lucy Chaney has no right to *say* so. I couldn't *let* her say such a thing about my family! You'd feel the same way, Aunt Linda! Of course, I had to beat her up, and all the other kids knew I had to. Even if I get 'spelled from school, I *had* to!"

She looked so little there in the dusky room, such a mite to take on the defence of her family. Loyalty of that size was too much to expect from so little a girl, and yet——

"You'd feel the same way, Aunt Linda."

Linda talked to Ann for fifteen minutes. There were methods of defending such things as family honour, she said. People like Lucy could be held in check in better ways than by fighting. Lucy had only been trying to needle Ann.

"But if you could manage to keep from showing that you were needled, Ann, she'd stop. When you get down and roll on the ground with Lucy, you're no better than she is, dear."

"She needed mussin' up!"

Yes, Linda thought, *Lucy had needed just that.*

But, eventually, she got Ann to agree that breaking school rules, and little girls fighting like boys, was not just what Mums would approve—or do. Was it?

"No—but I'm not smart like Mums."

"Oh, yes, you are. And besides, there's the matter of worrying her now. Here she's been telling me that she didn't need me to stay with her any more, that she had you, and Jim——"

Ann let Linda wash her face, comb her hair and pin up the hem of her skirt. She went down and mumbled an apology and promise to Miss Maggie, then returned to her classroom.

Linda told Miss Maggie what really had happened, and Miss Maggie, too, admired the child's loyalty.

It all took time, and strength. And Linda's crisp blouse was a wreck which she must remember to keep hidden beaneath her coat.

But she had a very fine story to carry home to Jasper—though he must be restrained from rewarding Ann! Could Linda make him know the exquisite essence of that fine story? That Ann felt—and had said!—that Linda was an understanding part of the Thornton clan, that she, too, would bristle defensively—and she would! There was the beautiful part! Linda felt as if a crown had been set upon her head, an accolade awarded!

She felt so good that she wished she hadn't to bother with her car. She wanted to walk. Oh, yes! Her tyres needed changing around. That was excuse enough; she would leave her car at the garage, cut across to the hospital and walk home with Alan, or ride with him. In any case, she'd see him, and talk to him. Maybe even tell him. Her step quickened.

So eagerly impatient was she that she burst breathlessly into Miss Adamant's office.

"Dr. Ernst is with him," said Laura; the secretary spoke almost indifferently. "But go on in."

The inner door was closed, but the latch had not caught; the light pressure of Linda's knuckles pushed the crack wide enough for her to see—and hear.

The two men did not look around. Alan was sitting behind his desk, Rupert Ernst stood before it, facing him. Both men wore hospital whites—duck pants, t-shirt, jacket, white shoes. Linda had never before, she thought, seen Rupert in whites. He was very handsome in them, smooth and slick.

Alan's garments were spotless, but they looked as if they

had done a day's work, just as his face showed lines of thought and concern—and anger.

Even as Linda touched the door she heard Rupert's accented voice telling the Chief Surgeon that he would like to resign his position at the hospital.

And Alan was looking up at him coldly. "I'm sorry that you feel that way, Ernst," he said icily, "because, of course, you may not resign. You must stay here and complete the year agreed upon."

Rupert's back and head drew upwards. "But, my dear Doctor! That is *not* what I want to do!"

"Who in hell," cried Alan loudly, "does what he *wants* to do these days! So you don't want to stay here! Well, I don't want to stay here, either!" He got to his feet, and leaned towards the shorter man. "If I could do what I want to do, I'd be in the Army—perhaps over where my nephew was killed—perhaps down the road here at the Fort. But I'd be in uniform if your rule were in effect. Great Lord Jehovah, man! I want to go into service! Except for being a specialist, I've never wanted anything so much and so keenly.

"But I am not a specialist, and I am not in uniform! It was argued to me that I had an obligation to my family, to what my father had done for me in building this hospital. . . ."

Ma'am was the one who had argued those things to him. Linda stepped inside the room, and closed the door behind her. "You should have gone anyway," she said softly.

Rupert's glance upon her was bright. Alan turned more slowly to look at her.

She spoke, still quietly. "Why, really, did you stay, Alan?"

"Because—I thought I was doing the right thing."

"Then," said Linda firmly, "you *did* do the right thing."

For a moment their eyes held, then—as if with renewed vigour, new faith in his position—Alan swung back upon Rupert Ernst.

"You are not going to leave, Dr. Ernst." His usually soft, drawling voice snapped the words like a whiplash, his eyes were lightning-green with anger. "You are going to stay right here, and do the job set for you. You came here to learn to be an American citizen and an American doctor. The citizenship, I know, means little to you except that you cannot be an American doctor without having it. You came here for a year, you've been here for three months—long enough to discover that this is no easy job which has been set before you. I knew, at first sight of you, that it would not be easy. I knew—I know now— that you could never take the place of an American doctor! But I said I'd try to do as good a job as possible with you. And now by God, you're going to try to do your part. I plan to see to it that it's a good try!

"You'll learn enough of American ways, of our skills and values . . ." He caught his anger in leash, straightened and spoke more calmly. "You know, Ernst," he said, almost pleasantly, "you're convinced that we provincials know nothing about a man like yourself. That's a big error, because, as a matter of cold truth, you're more like my mother than any of her own children. You mistake outward things for inward value. You think of names, and title, instead of what lies behind those things. Sometimes true worth is behind them, but not always—and you don't know how to tell the difference.

"Take your three months here in Valhalla Hospital. You came in our front door with a sneer on your lips. You've never lost it. This is a small-town hospital where you've been assigned to work. I, the surgeon-in-charge, am only a country doctor. You haven't learned in three months—you probably won't learn in your whole life's span, this one important truth —that a doctor, that *I*, in my professional life, can do just so much surgery, so much work of any sort. I can touch only a certain segment of humanity. It makes no important difference whether I work in the backwoods or in the city, and no difference at all if the work I do is good work. Then, wherever I live and practise, I become a good doctor. And that's all that any M.D. can say for himself when the time comes for him to knock on Peter's gate. I——"

His phone buzzed, and he broke off to answer it. "I'll come immediately."

"Wait," he said to Linda as he passed her, hurrying. She thought Rupert would go, too. He did not. He had turned, his shoulders lifted in a shrug, and now he took a step towards her. "You see," he said resignedly, "how little the individual means to your democratic husband?"

Linda's hands clasped together earnestly. "Oh, but you're

wrong!" she cried. "The individual is everything! Especially when that individual can be a man like Alan!"

Dr. Ernst stepped back, his face a mask. He bowed a little. "I misunderstood you!" he said politely.

"Yes!" cried Linda. "I am sure you did."

Alone in his office, Linda waited eagerly for Alan's return. She sat for a while in the chair, but she was standing at the window, watching the sunset, when he came in, as silent as a cloud. He came up behind her, spoke her name softly—she turned, and he took her into his arms. She clung to him, her lips against his mouth, her cheek soft against the roughness of his, her hand upon his dark hair.

"Love me, Linda," he murmured. "*Love* me!"

"I do, Alan! I do! I have always loved you. . . ."

It was dark when they started home, and in the car, switching on the lights, he sat gazing for a minute at the radiance upon her face, the gleam of her hair.

"I'm sorry," he said gruffly, "that you got let in on my blow-off to Ernst. But—there's always a time when a lecture is indicated. *That* was it!"

"It was a very good lecture, too," she said happily. "You were absolutely right. The individual is important! But only if he manages his relationship to others for the good of all." Her smile flashed. "I'm lecturing now," she said. "And somehow I don't think this *is* the time."

He chuckled. "The important thing is your understanding of me."

She sniffed. "More important, I hope, than *your* attempting to understand *me*!"

He made no comment, but on the way home she knew that he continued to glance at her, and excitement rose within her, happiness. He drove around the big house, to the rear steps, and when she got out, his arms again drew her close, and he kissed her. Linda held him tight, tight! This happiness—he was her lover, and her child! What woman could ask for joy greater than this?

Indoors they found the family group a bit upset. Linda was remembering that she should have stopped at the cottage—and

184

at her first word with Seretha, she also remembered that she'd told no one of Ann's trouble in school.

It appeared that Lucy's mother had just paid a call upon Ma'am which had plunged Seretha into despair. The whole family, she declared, seemed beset by grief and by disgrace. She certainly could not blame Linda for wanting to free herself.

Linda gasped, and looked appealingly at Alan. He smiled reassuringly, then managed to calm Ma'am a little—enough, anyway, that Linda could tell about her visit to the school.

"So much has happened since," she began, blushing prettily, "that I forgot—even my dirty blouse! You see, Ann comforted herself against it." Smiling, she looked at the others for a sympathetic understanding of her apology.

In one fireside chair sat Seretha, erect and uncompromising. Jasper was opposite her, his eyes sparkling. Alan stood slightly away from Linda, his head tilted downwards, his eyes watching her. Linda continued to look from one to the other as she told her tale—of Miss Maggie's call, of going to the school, of her talk with Ann.

"That baby's loyalty!" she concluded breathlessly. "And what she said to me—that I'd feel the same way! And I *would*!" Her pansy eyes were wide. "Oh, I *would*. That's how I know . . ." She turned full about to face Alan.

He was smiling—his contained, good smile, crinkled at the corners of his eyes, creased about his sensitive mouth. The crystal chandelier was behind his dark head; he stood quietly, one hand in his pocket, the other holding a cigarette—and he smiled.

Linda sighed. Everything *was* all right. She had escaped Seretha's tyranny. Now she and Alan—Linda did belong!

With this serenity upon her, she turned again to Seretha. "I hope that no one has gone to Margaret about this?"

Seretha's eyes were cold. "If Maurine Chaney can be conscious of Margaret's situation, *I* surely would remember it."

"Oh, I'm glad. Because everything has been straightened out. And in the first place, it was nothing more than a childish . . ."

"Linda!" Seretha's voice chipped out the name.

Alan took a step forward. Jasper's head lifted. Seretha's hand silenced him.

"Let me say this," she demanded. "I am grateful that Linda smoothed things over. But I cannot consider as 'nothing' one more evidence of the disgrace which recently has descended so fully upon the Thornton family. Margaret's behaviour with that man—that ridiculous performance of Arthur and Flora, and Ann now behaving like a common . . ."

"The Chaneys put in their two-bits' worth as well," growled Jasper.

Seretha ignored him. "Oh, dear, dear! Well, I give you that. I won't blame you, Linda, for deciding that you'd be well out of all this. . . ."

Linda crossed the room to her, and knelt beside the chair. "Oh, but, Ma'am," she cried, "I am not out of it, and I don't want to be. The family—remember what Ann said? The family needs me."

"What family do you mean, dear?" Ma'am could speak of the family disgrace; she was not ready to let another speak of it.

Linda laughed. "I mean the same family as you do. The Thorntons—my family!"

Seretha lifted her crisp handkerchief to her lips. "Oh," she said uncertainly, "the Thorntons. I thought perhaps there was something new. . . ."

Alan gave Linda a hand up; they both were laughing. "It *is* a new family for me," Linda told Seretha. "You see, I've just found out that the Thorntons—all of them—*are* mine."

So the morning came, ten years later, when men were again being called to the wars, and Linda had promised to talk to Manning Fowler in an effort to help him reach his own decision. She would, of course, tell him that there was no best way, no easy way. . . .

Her memories past, her thinking done, the golden sun an hour higher in the heavens, a tap on the half-open door announced Jacob—still the "young" butler in Ma'am's eyes—to tell Miss Linda that Manning was downstairs. And around Jacob's tall person came, breathless, a red-haired boy of eight; his green eyes were bright, his gap-toothed mouth grinning in spite of the message he brought.

"Mommie!" he called shrilly. "Aunt Flora says for you to

come—Uncle Arthur's sick as a horse!" His smile faded into anxiety. "That's bad, isn't it?"

She laughed as she rose to join her son. "Yes, Jappy," she told him. "In our family, it couldn't be worse. Especially if it's a good horse!"

Surgeon in Charge

by Elizabeth Seifert

For Amy Fleming, the German doctor, Josef, was willing to forfeit the trust of his wife. . . .

For Amy Fleming, Michael Barry was ready to give up his appointment as Staff Doctor . . .

But for Amy Fleming, only one man really existed. In all her travels, in all her hospital experience, among all the men she had ever known, Peter Mason was the first who could live independently of women . . . or, at least, one woman. Tall and rugged, red-headed, with the wicked blue eyes of a vital man, he seemed the sole man creature who could look at an attractive girl and not bat an eyelid. He was always Dr. Mason, Surgeon in Charge of the Amelia Cecilia Hospitals, greeting Miss Fleming, Director of the same.

But Josef was already married, Michael was just a boy, and the town was beginning to talk. . . .

FOUR ◢◣ SQUARE EDITION 3s. 6d.

Doctor of Mercy

by Elizabeth Seifert

Young, handsome Dr. Clay Walters thought he knew everything about medicine—and people. He had encountered every sort of case, every kind of person and hospital situation.

But that was before rich, beautiful Maria got her claws into him, and Clay found himself so tightly bound he thought he'd never escape with his reputation.

That was before Biddy came home to look after her dying father, the judge, and Clay discovered how much he needed her calm and happy presence . . . That was before the doctor became involved in a sensational court-case involving the charge of mercy killing after the old man finally died . . . That was before the terrible temptations Dr. Walters experienced, and the decision he must make between his love for Biddy and his duty as a physician 'to help the sick . . . but never with a view to injury or wrong-doing'.

FOUR ◨ SQUARE EDITION 3s. 6d.

Take Three Doctors

by Elizabeth Seifert

It didn't take Dr. Christy Johns long to settle into the little township of Greer. He soon found himself involved both with the people and their problems and foibles—with old-fashioned Dr. Jeff Moore and his hate of the rich city dwellers who were moving into Greer; with Dr. Webb Stokes, a brilliant dermatologist who seemed at first sight little more than a wastrel; with Norma Sims and her somewhat scarlet reputation; and with Jenny, whose small school turned out to be the storm centre of the crisis which so cruelly hit the town. But Jenny was someone with whom Christy was only too glad to be involved . . .

FOUR 🔳 **SQUARE EDITION 3s. 6d.**

Sister Morton's Protégée

by Margaret Aldridge

Ill-health and the advice of Dr. Gale persuade Helen
Morton to take a post as sister in a hospital on the West
Cornish coast where Julia, Dr. Gales's adopted daughter, is
training. He asks Helen to keep an eye on the young girl but
this poses difficult personal problems when Julia falls in love
with the house surgeon, Jerry Stacey. . . . Then Helen finds
herself in the unpleasant position of being in conflict with
the senior surgeon, Abel Akermann. She wonders why this
particularly brilliant man should bury himself in such an
out-of-the-way place. . . .

Sister Morton's Protégée is the heart-warming story of a
dedicated nurse who recognises that her first duty is to her
patients, but who determines to help a tormented doctor
recover his youth and happiness . . . and to share his close-
kept secret.

FOUR 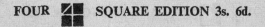 SQUARE EDITION 3s. 6d.

Doctor Grace's Dilemma

by J. L. Somers

When Dr. Vivien Grace first meets the ambulance man she discovers it is Frank, her first love.

Now he is married . . . but they both pretend he is free.

Urgently in love with each other, they take no thought of tomorrow.

Max Lacey, Resident Surgeon at the hospital seems severely critical of Vivien's continuing friendship with Frank. But his disapproval covers a more personal interest in her feelings.

Mavis Langley, the immaculate blonde 'Sister' whose devotion to nursing is focused more on Doctor Lacey than her patients, is fiercely hostile to Vivien.

These four people's lives interweave with increasing intensity until tragedy forces Vivien to recognise the lie she has been living.

FOUR ◪ SQUARE EDITION 3s. 6d.